Going home

Book Three in the *Norah's Children* Trilogy

by

Ann O'Farrell

To Rose, best wishes, Ann O'

Going home

Book three in the Norah's Children saga

Copyright © 2012 by Ann O'Farrell

ISBN: 146798843X
ISBN 13: 9781467988438

For you, Mum.

Also by Ann O'Farrell.

Norah's Children.

Michael.

Ann O'Farrell's Florida Memories.

Acknowledgments

Finally, I have completed the story I wanted to tell, the story of Norah's children, and especially of her youngest, Michael. My thanks to all of you who kept me on task.

Once again, Tom Coyne, eagle eye extraordinaire, has kept my chronology in order, my punctuation under control, and my story on track. Where would I be without you, Tom? In this book he was joined by my daughter-in-law, Jenny O'Farrell who finally had to be restrained from giving my writing so bright a polish I feared it would have far outshone the story.

I am so grateful to the Dunedin Library Writer's Group, my apologies that I cannot begin to list you all, there have been over fifty members over the last two years. My thanks also to Liz White in the Library's Adult Programming Department who looks after us so well.

My good friends Abe, Barbara, Jack, Lee, Susan, and Maureen in the POP group, (Publish Or Perish, can you believe?) have been invaluable in their advice, suggestions, and encouragement. Thank you, thank you.

I must continue to thank Pat and Harry McCarthy who started the ball rolling for me with the first book, and have been unwavering in their support ever since.

And finally to the man who reads, re-reads, listens, advises, and has the patience of Job as I write and re-write sections I have promised him I will not touch again! John, thank you, my love, this marathon is finally over and I give you my word ... No more trilogies!

Ann O'Farrell.

The story so far ...

When Norah Kelly died, in 1924, her five young children were separated. The eldest, Pierce, aged eleven, remained with his father in Glendarrig, a small village in the west of Ireland, whilst the four younger children were dispersed to different families. Mary, eight and the eldest girl, went to live with their great-aunt, Bridgie, in the neighboring village of Doonbeg. Colm, six years old, Sheelagh, four, and Michael, two, were shipped to England.

Colm was adopted by the Sinclairs, a wealthy family in London, and the two youngest were taken by Jim Porter and his wife to Bristol. When the traumatized Michael did not speak, Porter decided that he was retarded and fobbed the boy off on his spinster sister, Wyn. He and his wife kept Sheelagh.

On his Da's death, Pierce inherited the family haulage business. On Aunty Bridgie's death, Mary inherited her aunt's home and small store and married Joe Daly. Colm enjoyed his adoptive family's wealth, managed to avoid conscription, and dealt black market goods during World War Two. Sheelagh worked in her adoptive father's Haberdashery and Clothing Emporium. Michael worked in the same store before joining the RAF.

Thanks to Mary's persistent efforts the siblings were reunited after eighteen years. To seal the reunion, Michael and Pierce married on the same day though in different countries due to the war. Pierce married Maeve, the nurse who had cared for his father. Michael married Beth Howard, the sister of his best friend, Paul.

Bristol, England
January 1946

A New Life

B eth watched as Michael filled out the forms.

"Are you sure about this?" she asked.

He leaned toward her, kissed the tip of her nose. "I don't think I have much choice. The area manager almost made it sound like a requirement."

"I don't mean the policy, silly, you know I don't. I mean the job itself."

He put down his pen and shrugged. "It's a job. Who knows if I'll be any good at it? Never saw myself as an insurance salesman, but I can't sit around here all day."

"But …"

He rested a finger gently on her lips.

"Stop fretting, Beth. It's a new year, a new job. It's the start of a brand new life, and hopefully," he looked around the Howard's cluttered kitchen, "we will be able to move out."

"Mum loves having us."

"Yes, I know, sweetheart, but now that Paul and Evelyn have moved back home it's a little crowded. Paul shouldn't have to sleep on the couch; it's his home after all. You know I've always loved your family, Beth, but it's time to find a place of our own." He picked up the papers and waved them at her, "and this job is going to help it happen."

She smiled, "I still feel guilty I made you give up flying."

"You *didn't* make me. I promised."

"But still …"

"No, Beth. You're far more important to me than flying. I promised you I'd stop when the war was over. It is, and I have. *This* is what I'll be doing now." He studied the document, signed it with a flourish, waved the final page in the air, and smiled. "Look, I just sold my first policy!"

She loved his smile. Even his eyes, his beautiful, brown eyes, seemed to smile. Beth studied him. He seemed to get more handsome as he got older. Only twenty three, but already his dark hair had flecks of grey at the sides. Whenever she commented on them he laughed and called it his 'extinguished' look. Her friends said he looked just like Cary Grant. Beth secretly agreed, but she didn't say so.

"What are you staring at, Mrs. Kelly?"

"You." She felt herself blush; it was like he could see what she was thinking. She reached over to the clothes horse beside her, began tugging off socks, checking if they were dry, pairing them. "It *is* nice having you at home all the time." she said. "It's going to seem strange when you start work. I've got used to having you around."

"It's been nice to be here."

"I'm just afraid you're going to be envious of Paul, now that he has a flying job. I don't want you blaming me for keeping you away from it."

"That's all he's ever wanted to do, Beth, to fly. But not me. The war is over. No more flying for *me*. So stop worrying."

She wasn't convinced. Beth knew how much flying had meant to Michael, *and* that she'd probably coaxed the promise out of him. She'd worried about him constantly since he'd enlisted, jumped every time she heard a knock on the door, and was filled with dread whenever she saw a telegram boy coming down the road on his bicycle, fearing that one of his buff envelopes was for her.

No, she was glad he wasn't flying any more. He was right; selling insurance was only a beginning. He could get a better job later.

She watched as he slipped the papers into the envelope, closed it, stuck on a stamp, and tucked it into his breast pocket.

"I want to pop this in the post this evening," he said. "Make sure they have it before I start on Monday. Do you feel like a walk to the postbox with me?"

"Of course."

Michael collected their coats and scarves from the hallstand.

Beth called, "We're just going for a walk. Back soon, Mum."

"All right, darling."

The living room door opened. Paul stood grinning at them.

"Are you two going for a drink while you're out?"

"No, just posting a letter."

Michael smiled, waved his friend back into the room, and hustled Beth out of the front door.

They tried to stifle their laughter as they hurried down the pathway.

"And that ..." said Michael, as he held the gate open for her, "is why we are getting our own place, and soon!"

"I know, I know."

They walked hand in hand down the street toward the postbox.

* * *

Once Michael started his new job, Beth began scouring the local papers, searching *For Rent* notices there and in their local shops. They decided they would have to rent a flat to begin with, but that as soon as they had saved enough money they would try and buy a house.

After weeks of searching, number three Wooleton Road was the best she had seen. It was a cramped, ground floor flat with one bedroom, a sitting-dining room, and a tiny kitchen. But they had their own bathroom; they wouldn't have to share.

"I know it's all a bit dingy," she told a doubtful Michael, "But I can make it cozy, really I can."

They were almost three years married, the war was over, and it was time to have a home of their own. They had looked forward so much to all the things they would have, and do, once the war was over. Everything they'd spoken about and planned had begun with the words "once the war is over."

"Once the war is over, we'll have our own house."

"Once the war is over, we can start a family."

"Once the war is over, everything will be all right."

The landlord seemed nice. They thought the rent was probably affordable on Michael's commissions, and the demobilization money Michael had saved would pay for the first month.

They signed the lease and the entire Howard family helped them move. Maggie gave them table and bed linen; her husband borrowed a friend's van. Ev helped clean the bathroom and kitchen and re-painted an old table and chairs they'd found in a second-hand furniture shop. Mrs. Howard gave them a few pieces of furniture, including her late husband's armchair.

"It reminds me too much of your dad," she'd said when Beth protested. "Better you and Michael should have it now."

Paul bought them a new bed and helped Michael assemble it.

It was fun, and exciting, and it really did seem that now that the war was over things *would* be all right. Beth cleaned and tidied until their new home shone. She spent hours deciding on what kind of lampshade she should buy for the standard lamp behind Michael's chair, or where an old coffee table of her mother's should go. Though she'd never been much good at sewing, she borrowed her mother's machine to make cushion covers and curtains, so that she could get rid of "those horrible old blackouts." The new ones were not a great success, the pattern uneven, and the amount of material inadequate. She wished she could ask Michael's Aunty Wyn how to do it, but the old lady was as stubborn as ever. She would have nothing to do with either of them.

Michael worked so hard, such long hours. Beth spent a great deal of the day on her own. Even though she tried to keep busy, she missed him and was lonely. She thought that perhaps if she were working it would be better. She searched the paper for jobs, but there were so many unemployed men since the war ended, nobody wanted to employ women any more. She took long walks, joined the library, visited her mother, her sisters, and her friends.

In the evening she would set the table for supper with a fresh tablecloth, fresh napkins, and maybe a small vase of flowers. She would change her dress, brush her hair, and even put on a little lipstick. As they ate, she would tell him about her day, try to make it sound interesting or fun. He listened in silence to her chatter, but didn't seem to notice if she tried a new hairstyle, freshened up an old dress with new buttons, or even put a dab of her mother's perfume behind her ears.

When they'd eaten he would help her with the dishes before taking the newspaper and collapsing into the sagging armchair. There he would open the paper, create a barrier between them, and read. Every evening Beth sat, sewing or reading a book, waiting for him to finish. More often than not, when he did, he would close and fold the newspaper, stand, stretch, yawn, and say he was ready for bed.

Soon Beth admitted to herself that married life in their new home was *not* how she imagined it would be, and she knew in her heart that a large part of the reason was because of Michael's job. He had grown quieter, looked tired, his face drawn. She missed the sparkle in his eyes. When she tried to talk to him about it all he was brusque, told her he was still looking for a better job, said he was tired, not used to all the walking, door to door, street to street, all day long. He promised her it would sort itself out in time. That was always the end of the conversation.

The war *was* over, but they were not happy. And she wasn't pregnant.

* * *

It was early summer before Michael acknowledged that things were not going well. He'd arrived home late that evening, ate his supper in silence, pushed his chair away from the dining table, and retreated to his armchair, as usual. But this evening, instead of opening the paper as he usually did, he unlaced his shoes and tugged them off. He examined the sole of one and waved it at Beth.

"I'm not sure I'm cut out to be a salesman," he said, smiling ruefully. He poked his finger through a small hole and waggled it. "I think I'm using up more in shoe leather than I make in commission. I only got this pair re-soled a month ago."

He dropped the shoe to the floor and sighed. They were quiet for a moment. Beth watched him. He frowned, continued to stare at the shoe. "I don't mind knocking on door after door. I don't mind asking if they want insurance but, damn it all, Beth, I *hate* all that heavy pressure stuff they want me to do." He looked up at her. "If a person can't afford it, I shouldn't have to try and persuade them," he said, "just to make the bloody company more money, or so that I get my commission."

Beth put her knitting into the basket by her feet. "But you told me everyone needed insurance. You said it was important. That's why you signed up for ours."

"Yes, I know I did. But sometimes I feel I'm just pushing people too hard." He sighed again. "Like today. There was an old lady, Mrs. Morgan. To start with she said she didn't want any insurance. But I kept talking. And I talked her into one. A life policy! I told her that even if she didn't need it herself, it would be a nice nest egg to leave for her children. I pushed. I told her if she was insured, when the time came, they wouldn't be burdened with funeral expenses or whatever." He bowed his head. "I felt downright bloody ashamed when she signed the papers."

Beth went and knelt in front of him. She took his hands. "Then, why don't you try and find another job, Michael, my love?"

He pulled his hands away, "Oh, for God's sake, Beth. There aren't any. You know that. Too many of us got let out of the service at the same time." He looked down at her and shrugged. "Anyway, they've got used to women doing the jobs. Nobody needs us men anymore."

"That's not true, my love. I'm out of a job too, don't forget. Mr. Atlee says it's going to take time for the country to get back on its feet. Things will get better. He says it will. I know it will. Perhaps we can ask at Thristle Engineering?"

His laugh sounded hard and nasty, not like it usually did. "Just because you worked there during the war doesn't mean you have any influence, my love. According to the paper they're still laying people *off*, not taking people *on*." He squeezed his eyes tight shut, shook his head. "I'm sorry, sweetheart." He looked down at her and stroked her face. "I know I haven't been much of a husband recently. I just don't think I'm cut out to sell insurance." He shrugged. "Not ruthless enough, I suspect."

They sat in silence for a while, Beth on the floor at his feet, Michael leaning over her, stroking her hair.

"You have to do something, Michael. You're miserable and that makes me miserable. Could you go back to flying?"

He shook his head. "No. I'm finished with flying. We've been through that. Anyway, a promise is a promise." He sat back in the chair. "Sorry, I didn't want to sound so gloomy. Things will improve. I keep looking in the paper. Maybe I'll find something else."

They were quiet for a while longer then he stood. "Come on, let's get to bed. It's late."

She looked up at him. "I meant it, about the flying. I don't mind, Michael, really I don't. I know you miss it."

"Thank you, my dear, sweet, Beth. But believe me, I'm finished with flying. We both agreed I must have had more lives than a cat to get through the war in one piece. I don't need to tempt the fates. Now, come on, I'll race you to bed." He stretched his hands out to her, helped her stand, then pulled her to him and kissed her.

She smiled and hugged him tight. "I miss the old Michael," she said, snuggling into his chest.

He tip-tilted her chin, and kissed her again, more gently. "He's still here. Come on, Mrs. Kelly, I'll show you." He took her hand and led her to their bedroom.

But she knew the other conversation wasn't over.

Command

Paul had known for three days, but he wanted to tell the family when they were all together. Evelyn was late home, so he waited until she arrived and the commotion of getting the tea was over. Now he stood in front of the fireplace in the Howard's living room, feet apart, hands behind his back, grinning.

"I'm getting a command. They told me on Monday. I begin training next week."

He waited for their reaction. His mother was the first.

"You're going to be a captain?"

He nodded.

"But you've been with them less than a year!"

"I know, Mum, but they're screaming out for pilots. Everyone who has money wants to travel now that the war's over. And I'm an expert, remember?"

His mother sniffed. "Maybe with fighter planes, but you're in a civilian company now, dear. Are they sure you're qualified?"

Everyone laughed. Evelyn leaned down over the back of the couch to hug her mother. "Stop worrying, Mum. Of course he's qualified. Anyway, you just heard him say they're going to train him."

"Yes I know, but ..." Margaret Howard looked up at her daughter, then turned to her son and shook her head. "Why couldn't you have taken a nice, safe job, Paul, like Michael, so that I could stop worrying about you?"

Nobody looked at Michael. There was almost a communal holding of breath. Michael laughed, "He'd go crazy if you tried to keep him on the ground, Mrs. Howard. He was born to fly." He continued as he went to his best friend and shook Paul's hand. "Congratulations, Paul, you'll make a great skipper."

"Thanks, Mike, I appreciate it."

Maggie, sitting tucked into the corner of the couch beside her mother, smiled up at him. "Congratulations, little brother. Dad would have been proud of you. I'd give you a hug, but I don't want to wake her." She indicated the tiny baby in her arms. "Come on, Mum, time to crack out the sherry. Time for a toast!"

Paul laughed again. "Hang on, how about we wait until I pass my command checks, shall we?"

"Spoil sport," said Evelyn. "We're only looking for an excuse to get into Mum's secret sherry stash."

"It's not a secret stash," Margaret Howard pretended to take offence. "You know very well it's only one bottle. And I was just being careful, that's all. I didn't know when the war would be over. It was for emergencies."

They all laughed. Their mother had kept the bottle since the first days of the war, and no family event had yet convinced her to open it, neither funerals, nor weddings, nor christenings. It was a family joke as to exactly what occasion would ever be special enough.

Beth laughed with the rest of her family, but she also watched. She watched her brother, saw how happy he was with his promotion. She watched her sister Maggie, so happy in her marriage, with her two beautiful children, little Georgina and now the new baby. She watched Evelyn, who would be starting a teacher's training course next year and who had vowed she would not be like all the teachers who had ever taught her. And she watched Michael. She saw the fleeting expression on his face when Paul made the announcement. Disappointment? Envy? He looked forlorn.

Beth went to her brother and gave him a kiss. "Congratulations, Paul. You deserve it."

He hugged her. "Thanks, Sis." Then he whispered in her ear. "Sorry."

She nodded, smiled, and returned his hug.

Evelyn began collecting the tea things and loading them on a tray, "Well done, little brother. I suppose that means you'll be too grand to help with the dishes now?" she indicated the tray.

Her mother stood and opened the door for her. Evelyn thanked her, then turned in the doorway. "Hey, does that mean you will be moving into your own place now? Your room's bigger than mine."

Paul laughed. "That's great; that's all it means to you, is it, getting a bigger room? I'm only just getting used to it, since Beth and Michael moved out." He protested. "No, I won't be moving, not for a while anyway."

Evelyn pulled a face at him and left.

Beth continued to watch her husband. Despite his smile he looked awkward, uncomfortable, and even though he was smiling his eyes were sad. She reached out and touched his hand. "Let's give Ev a hand with the washing up," she said.

He nodded.

Paul hadn't seemed to notice his friend's discomfort. He was hugging his mother, still laughing, still enjoying his family's response to his announcement. "Stop worrying, Mum. I'll be fine. I've to go to London for the training, but I hope to get posted back here afterwards. They want crews to work out of the regional airports. London is still knocked about a bit; there's an awful lot of bomb damage."

"I think it's great news," said Maggie, trying not to wake her baby as she eased herself out of her seat. "I'd better get going; I promised James I wouldn't be late. Sorry he couldn't be here to hear the news himself, Paul. Working overtime, as always. Still, at least he has a job." She looked toward her older daughter, engrossed in playing with her dolls. "Come on, Georgie, put dolly in her pram. It's time to go."

"Don't call her that, darling, Georgina is a lovely name," said her mother. She took the baby and gently rocked her.

"Sorry, Mum, it's sort of stuck, now." Maggie smoothed down her dress, picked up the bag of baby things from beside the couch, and gave Beth a quick peck on the cheek. "Thanks for the little jacket, Beth. It will look lovely on her. Your knitting is getting better all the time." She took the still-sleeping baby from her mother. The infant opened her eyes, whimpered softly, then settled back to sleep. "See you all soon, with James next time, I hope. Georgie! Hurry up darling." Maggie looked at her mother, "Sorry, Mum, Georgina!"

Evelyn hurried back from the kitchen as the family said their goodbyes. She hugged Maggie, kissed the baby's forehead very gently, and lifted Georgina to hug and kiss her goodbye.

"Bye bye, big girl, mind your baby sister. I'll be 'round to see you soon."

The whole family stood at the door while Maggie settled the baby into the pram. Paul ran to hold open the gate, and they all waved a last time as the young family set off down the road.

Once the front door was closed, Paul and his mother returned to the living room and Beth and Michael went to the kitchen to help Evelyn with the dishes. Then they thanked Mrs. Howard for the tea, congratulated Paul again, and left.

Hand in hand they walked back toward the flat, saying nothing. It was Beth who finally broke the silence.

"That's great news, isn't it, about Paul?"

"Uh huh," Michael kept walking, head down.

She waited, but he said nothing more. She grew angrier and angrier as they walked, though she wasn't really sure why. Maybe she *was* angry at her brother. *Why did he make such a big fuss about his promotion? It was bad enough he was flying. Did he want to make Michael jealous? No! That wouldn't be like Paul; he simply didn't think. Maybe he hadn't realized how it would affect Michael? But he did know, he said he was sorry.*

Perhaps she was a bit angry with her husband too? Why couldn't he find a job that he liked? Why did he have to look so damned miserable all the time? She shook her head; she knew she wasn't being fair, or reasonable. He was always looking in the paper. There just weren't jobs available. He missed flying, she knew he did, despite what he said. He'd never complained about her asking him to give it up. She was being mean, mean and selfish!

She took a deep breath, "I wish it was you," she said.

He stopped and turned to her. "No, you don't, Beth." He turned and continued walking. "I know how you were when your father and brother died. I don't want you worrying that something like that might happen to me. It isn't worth it." He stopped again and turned to her. "You're more important to me than flying, Beth."

"But you're not happy, Michael, in fact you're downright miserable. I can't stand you being like this."

He shook his head, waved her comment away, and continued walking.

Beth hurried after him. She caught his hand. "*Please* go back to flying. I know it's what you want to do. I've seen you when Paul talks about it. I saw you tonight. Please, Michael, for me, for us?"

"You don't mean that. You just think I envy Paul."

"No, really." She tugged him to a halt and waited until he turned to her.

"*Really*," she said more emphatically.

She waited until he nodded that he believed her.

Michael bent and kissed her on her nose. "We'll see," he said. He shook his head in mock despair. "And I *swear* I will never *ever* understand women."

She smiled, shrugged, and they continued their walk home. She felt a familiar tension in the pit of her stomach. She swallowed hard. What had she done? Was she mad? Beth rammed her hands into the pockets of her coat and clenched her fists tight. She meant it. She *did* want him to fly again; she would just have to get over her fears. It was more important that Michael was happy, and right now he clearly wasn't.

* * *

For weeks nothing more was said about flying. Michael continued working for the insurance company and reading the 'situations vacant' column in the newspaper in the evenings. It was over a month before he mentioned their conversation again. He'd come home earlier than usual, ate very little of his supper, and retreated behind his newspaper. Beth wondered if he was ill. She sat knitting, and waited for him to finish reading. The only sounds in the room were the ticking of the clock, the clacking of her knitting needles, and the rustle of the newspaper as he turned the pages.

Then, suddenly, "A new airline is setting up. They're looking for pilots," he said.

She rested the knitting in her lap, felt her heart beat a little faster. Michael was still hidden behind the newspaper. "Really? Where? Show me."

"It's not in the paper, actually." He lowered it, just enough so that he could look at her. She could just see his eyes. "Paul told me about it when we were over there last weekend."

"And you waited until now to tell me?"

"I wasn't sure."

"What do you mean you weren't sure?" She tried to sound calm. "Sure about what?"

"About whether I would mention it to you."

"Why wouldn't you? We've never kept secrets from each other." She could hear the sharpness in her voice. She couldn't help it.

"Gently, Beth. Anyway, I wasn't sure if I really wanted to do it."

"But I told you I didn't mind." She tried to soften her tone.

"I know, but still ..."

She stared at him for a minute, trying to control her fear and anger. She finally put her knitting to one side and went to him.

"Sorry. I didn't mean to snap."

He folded the newspaper, dropped it beside the chair, and pulled her gently onto his lap. "Look, Beth, are you really, really, sure about this? It's a big decision."

She smoothed the frown lines on his forehead with her finger and nodded. "I am quite, quite sure. Tell me about it. Is it with Paul's company? That would be funny if you both ended up flying together, after hardly seeing each other all the way through the war."

She just needed time to get used to the idea.

He paused briefly before answering. "It's in Ireland."

She knew he was watching for her reaction, studying her expression. "Ireland?" It had caught her by surprise. *Ireland! Leaving Bristol. Leaving her family and friends! For Ireland!* "Wow, Michael!"

He was grinning now. "Yes, I'd be back in Ireland, after all these years."

She returned his smile. How could she deny him? It was the career he wanted. It was his country, too. His family was there. Well, some of them were. "Sheelagh and Colm will be jealous of you."

He shook his head. "No, I don't think so. Sheelagh has always been happy here. As for brother Colm, I don't think Ireland is big enough for him!"

She smiled. "You'd be closer to Mary and Pierce."

"And you will too, Beth. You'll love Mary, I know you will, and Joe, and little Norah. And we'll be able to see their new baby, Michael."

She would have to let him do it. How could she say no? "So, have you applied?"

"Of course I haven't. I wouldn't do anything without talking to you about it first." He indicated she should get off his lap. As she stood he continued, "But Paul got an application form. He thought I might be interested, so he sent for one for me."

Thank you, big brother! "Well, well, good for him." She watched her husband delve into the inside pocket of his overcoat and produce the envelope. He waved it at her, smiled, opened it, and spread the contents on the table. She joined him.

"You see." He pointed to the first page, "They want pilots, starting immediately." He sorted through the pages and selected another to show her. "And look what they say here; with my flying experience, I could even be a captain within six months, just like Paul, once I completed the basic hours on type." He turned and hugged her. "Oh, Beth." He put her at arm's length, studied her face. "Are you quite sure you're happy with this?"

She took a deep breath, smiled and kissed him. "Certain, sure, and positive! Now get busy filling out that form and we can have it in the first post in the morning."

He returned her kiss. "I might not even get it," he said. "There're a lot of pilots looking for work. It might not happen." Despite what he was saying, he pulled a chair out from the table, sat, took a pen from his top pocket and began to scan the document. He was smiling.

Beth went back to her chair and watched him.

Good News

Beth had delayed and delayed visiting the doctor until she was sure; until she was truly convinced that the queasy feeling in her stomach couldn't *all* be blamed on Michael's application to go back flying.

She was pregnant! At last! It felt like she'd been waiting forever.

Beth decided she wouldn't tell Michael, not until she had confirmed it with the doctor, not until she was quite, quite sure.

The morning of her appointment she was making breakfast, and Michael was in the bathroom shaving, when she heard the post arrive. It was an official-looking buff envelope, addressed to Mr. Michael Kelly. And it had an Irish stamp.

Not today! Why did it have to arrive today?

"Post?"

Michael was standing behind her. She nodded and handed it to him. He ripped open the envelope, scanned the contents, and gave a loud whoop. Beth's stomach churned but she forced a smile. Perspiration formed on her top lip.

He lifted her up. "We're going to Ireland," he shouted as he swung her around, then he laughed, and put her down. "Thank you, Beth." His face suddenly became very serious. "Thank you."

All laughter was now gone. He took her two hands in his and held her gaze with his. "I'm going home, Beth. Finally, I can go home. To stay! Thank you, my love." He released his grip and stepped back, looking a little embarrassed.

Beth didn't know what to say, she studied his face. His grave, earnest face. What could she say?

Michael gave a wry smile, and glanced at his watch. "I'm late, I have to rush. We'll celebrate this evening. Thank you, sweetheart."

How could she not be happy for him?

"What about your breakfast?"

"I'll be fine." He tucked the letter into his jacket pocket, "Bye, love, see you later." He kissed her. "Oh, Beth, we're going to Ireland!" He opened the door. "I'll try and finish work early. Love you!"

He was gone.

Celebrate! She sighed and closed the door.

After seeing the doctor, Beth slowly walked home through the cold November morning. A whisper of snowflakes danced in the air. The first snow of winter, she thought. But that was all. She hardly noticed as the flakes gathered in intensity, moistening her face and dampening her hair. She was too preoccupied, not sure if she felt happy or sad, nervous or excited. So much to think about, to decide.

Once home, she made herself a cup of tea, sat at the table, and tried to clear her thoughts.

Celebrate!

The word kept pounding in her head. Now that she had the news about the baby it *should* be a double celebration, but ever since she'd left the doctor's office, all she could think about was the possibility of having her first baby in a foreign country. Leaving Bristol! Leaving her family! *And* Michael would be back flying. He'd left in such high spirits that morning, how could she tell him the huge muddle of feelings she had? Of course she was happy for him, and about the baby but ... *Could she really do all this? His new job, them moving to Ireland, her first baby. Could she cope? Having the baby was the most important thing, wasn't it? Perhaps they should put off moving to Ireland? He could apply again later.* But he had the letter. *So how could she disappoint him now?*

She would talk to her mother and see what she thought, but she had to tell Michael about the baby first.

All day she paced the flat, torn between her excitement about the pregnancy, and her concerns about their new life. *But the baby comes first.*

By the time Michael arrived home, she was ready. She would tell him about the baby, then they would decide. He would understand.

* * *

She stood at the window watching for his arrival. When she saw him, she'd opened the door before he was at the gate. She barely gave him time to remove his coat before she tugged him into the living room and made him sit at the table. Then she stepped back feeling a little awkward and shy.

"We're going to have a baby."

Michael was stunned into silence. She saw it was a moment before he fully understood what she had said; then an enormous smile lit up his face.

He jumped up. "Beth, this is wonderful." he said, hugging her tight, kissing her. "We have to go and tell your mother, and Paul, and Evelyn. Everyone!"

For the second time that day he lifted her off her feet and whirled her around. "Oh, Beth, it's a whole new life. A new baby, a new job, a new country."

"Michael, stop it, we'll break the furniture," she said, laughing.

He stopped twirling her immediately and, oh so gently, lowered her until she stood, a little unsteadily, in front of him. "Oh, Beth, I'm sorry, so sorry," he tenderly rested his hand on her stomach. "I'm sorry, baby; I didn't mean to make you dizzy." He bent and kissed her stomach, then looked up at her. "When, Beth? When? How long do we have? We have to be settled in; we have to have a house. Will your mother come over? You can't have a baby without your mother being there. How are you feeling? You didn't say anything this morning. How long have you known?"

He dropped into his armchair and stared up at her in amazement, clearly trying to absorb all the implications of her news.

"I just saw Dr. Crosby this morning," she said, "after you went to work. I wanted to be sure."

"What did he say, exactly?" Michael jumped up and pulled her chair closer to the fire. "Sit down, Beth; you have to take it easy. Mind yourself. Can I get you anything? Would you like a cup of tea?"

Now she was *really* laughing. His excitement was infectious. "Stop it, crazy man. I'm fine." He gestured to her chair, mock frowned, so she sat. "I've been feeling a bit sick, but only in the mornings; it's usually gone by lunchtime."

"Why didn't you tell me? Can you take anything for it? Are you all right now? Do you want to go to bed for a rest?"

"Michael Kelly, sit down and stop fussing."

He sat opposite her, leaned forward on the edge of his chair, his hands gripped tightly together. She could see he was trying hard to contain his excitement. "So can we tell people? Can we write and tell Pierce and Mary? ... And we have to tell Sheelagh. And Colm, I suppose. Have you told your family?"

"Stop," she said holding up her hand. "Too many questions; give me a chance." She sat back, and smiled at him. "No, of course I haven't said anything to anyone yet. *You* had to be the first; you know you did. I thought you'd never get home from work." She paused. "I really don't know if we should tell anyone else for a little while, Michael, just to be sure." She saw the disappointment in his face. "On the other hand I don't think either of us are going to be able to keep it secret for long." She smiled again, and shrugged. "So maybe we could go over to Mum's tomorrow night, when you get home from work?"

Michael glanced at the clock on the mantelpiece. "Why can't we go over this evening? It's only eight o'clock. We can be there in half an hour. They'll still be up, you know they will."

"But you haven't eaten yet. Your dinner is ready. I just have to heat it up."

"Do you think I can eat? Are you mad, woman?" He jumped up. "Let's go and tell them." Then he stopped. "Unless you'd rather stay in and take it easy? Are you sure you don't want a cup of tea?"

He knelt in front of her and caught both her hands in his. "Beth, I am just so happy. I love you so much."

She leaned forward and kissed him. "I love you too. All right ... " she stood and tugged him to stand up. "Come on, let's go to Mum's."

"You stay right there; I'll get your coat, and a scarf. It's snowing out there, you have to stay warm."

She watched him hurry out into the hall. They would have to talk. Perhaps they could put off going to Ireland, just for a while, just until she had the baby. But not tonight. She could wait. Tonight they would go and tell her family.

Plans

The Howard family was thrilled with the double good news. No one seemed to think that moving to a new country when expecting your first baby was a problem. Beth's mother promised that nothing would prevent her from being with her daughter for the birth. Reassured and incapable, she realized, of disappointing Michael, Beth finally accepted that she and Michael would begin a whole new life very soon. With everyone in the family so happy for them, how could she bring herself to tell them what a coward she was? And she couldn't go back on her promise, ask him to forfeit his chance to fly again. He was so excited about it all.

* * *

Things were happening so fast that Beth's head was in a constant whirl. The airline wrote to say that they wanted Michael as soon as possible, and after an intense evening of discussion, he and Beth agreed that Michael should travel on ahead to begin training and find accommodation. Beth would follow once she had found a moving company to pack and transport what little furniture and clothing they had. Michael made her promise she wouldn't carry any suitcases when she travelled.

The night before Michael's departure, Paul arranged a farewell party in the Carpenters Arms, their local pub. During the evening Michael finally found an opportunity to speak to Colm. He'd been trying to get hold of him for days, but his brother always seemed to be busy or unavailable.

"I have a favor to ask of you, Colm."

"Sure, what is it?"

As soon as his brother spoke Michael realized that Colm was more than a little 'worse for wear' with the drink. Michael had tried to contact him a couple of times, but Colm was never at home. Sheelagh had promised to make sure he came to the farewell, and he did, but Michael suspected he had already been drinking. This wasn't the right time, even though he was leaving the next day.

"Perhaps not tonight. Could you call around to the flat tomorrow before I leave? Or I could call over to your place if that suits you better?"

Colm held his hands up in mock alarm. "No, no, I can come over to you, just as long as you don't want me there too early, eh?"

"I've to be at the railway station for four o'clock."

"That's all right then." Colm indicated a blonde woman in a low cut blouse sitting at the bar, her hands cupped around a large brandy glass. She was smiling invitingly at him. "I've a little business to attend to tonight," he continued, "and I don't want to be leaping out of bed at the crack of dawn, now do I?" He raised an eyebrow at his brother.

Michael ignored the implication. Colm always seemed to have a woman close by, and rarely the same one twice. "That would be fine. Come round at lunchtime, will you? We may even be able to come up with something to eat, though the flat's in chaos."

"Ah, yes, off to the land of milk and honey then, aren't we? Weren't the Irish the clever people not to get mixed up in the nasty old war then? No shortages over there, I suppose. I hear you can have all the eggs, and cheese, and meat your heart desires."

"No, I don't think so. Mary says they have shortages in Southern Ireland too; it just isn't quite as bad."

Colm hardly seemed to be listening. "I should take a little trip over there myself," he continued. "I bet I could make a pretty penny bringing back a side or two of bacon. Do you have any idea how much that would make in the market? A pretty penny, I tell you." He nudged Michael and laughed. "But I suspect it would be a bit difficult to stuff a load of eggs down my trousers, wouldn't you think?" He laughed again and staggered slightly.

Michael didn't like his brother when he drank. He also hadn't liked that Colm dealt in black market goods during the war, and that he was probably still doing so. Colm always said they weren't black market goods, just 'difficult to get' items that he was able to 'locate.' Despite his misgivings, Michael knew family was important and, especially for his sister Sheelagh's sake, he tried not to make judgments about their brother.

He avoided making any critical comment now. "Tomorrow, then? One o'clock?" he said.

"I'll be there." Colm punched Michael gently on the shoulder, "Can't refuse a request from the baby of the family, can we?"

Michael wondered if he'd made the right decision. He didn't have much choice. Sheelagh still lived at home and he didn't want to involve Jim Porter in any of his business. Anyway she only got a small wage from her stepfather, even though she was now managing "Porter's Haberdashery and Clothing Emporium" whilst the old man recovered from his 'heart problem.' Michael didn't want to ask any of Beth's family for any more favors either, and Paul was away so much.

No, it had to be Colm. He just hoped his brother would be able to help.

* * *

It was half past two before Colm arrived. When Beth answered the door, she noticed he was wearing the same clothes he'd worn the previous evening in the pub. Her brother-in-law looked as if he hadn't had much sleep either. Beth could never understand why Ev thought he was so good-looking. Well, perhaps he was, in an Errol Flynn, greasy, sort of way, especially with the thin moustache he had now. She didn't like Errol Flynn. Far too smarmy.

He smiled and leaned forward to kiss her on the cheek.

"Hello, beautiful. Is my brother here?"

"Hello, Colm." She stepped back but was still almost overwhelmed by the strong, stale, odor of cigarettes and beer as he passed her in the narrow hallway. "Michael, Colm's here," she called. "Go on into the living room, Colm. He'll be in directly." She excused herself and hurried to the bathroom.

Colm did as she asked.

Michael came out of the bedroom, "Sorry Colm, didn't hear your knock, just finished my packing. Thanks for coming." He looked around the cluttered living room. Piles of clothing, kitchen utensils, books, and assorted half-filled boxes were everywhere. "Here, sit here," he said, lifting a pile of neatly folded laundry from his armchair.

Colm eased himself gingerly into the chair. "Thanks, Mike. The old head's banging a bit. Might have had a drop too much to drink last night." He leaned back and looked up at his brother. "So, what can I do for you? Want me to look after your little lady after you've gone?" He leered.

Michael tried to smile at his brother's tasteless joke. "No, I think she'll be fine with her family looking after her, thank you. ... Umm ..." *Damn, he wished he didn't have to do this. It was awkward, and it was embarrassing.* "I have a favor to ask Colm."

"Yes, so you said last night. Come on, man, spit it out. You look like you've swallowed an extra-nasty pill."

"Well. I have an insurance policy; a life insurance policy."

"Good for you! I'm glad one of us is taking his responsibilities seriously."

"Well, yes. I took it out with my own insurance company when I joined."

"Yes, ... so? Well done?"

"Well, ... it's just that I would like to keep it up, even though we're moving to Ireland. What with me going back flying, and with the baby on the way, you know. Just in case. You know what I mean?" Michael smiled sheepishly. "It's just that ... well, it's supposed to be paid monthly ... and I'll be away ... I'll have to make arrangements to pay it when I start getting paid. But ..."

"Good God, Michael. Just tell me what you want, will you? I've never seen you so damned fidgety. You're making me nervous."

"Well, with the move and everything, and having to rent a place when I get over there I don't actually have enough to pay for the next month or two. Just 'til I get settled."

"Oohh ... you need some cash." Colm reached into the inside pocket of his jacket. "No problem, little brother. Happen to be flush right now. How much do you need?" As he spoke he removed money from his wallet and thrust it at his brother.

Michael took a step back, held up his hands and shook his head. "NO! ... No, thank you. That's fine, no, thanks, Colm. It's just ... could I ask you to pay the premium, just for a couple of months, just 'til I get sorted over there?"

"Of course I will. But why don't you take the cash, give it to them yourself?" He again held the money up to Michael.

"It's not the way they do it. They come and collect every month. I asked if I could post it to them. They said they need the book signed every month. I knew that really. Look, Colm, I don't want to worry Beth. She's nervous enough about my going back flying, without bringing up my life insurance." He took an envelope from his pocket, "It's quite straightforward, really, if you could just tide me over until I get my first pay check, or so." He took out a document and a small booklet and handed them to his brother. "The new man, Pete Williams, will be taking over my customers. He said he can call to you to collect the money each month, if that's all right with you. Whenever it suits you."

"Fine, I can do that." Colm flipped through the pages of the booklet. "That's certainly not going to break the bank."

"I'll pay you back the couple of months you put in as soon as I can. After that I can send you a regular cheque. If you could keep paying it for me? I did ask the company, but they don't have agents in Ireland. It keeps people in jobs, I suppose, having it collected every month."

"Relax, Michael, for God's sake. Consider it done."

"It's important, Colm. The policy will lapse if it's not paid every month."

"No problem, old chap. Not *that* hard, is it?"

"Thank you. I really do appreciate this. I didn't want to ask, but I'm just a bit stuck at the moment."

""Don't give it another thought. Might even take one out myself. The folks are always saying I should get a steady job, settle down, all the usual stuff."

"How are they?"

"Not doing too well actually, old boy. Father's business pretty much closed down during the war ... not a lot of call for bespoke tailors when everyone's in uniform. But it hasn't picked up much, what with the government giving out those bloody awful, free demob suits to everyone."

Michael looked down at his own government-issue demobilization suit.

Colm laughed. "Sorry Mike, no reflection on you."

Michael shrugged, "Well, thanks anyway. For the loan, I mean."

"My pleasure. Your agent friend knows where I live, does he?"

Michael nodded, "I gave him your address."

Michael heard the bathroom door open. "Beth is a bit wound up," he whispered hastily. "I haven't discussed this with her yet."

"Understood. Understood." Colm took the envelope, put it in his pocket and struggled to his feet. "As good as done, Mike, as good as done. Well," he thrust out his hand. "Good luck in the new job. I suppose you'll get to see the Irish side of the family a bit more now eh? Beats me how you understand that accent of theirs. Still, you don't seem to mind."

The two brothers shook hands as Beth joined them. She looked a little pale.

"You look almost as bad as I feel," laughed Colm.

Michael put his hand out to his wife. "Are you all right, love?"

Beth took his hand, nodded, and managed a faint smile. "Sorry, Colm," she rested her hand on her stomach. "Still not used to the baby, I suppose."

"Understood. Pretty rough I hear. Hope you're feeling better soon."

When they reached the front door Colm shook Michael's hand again. "Just mind yourself, Mike; you'll be flying passengers now, not bombs."

Michael frowned a 'say nothing' warning as Colm laughed again and turned to Beth.

"I'll probably see you again before you go, Beth. Meantime, take care, mind yourself." He hugged her, and gave her a moist kiss on the cheek. He winked at Michael and patted his breast coat pocket. "And I'll take care of that little job for you, never you fear."

As he walked to the gate Beth looked quizzically at her husband.

Michael shrugged. "Just some bits of paperwork I didn't get done on a policy. He's going to look after it for me." He gave Colm a half wave and closed the door. "Now, I had better get going myself or I'm going to miss my train."

In the bustle of Michael's departure, Colm's visit was not mentioned again.

Moving In

"Michael, don't be silly. I'm too heavy, put me down."

"I will not, this is our first real home and I'm going to carry you over the threshold, whether you like it or not, Mrs. Kelly."

He pushed the door wider with his foot and carried her into the hallway, nudged the door closed with his shoulder, and continued to carry her all the way to the kitchen where he lowered her gently in front of the kitchen sink.

"There you are. And there you will stay, wife, for the next ..." he paused in thought for a moment "... oh, about fifty years." He rested his forehead against hers. "Do you think you could put up with me for another fifty years, my dear, sweet, Beth?"

"Not if *this* is where I have to stay! Tied to the kitchen sink!" She laughed and pushed him away.

"Oh, all right, you can have time off for good behavior, *and* good cooking ... and I'll give you some time for your other wifely duties, too. Very important, those wifely duties."

Beth smiled at him and turned to look out of the back window.

"The garden's a bit of a wilderness." She rubbed her hand over her slightly swollen stomach, "I wish this bump wasn't in the way. I could get out there and do some digging."

"You will do no such thing! That does *not* come under the heading of wifely duties. If there is any digging to be done, *I* will be the one to do it. Though, now I come to think of it, I'm not sure with what. We've no gardening tools yet, have we?"

He had followed her to the window and now stood behind her, viewing the weed-clogged and rubble-strewn garden. "Unless you think a knife and fork might be enough? Anyway ..." he reached both arms around her and tenderly placed his hands on top of hers. "This bump isn't in the way. You have a few months to go yet, Mrs. Kelly. It's only when you can't fit in through the front door any more that we'll know you're ready. I'm telling you, Mary was so big with her last baby I thought it would be triplets, at least."

"But your sister was big to start with, wasn't she? She was quite big, well wide, when I saw her last, and she wasn't even pregnant then."

Michael smiled. "Yes, bless her; she's a lot bigger now than when I first met her. Slip of thing she was then, just like you. However," he turned, "Speaking of the front door," he pointed along the hallway. "That's the first thing that's going to get done, before we tackle the garden. I hate black. Let's paint it a nice bright color."

"That's fine with me, as long as you are doing the painting. How about blue?"

"Blue it is."

He turned back to look at Beth, raised a hand to her chin, and tugged her toward him. "I love you, Beth. Thank you for coming to Ireland. Thank you for letting me take this job." He traced her lips with his finger. "And thank you for being you."

He kissed her, softly, slowly.

"I'm glad we came. I love this house." She said, kissed him in return, and hugged him close. She stepped back and caught his hand. "Let's look at the rest of it, shall we?"

He laughed and agreed. She led the way out of the kitchen and into the hall.

"It's going to be lovely, isn't it, Michael?" She opened the door to the first room. "This is going to be the dining room." She turned back to him. "Is that all right? I want the sitting room at the front; that room gets the most sunshine."

"Whatever you want is fine with me. We have so much more space than in the flat, so it's going to be a while before we have enough furniture to fill it all. We'll be eating at the kitchen table for a few months yet, so you can call this room anything you like."

"Dining room it is!" she laughed and Michael followed her back out to the hall and into the front room. "See what I mean?"

The spring sun streamed into the empty space, sparkling the drifting dust motes. It also exposed the grubbiness of the wallpaper and highlighted the chipped paintwork. Michael went to a clean square on the floral wallpaper.

"Do you think we could find a bunch of pictures the same sizes as these?" He indicated the other ghost shapes around the room, where pictures had been, "So we don't have to redecorate?"

"No, sorry, the wallpaper has to go." Beth pulled a face. "It didn't look half so dirty when the agent showed us around."

"I know, but houses always look better with furniture. You know I looked at lots of houses before you arrived, Beth. This really was the best we could afford. Don't worry, love, it will be fine once we move in. I promise."

"I know. Let's go upstairs, shall we? I want to see the nursery."

"Lead on Mrs. K. I'm right behind you."

On the way they looked into the bathroom on the half landing. It was small, and the ceiling sloped low over the bath.

"We're going to have to mind our heads climbing into this," he said, as he leant over the grubby enamel tub, "and it looks like the tap drips too," he added, pointing to the rust-brown stain that ran from tap to plug hole.

"I'll write to Mum and ask her how we can get the stain off. It'll be fine." Beth tugged at Michael's arm. "Come on, nursery!!"

He followed her up the last four steps and into the back bedroom.

"Oh, my!" he said looking around the gloomy room. "This will definitely have to be re-done."

"I know, and I'll help. I know exactly what I want."

"Do you now, madam?"

She smiled at him. "I do sir, and it's our first job, well, after the front door. I want lemon paint on the wood, and pretty wallpaper, with animals on, but it has to be green and lemon."

"Does it really? And why would that be?"

"'Cos we don't know what the baby is yet, so we can't do it pink or blue and anyway this room doesn't get the sun like the front of the house, so the yellow will make it seem more sunshiny, and yellow and green can be for a boy or a girl."

"You know, you've become very bossy since you got pregnant, Beth Kelly. I'm going to have to sort you out a bit."

"Are you indeed, Mr. Kelly? With whose help, may I ask?"

"With the help of my son," he said firmly, pointing at her belly, "Do you hear that, young man?"

They both laughed and Michael took Beth by the hand. "Now for the most important room," he said, as he led her into the front bedroom.

They stood in the center of the room, arm in arm, smiling, and saying nothing.

New Arrival

Kelly. Michael and Elizabeth
Kelly are proud to announce the
arrival of their beautiful baby
daughter, Ellen Mary Kelly. Born
June 10th at The Talbot Nursing
Home, Drumcondra Road, Dublin.
Mother and baby are well.

"Did you ask them to put it in the Bristol papers, as well, Michael?"
"I did, my love."

"It seems a bit grand, putting it in the paper."

"But everyone will want to know, and it's the quickest way."

She studied the newspaper notice again. "I still think we should have put Captain Michael Kelly."

"That would have been showing off!"

"When do you think Mum will arrive?"

Michael laughed. "I only sent the telegram a couple of hours ago, my love. I think you'll have to give her a day or two to get herself organized. Sister O'Brien says you will be here for the rest of the week anyway, so there's no rush."

Beth smiled down at the tiny baby cradled in her arms. "I know. I just can't wait until Mum sees her. She is beautiful, isn't she?"

"Yes, she is." He laughed again.

Since he arrived back in the nursing home after sending telegrams, buying flowers, and delivering the announcement into the newspaper office, he and Beth had taken turns holding the infant and telling each other how beautiful, and perfect, she was.

He leaned over and gently stroked the baby's tiny hand. "Even her finger-nails are beautiful."

"When are you flying again?"

"I'm on 'earlies.' The lads were very good, said they would swap, do whatever I wanted. I thought if I did 'earlies' I would be able to come in and see you and the baby at both visiting times."

She lay back on the pillows. "The flowers are beautiful, thank you."

"You're welcome, Mrs. Kelly. Now would you and our daughter please get some rest. I have a few things I need to do."

"Like what, Michael Kelly. What's more important than us?"

"It's a surprise."

"Oh, that's not fair, you have to tell me."

"No, I don't. It wouldn't be a surprise then."

Sister O'Brien peeked her head around the door. "Baby's feeding time, Mrs. Kelly. Time for you to leave now, Mr. Kelly. Mammy and baby's quiet time."

Michael nodded, and stood. He kissed Beth, then the baby. "See you tomorrow. Love you."

"Love you too."

* * *

It was Sister O'Brien who walked with Beth and her new baby to the front door of the nursing home. Michael hurried ahead, "to open the taxi door," as he said. But when she arrived on the steps Michael stood holding open the passenger door of his surprise; their first car.

* * *

Despite her fears, Beth loved their new life in Dublin. It was all so different from the dingy flat in Bristol. They had settled in quickly, and she found she enjoyed all the painting and decorating, gardening and housekeeping, even though Michael fretted through her entire pregnancy that she was doing too much.

She did miss her family sometimes, but the neighbors were mostly newly-weds like themselves, and they soon made friends. When Beth went into 'The Talbot' again two years later, this time for baby Brendan, it was Oonagh and Liam next door who looked after Ellen. Neighbors became their family, life was good, and Michael was so happy to be back flying.

Eventually, even when Michael arrived home hours late from work because of weather, re-rostering, or 'technical glitches' as Michael called them, Beth learned not to get into a panic, not to imagine the worst. She finally accepted the delays as part of his job. It wasn't like in the war. There was no fighting, no enemies, no danger.

1954

The Wake

O nly Mary's mournful keening disturbed the quiet in the crowded room. She rocked back and forth, eyes closed, oblivious, her face moon-pale. She was dressed in black, entirely in black, as were all the women. The men wore their Sunday suits, pressed shirts, stiff collars, black ties and armbands. The women sat on straight-backed chairs in the dim, curtained half-light. They sipped tea, balanced plates on their laps, and accepted or declined food with an almost imperceptible nod or shake of the head. Their husbands stood behind them nursing small glasses of whiskey or clutching tumblers and bottles of stout. They looked distinctly ill at ease in this house of mourning. No one spoke. No one knew what to say.

All eyes went to the door when Ellen ran in, calling for her mother. Seeing so many people turn toward her, she came to an abrupt halt.

A woman reached out her hand to the child. "I think your Mammy's gone upstairs for a rest, alanna."

Ellen backed away from the stranger, thrust her hands behind her back and shook her head. She ran from the room. "I want Mammy!" she wailed as she climbed the stairs.

"How old is she?" whispered an older woman, her voice barely audible over the keening.

"Six, I believe," said another.

They shared sorrowful glances and shook their heads in tragic disbelief. One fumbled in her pocket, pulled out an already sodden handkerchief, and dabbed at her eyes.

"I live at the other end of the road," the older woman explained. "I only heard this morning. I don't really know them very well, but I came to pay my respects."

"She has a young fella as well, Brendan, and he barely four," another woman said, "Their grandmother has taken him out for a walk, to get away from all this for a while."

A young woman came from the kitchen carrying an empty tray. She circled the room, collected discarded cups, plates, and glasses, asked each woman in a low voice, "Can I bring you anything else? A nice fresh cup of tea … or a drop of sherry, perhaps?" Everyone shook their heads. She returned to the kitchen, carefully balancing her laden tray.

After a while, Mary's keening quieted, though she continued to cry, rocking back and forth with her face buried in her hands. Sheelagh sat beside her along with their sister-in-law, Maeve, silent in their shared mourning. When Mary's cries eased Sheelagh put her arms around her older sister and hugged her close. Mary turned her face into the comforting shoulder.

"Why? Why?" she sobbed, her words muffled. "It's not fair, Sheelagh. Not right. Not after all that has happened. What will become of the childer? How will Beth manage? He was too young."

"They will be fine, Mary, I promise. We'll make sure of that." Sheelagh gently raised her sister's chin. "We will make sure of that, won't we?" She held Mary's gaze until the woman's sobbing eased and she nodded.

When she was sure Mary had calmed a little, Sheelagh gave her sister a reassuring smile. "I'm going to see how Beth is. Can I get you something to eat before I go?"

"No, not just now, Shee, thank you."

"You have to eat, Mary. You've had nothing all day. You'll be no good to anyone if you don't. Now, I'll be back in a minute, and I'm going to make you have something then, whether you want to or not." She gave her sister another hug before she left.

Sheelagh stepped into the hallway and glanced towards the kitchen. It bustled with activity; women making pots of tea, washing and drying dishes, slicing and buttering bread, carving ham, and arranging sandwiches and thick wedges of fruit cake onto plates.

She sighed. People had been so kind. Everyone who came brought something; cooked meat, fresh baked bread, pies, cakes. Mary explained that it was so the family would have enough to offer mourners at the wake and to be sure the family did not want in the days after the funeral.

So different in Ireland, thought Sheelagh. In Bristol, when her father died, her mother put 'house private' in the newspaper announcement and asked Sheelagh to arrange a luncheon for the mourners at a local hotel after the funeral. No one came to the house with food or to sympathize. Sheelagh arranged another luncheon when her mother died, thinking that's how things were done.

A woman came from the kitchen carrying a teapot and milk jug. Sheelagh stepped out of her way. It seemed so unnecessary, so much to eat and drink, at a time when nobody felt like it. Still, maybe it gives them something to do. Everyone feels so helpless, so hopeless. She sighed and started up the stairs, following the faint chatter of Ellen's voice and Beth's subdued replies.

She knocked on the bedroom door. "May I come in, Beth? It's me, Sheelagh."

Beth said something quietly, and she heard Ellen's light footsteps coming toward the door. The child fumbled with the handle and the door opened.

"Mammy says come in, Aunty Sheelagh." The young girl opened the door wider and stared up at Sheelagh, her large, blue eyes peeking from below a thick fringe of dark hair. Such a beautiful child, Sheelagh thought. God love her, she looks so confused. She *must* be so confused by everything happening in the house. Sheelagh hadn't agreed with Beth's mother's suggestion that the children should not be told what had happened. "Not yet," she'd said, "not until Beth is better able to help them deal with it." Sheelagh didn't think it was a good idea, thought they should be told, but Beth had agreed with her mother, and Sheelagh accepted their decision.

"Thank you, sweetheart." Sheelagh stepped into the room, rested her hand on the little girl's head and looked beyond her to where Beth sat on the edge of the bed, her head bowed, her hands clutching a wadded handkerchief.

"Can I do anything for you, Beth? Can I get you anything?"

Beth shook her head, but didn't look up.

"Do you want me to get rid of the people downstairs? Would you like to have the house to yourself for a while? Give you a break?"

Beth shook her head again. "No, it doesn't matter. I know they mean well, it's the way they do things here." She looked up at her sister-in-law and gave a rueful smile. "But I'm glad Mary has stopped making that noise."

Sheelagh smiled too. "Keening, she calls it. It's the first time I've heard it. It's a bit spooky isn't it?" She crouched in front of her sister-in-law and rested her hands over Beth's clenched fists. "Would you like to go for a walk, get some fresh air? Your mother has already taken Brendan out."

Beth took a deep breath and nodded. "That would be nice."

Ellen ran to her mother, "Can I come too, Mammy?" she pleaded. "Can we go to the park? Can I go on the swings? Can I? Can I?"

"We'll see, my love. Go downstairs and get your coat on. I'll be down in a minute."

Sheelagh stood and the two women watched the little girl run from the room. They heard her clatter down the stairs as Beth eased herself off the edge of the bed. The size of her belly made any movement awkward. She stopped, mid-rise, and grimaced. Sheelagh quickly stepped forward, held out her hand, but Beth shook her head, "I'm fine." She took a deep breath and straightened. "He has a strong kick," she said, and smiled, but tears welled in her eyes.

"You're so sure it's a he?"

"Oh, yes," she placed both her hands on her stomach. "This is baby Michael."

The Service

A sea of black-clad mourners sat or knelt in the crowded pews. All were pale-faced, red-eyed, and silent. The somber organ music reverberated to the high vaulted roof of the pro-Cathedral, and its base notes trembled the delicate flowers in the wreaths and floral tributes that covered the altar steps. The priests and altar servers, clad in their black and white soutanes and cassocks, moved silently back and forth across the altar, genuflecting as they passed the tabernacle. Beth remembered when they were young and Michael and her brother were altar boys together. *He was so good-looking even then, everyone said so.* She blinked away her tears and continued to watch the young men as they checked that everything was ready. The priests supervised, not yet time for them to don the purple of their mourning vestments and begin the solemn service, and remembrance, of the deceased.

Beth sat in a front pew with her mother, Margaret, on one side and her sister, Evelyn, on the other. The rest of Beth's and Michael's families filled the remainder of that pew and the two behind. She knew family members of the other deceased sat in pews that stretched back to the open doors at the rear of the church. *So much sadness, so many deaths.* There was little room inside for friends. Outside, friends, neighbors, colleagues and members of the public, all those who wanted to share in the collective grief and mourning of the day, stood in the misty drizzle of a damp, early February morning.

Only Michael's brother, Colm, was missing from the family group. No one had been able to locate him, though Sheelagh had tried. It had been decided that Ellen and Brendan should not be at the ceremony.

"They wouldn't understand, they're too young," Beth's mother had said, "It wouldn't be fair on them, or Beth."

Beth hadn't argued, so earlier that day, before the funeral cars arrived, Maeve took them to a neighbor's house until it was all over. The neighbor, Oonagh had two children of her own, almost the same ages as Ellen and Brendan, and she'd readily agreed.

"It would be the best place for the poor little gosters," she'd said when Maeve asked. "Of course they can come. Why should they suffer any more than they have to? Time enough for them to mourn when they have a better understanding of their loss."

* * *

The Requiem Mass was long and concelebrated by five priests. Every now and then Beth felt the baby pummel and pound at her stomach. She sat for a great deal of the service. The smoky pall of incense that continually wafted from the thurible clouded the altar in a soft grey smoke, and its heavy perfume cloyed at her throat and made her feel ill. Occasionally she heard muffled thuds and shuffling behind and knew that the oppressive air was causing more than one mourner to succumb and be helped to the rear of the church by unctuous attendants. She bit her lip hard, determined not to seem weak and not to faint.

There were no caskets on the altar. The Company had said that no remains had yet been found since the aircraft's deadly plunge into the Mediterranean and that they didn't expect that to change. In the days since the crash Beth had read in the papers over and over again that only small fragments of cloth and debris had been found floating on the oily waters. Her mother had eventually taken the newspapers away from her.

No, this was a memorial service, not a funeral. *And the only formal farewell we will probably ever have*, she thought. *Oh, Michael! My dear, sweet, Michael! After everything! After you survived the war. It's not fair. I shouldn't have let you fly again, I should have stopped you. I could have!* She clenched her fists until she felt her nails dig deep into the palms of her hands. *Oh, Michael!*

* * *

44

Beth remained seated when the service was over. Dazed and numb, she sat as an interminable line of people waited patiently to shake her hand, sympathize with her loss, and murmur consoling words. She couldn't cry. There were no tears left, just a deep ache and loneliness. She didn't recognize most of those who spoke to her and found it hard to respond to their expressions of sympathy, but she nodded, did her best to smile her thanks, and fervently wished the nightmare would end.

When it was over and the line ended, Margaret helped Beth stand. She wrapped an arm protectively around her daughter's shoulder. White-knuckled, trembling, Beth gripped her mother's hand. They stepped into the aisle and followed the priests and altar boys back past the mourners who had now returned to their pews to witness the solemn procession. At the entrance to the church the altar boys filed silently away down the side aisles. The priests remained and stood on either side of the open doors to sympathize one last time with the bereaved as they left the church and descended the shallow flight of steps to the street.

* * *

A long line of black funeral cars waited at the curbside. A dark-suited man held open the door of the first car. Beth flinched as cameras flashed from amongst the small cluster of newspaper reporters and photographers gathered to one side. Her mother and Evelyn quickly helped her into the car and took their places on either side of her. Her sister Maggie followed and her brother Paul sat in front. The driver gently closed the doors, took his own seat, and eased the car slowly away from the curb. The crowd lining the narrow street crossed themselves in silence as the cortege passed. On leaving Marlborough Street, the mourner's cars went in their different directions; there was no cemetery, no burial, no closure, and no 'after' gathering of mourners.

Decisions

Margaret sat on the couch beside her daughter, gripping Beth's hand. Now that the memorial service was over and most of the friends and family had left, only Margaret and Sheelagh remained in the house. Margaret had promised Beth she would stay in Dublin as long as her daughter needed her, but now that the house was quieter and the service over, she was anxious to persuade her daughter to move back to Bristol. She was convinced it was the best solution.

"You can't stay here, Beth, *really* you can't. Come home, come back to Bristol, dear. At least there you'd have your family around you. You *know* we'd love to have you living closer, especially your brother. He was Michael's best friend after all. You know he'd do anything for you, and the children. The baby's due in less than three months. You can't possibly manage on your own, not with two small children *and* a new baby. If you were in Bristol, we could all help."

"I don't know, Mum. Dublin is my home now, I *like* living here. It's seven years since we left Bristol. A lot of people have forgotten me over there. Here I have friends. And it's the children's home."

Margaret squeezed Beth's hand. "Just think about it, darling, that's all I'm asking. You'll have three children! That's an awful lot to cope with on your own. When you children were young I had your father with me, Lord rest him, and I *still* found looking after all of you hard work."

Beth turned her face to her mother, her eyes sparkling with unshed tears. "How did you manage, Mum, you know, when Dad and George died? I can't imagine how you did it. I can't even imagine life without Michael." She shook her head, "But you lost your husband *and* your son." She gripped her mother's hand tight, pleading, "Tell me how I can do it, Mum. Help me, please."

Margaret smoothed Beth's hair back and brushed away the tears that fell unheeded on her daughter's cheeks. She had to take a deep breath to steady herself before she answered. "You'll manage. You have to, dear." She blinked away her own tears and took another deep breath. "Your children need you, Beth; you just *have* to do it. One day at a time, my love, one day at a time."

The door opened with a bang. Brendan held it open as Sheelagh followed carrying a loaded tea-tray. His aunt smiled down at him as she passed.

"Thank you, darling." She put the tray on the coffee table in front of the couch. "Here we are; a nice, fresh cup of tea, as promised." She saw Brendan eyeing the plate of biscuits and smiled, "Would you like one, sweetheart?" She offered him the plate. He chose a chocolate finger.

"What do you say?" prompted his grandmother.

"Thank you."

"You're welcome, sweetheart. I think those are your favorites, aren't they?" He nodded.

"You may take another. Will you take some for your sister? I think Ellen may be out in the kitchen, or else she's gone up to her room."

The child nodded again, quickly thrust the chocolate finger into his mouth and took the extras his aunt offered, two in each hand. Sheelagh smiled, held the door open, and watched him run down the hall to the kitchen. "Mind you don't fall," she called before closing the door and turning back to the two women.

"I know what your mother's been saying, Beth, and she's right." She sat on the edge of an armchair opposite Margaret and her daughter and poured a small amount of milk into each cup. "Two children and another on the way is just too much." She poured the tea. "I've been thinking about it." She handed the cups to Margaret and Beth, considering her next words carefully. She stirred her own tea as she continued, "You know I have to get back to the business. My Richard is a love, but I get nervous when I leave him looking after the shop for too long." She looked up and smiled, "I don't think my husband, bless him, is the greatest manager in the world, not like Daddy was." She lifted her cup and carefully settled back into her chair. "Anyway, Beth," she said, more firmly, "I've an idea. How would it be if I took Ellen and Brendan back to Bristol with me? I could look after them for as long as you wanted, at *least* until you had the baby, until you have time to decide what you'd like to do." She leaned forward, and smiled encouragement at Beth. "What do you think?"

Margaret looked at the elegant young woman sitting with such poise oppo-site her. "That's a wonderful idea, Sheelagh," she said and turned back to Beth. "Don't you think so, darling? And I could stay here and help you, while we sort things out."

Both women were now looking expectantly at Beth.

"But you don't know how … I mean … you don't have children … I mean … they're hard work, Sheelagh, and you're so busy with the shop. They're a lot of work."

Sheelagh nodded, "And that's exactly what we're saying, Beth."

Margaret nodded her agreement.

Beth slowly placed her cup and saucer back on the coffee table and stared at them. Sheelagh and Margaret watched her, but remained quiet. Finally Beth turned to her mother.

"What about school? Ellen's happy where she is and Brendan's supposed to start infants soon."

Sheelagh hastily put down her cup. "We can work that out. They'll be fine. It won't be that long. I know I'm not used to looking after children, but I'm learning since I've been here, and I'll get better. I promise, Beth. You know I adore them." She clasped her two hands together, pleading. "Oh, Beth, *please* say yes. You *know* I'd love to have them."

Beth thought for a while, took another sip of her tea. "I don't think so. I'm sorry, I know you mean well, but I'd miss them too much."

Margaret again put her arm around her daughter's shoulder. "Of course you would, darling, but you have to think of the new baby. You have to look after yourself. Yourself, and the house, and all the things that will have to be re-organized, will be quite enough for you right now."

Beth looked up at her mother, then Sheelagh. "I don't know … they've been through so much this past two weeks … I don't know if they could cope."

"We'll tell them it's an adventure, with a trip on a boat, and a train! They'll love it. And you know that Richard and I will take good care of them."

"What about your shop?"

"Don't you worry about that. As long as I'm close by, Richard can always fetch me if he has any problems."

Again, there was a pensive silence in the room. The children were squabbling in the distance, but no one moved. Margaret sipped her tea. Sheelagh reached for a biscuit and nibbled on it. Suddenly Beth slammed her cup back onto the tray and stood.

"Everyone is trying to tell me what to do." She stepped to the curtained window, "And no one has any idea what it's like." She turned to her mother. "*Nobody* knows how I feel. You're all making plans behind my back. You're deciding for me. It's too quick. I'm not ready. It's not fair to make me do things. I don't want to lose them." She turned to Sheelagh. "Don't you remember, Sheelagh? Don't you remember when you were taken away? Brendan and Ellen aren't much older than you and Michael were. How could you ask me to do it to them? You have to remember what it was like!"

The room was very quiet. Sheelagh and Margaret put down their cups and Margaret hurried to her daughter. She tried to put her arm around Beth's shoulder, but Beth shrugged it off.

"No, Mum, just leave me alone. I want Michael. I just want Michael." She sank to her knees, sobbing.

"Oh, Beth, my poor Beth." Margaret knelt beside her daughter. "I know, I really do. I lost your father, don't forget."

"I'm sorry, Beth." Sheelagh spoke very quietly. "I do remember. I'm sorry."

The door burst open and Ellen rushed into the room shouting and waving a ragged piece of newspaper. "Mammy, Mammy, Look what I found. It's a picture of Daddy. I found it in the paper. I've torn it out, I'm going to show Daddy when he comes home. Brendan wanted it, but I found it first."

The child stopped when she saw her mother and grandmother kneeling on the floor and all three women staring at her. Her mother burst into tears and covered her face with her hands.

Ellen looked to her grandmother, "Why is Mammy crying again?" she asked.

Margaret shook her head, but her lips were pressed tight and she couldn't answer. She gently helped Beth to her feet. The little girl watched them in puzzled silence and handed the roughly torn page to her grandmother. Margaret looked down at a grainy photograph of Michael in the center of the page under the banner headline that read,

All Perish in Devastating Air Crash.

She wondered where the girl had found the newspaper. She had been so careful to hide them all.

Sheelagh quickly went to the little girl and put her arm around her shoulder. "That is a nice idea, Ellen." She gently took the ragged piece of newspaper from the older woman. "Let's go and put it somewhere safe, shall we?"

* * *

It was several days before the subject of taking the children to England was mentioned again, though both Margaret and Sheelagh continued to discuss it between themselves. People were still calling, offering their condolences, crying.

"It's not fair on them. There's too much sadness in the house and they don't understand," said Margaret to Sheelagh as they dried dishes one day after lunch.

"Perhaps we should explain to them, now. Ellen keeps asking when her daddy is coming home."

"No, not yet. Beth can hardly cope with her own grief; she's not ready yet, and the children are too young."

Margaret remained adamant on the subject, as she had been from the start. Beth agreed, though Sheelagh thought that was only because she couldn't bring herself to tell them. Maybe she felt it would make everything too final somehow.

Eventually, a week after the memorial service, Beth brought up the subject herself. It had been a particularly trying day, with too many visitors, and the children had been particularly fractious.

"Maybe it would be a good idea to send Ellen and Brendan to Bristol. Just for a short time," she said that evening, when the children were in bed. "Just until I sort myself out." She added hastily, "I'm not saying yes ... and we'd have to ask them. If they are not happy with the idea ..."

"Oh, they would be, I promise you." Sheelagh broke in. "I would make it sound like the best holiday they ever had. I would make it the best holiday they ever had, I promise. I really would do my very best, Beth."

"I'll see." Beth still sounded doubtful. "I have to think about it." Her eyes filled with tears. "I'd miss them so much."

Margaret hugged her daughter closer. "It would only be for a little while, Beth darling, just a couple of months. Just until you have the baby. Remember, your sisters would be there too, as well as Paul, and you know Sheelagh and Richard would take great care of them. The children would be fine. In fact, I'm sure they'd be quite spoiled."

Beth gave a faint smile through her tears.

"I'll see." She took a deep breath and changed the subject. "I got a note from our lawyer, Mr. Timmons, this morning. He said he'd like to come and talk over a few things with me, when I'm ready. I suppose it's about money. I've no idea how we're fixed financially. Michael took care of all of that." She paused, struggling to hold back the tears. "He took care of everything." She turned to her mother. "I'll think about it ... about the children, Mum ... perhaps I *should* let them go away for a while.

Permission

Sheelagh pushed coin after coin into the slot. "Hello? ... Hello? ... Doris is that you? ... Is Mr. Hudson there?"

A passing car backfired. There was more beeping on the phone. Sheelagh pumped in more money. "Sorry? ... Doris? ... Look, find Richard and ask him to call me back right away, will you? ... Sorry? ... Yes. It's a telephone box, but I'll wait here. ...Tell him I need to talk to him. Take down this number, will you?"

She called out the numbers, there was more beeping. "I'll hang up and wait, Doris. Thank you. 'Bye." They were cut off.

She hung up and looked around her. The phone box was dirty and it smelled. There were cigarette stubs, ash, and stains on the floor, and the directory was well-thumbed and dog-eared. She could wait outside; she would hear the phone ringing there just as easily. She tugged the door open.

A woman, pushing a pram, arrived. "You finished?" she asked, as she put the brakes on the pram.

"I'm expecting a long distance call."

"I need to call our doctor. My husband's sick."

"Could you wait, just for a minute? He's going to call right back."

"I won't be long. If it's engaged, he'll call again." She reached past Sheelagh and pulled the door open. Sheelagh stepped away. She watched as the woman took a piece of paper from her pocket, pushed in her money, dialed the number and pushed the button. She was shouting down the phone. Sheelagh couldn't help hearing.

"Yes, the coughing is worse. Yes, it's bright red ... he looks dire, very pale .... When will he come? Fine, thank you Miss."

When she hung up and opened the door, the woman was near tears. She looked at Sheelagh and shook her head. "He's going to the sanatorium. Signs on it. I know he is."

Her tears spilled over as she unlocked the brake on the pram and returned the way she came.

The phone rang. Sheelagh hurried to answer it, then paused, took a handkerchief from her pocket and wiped the mouthpiece. She could hear him shouting.

"Hello, Richard?"

"Of course it's me. Who the hell else would be calling a bloody phone box? Could you not hear me yelling?"

"I had to wipe the mouthpiece. A woman was just using it, and it sounded like her husband has TB."

"What? For God's sake, Sheelagh, what the hell is going on there?"

"Nothing, look, I'm sorry Richard. I have a question for you."

"Go on."

"Would you mind if I brought Michael's children back with me?"

"What? Why?"

"Well, Beth needs a break, and Margaret is trying to persuade her to come back to Bristol, and it would be easier if the children were already there."

"For how long?"

"Just for a visit, a little holiday for them; it has been pretty awful here."

There was a pause. "Well, if it means you're coming back, fine."

There was another pause. "You've been gone for ages, I miss you."

"It just seems like ages. I miss you too."

"How is she?"

"She's coping."

"All right, well, … come on home. I'm sure we can manage for a short while."

"Oh, thank you, Richard. I knew you wouldn't mind."

"Fine, just hurry home, will you?"

"I will. I'll send you a telegram when I've booked the tickets."

"Good. Now get off this phone. You're costing us a fortune."

"Love you."

"Me too."

He hung up.

The Journey Begins

Ellen didn't like the room on the boat. Aunty Sheelagh called it a cabin. It wasn't very big and it smelled nasty. The four beds, two on either side, were more like big shelves than beds. Aunty Sheelagh called them bunks. Everything was strange about the room, even the door. It was metal, nearly round, and it looked like it was cut out of the wall. They had to step over a ledge to get in.

There was a tiny wash basin sticking out from the wall, with a little mirror over it. Beside the mirror, close to the low ceiling, there was a small, round window. At least, Ellen thought it was a window, though it looked like it was fastened to the wall by huge screws. It was shiny like glass but like a mirror as well, because Ellen could see a reflection of the cabin. She couldn't see anything outside. If it *was* a window, Ellen wished it was open. She was used to her mother always having the windows open, unless it was the winter time and it was very cold.

The man in the white jacket had left the cases in the narrow space between the bunks so that there was hardly any room to move. After he left, her aunt lifted her polished brown suitcase with the wide strap and gold locks up onto a lower bunk. She pushed it down to the very end, then lifted up their old battered suitcase to put beside it, the one with the scratch marks that Ellen had watched her mother pack earlier. Their suitcase looked very dingy beside their aunt's. Hers looked like Ellen's shoes looked after her father polished them before Mass on Sundays.

It was strange that this lady was her daddy's sister. Everyone said Ellen and Brendan looked like each other, but Aunty Sheelagh and Daddy didn't look like each other at all. Her daddy had dark wavy hair with just a little bit of white at the sides. Aunty Sheelagh's hair was reddish with lots of curls, and her eyes were a pretty bright blue, like Nanny's ring. Her daddy's were dark brown like chocolate. Aunty Sheelagh's smile was a bit like her daddy's though, and so was her chin, the way it went all dimply when she drank a cup of tea.

"I think we can take off our coats, darlings. It's a little stuffy in here, isn't it?"

Neither child answered. Ellen unbuttoned her coat, shrugged herself out of it, and laid it on the bed. Her aunt helped Brendan with his, and then she opened the battered suitcase and took out his pajamas. "Come on, Brendan dear. Let's get you into your PJ's and into bed, shall we?"

"Mammy always makes sure he goes to the toilet before he goes to bed."

"Oh, yes, of course, silly me. Thank you, Ellen. It's easy to see I'm not used to children, isn't it? Come along then darlings. Let's all go and find the toilets."

Their aunt opened the door and, taking each child by the hand they stepped over the ledge and she led them along the corridor. The walls, ceiling, and floor were metal, which made the corridor very echo-y. There was a thud, thud, thud noise, and Ellen wondered if that was the engine and if the boat was moving yet. She wished there were windows in the passageway.

Aunty Sheelagh opened to door to the toilets. As they stepped over the ledge, Ellen smelled a nasty mixture of sick and the disinfectant Mammy used in the bathroom. It made her feel a bit sick too, and she didn't want to stay, but she was too nervous to go back to the cabin on her own. Anyway, she'd only want to go later. She was as quick as she could be and told Brendan to hurry up too, then asked her aunt if they could wash their hands when they got back to the cabin. Aunty Sheelagh agreed and they hurried back.

Once in their cabin Ellen leaned on the edge of a bunk and watched her aunt help her brother out of his clothes. She tugged hard at his jumper to pull it over his head and Ellen saw Brendan make a face as the jumper pulled his ears. He didn't say anything, he didn't even cry. He just stood very still and quiet as Aunty Sheelagh finished undressing him, put on his blue and white striped pajamas, tied a knot in the cord in his pants, and buttoned and tucked in his jacket. She folded down the bedclothes on the lower bunk.

"Now, climb in there, darling. I'm sure you'll be asleep in no time."

Brendan climbed into the bed and watched his aunt as she tucked the bedclothes under his chin.

"May I have a kiss goodnight, do you think?" she asked.

Brendan said nothing. Aunty Sheelagh bent down so that she wouldn't bump her head on top bunk and kissed him on the cheek. It left a red smudge. As her aunt stood and turned, Ellen saw her brother sneak his hand up from under the bedcovers and rub away the kiss.

Aunty Sheelagh smiled down at her. "All right, let's get you ready now, shall we, sweetheart?"

Ellen watched her aunt take the pink nightdress from the suitcase and shake out its folds. It was Ellen's favorite, the one with tiny, white daisies sprinkled all over it. When they'd seen it in the shop, Ellen had told her mother they looked like flowery snowflakes. Mammy had packed it at the top, "because," she had said, "you will be sleeping on the boat tonight, Ellen. Isn't that exciting?" Ellen wasn't sure and her Mammy didn't look very happy about it.

"Aunty Sheelagh thinks it would be better if you got a proper night's sleep. I do too. They'll let you stay on the boat until the morning, even though it's docked," she'd said. "And in your favorite nightie, and with Mandy to snuggle up to, you won't feel too lonely," she'd said, hugging Ellen really tight.

Aunty Sheelagh told them it would all be part of the adventure, sleeping on a boat, but she didn't like the tiny cabin, or the smells, or the noises, and she wasn't even sure she liked her aunt, now that she was in charge of them and her mother wasn't there.

"Can I help you, darling, or are you big enough to do it all yourself?"

"I can do it. I'm nearly seven." Said Ellen, even though she wasn't. She half-turned away and unbuttoned her cardigan.

"Yes, of course you are. Good girl."

Out of the corner of her eye Ellen saw her aunt close the suitcase on Mandy's face. She nearly said something but decided to just finish getting undressed instead. Maybe Mandy would like it better in the suitcase; Ellen knew she wouldn't like the smells either.

She had never slept without her doll before. She watched as her aunt pushed the case to the bottom of the bunk again and sat down where it had been. She opened her handbag and took a cigarette from the shiny silver cigarette case Ellen had seen so often since their aunt's arrival in Dublin. She then fiddled around in her handbag and pulled out her silver lighter. Ellen secretly went on watching her aunt, as she finished undressing. She watched her click the lighter and bring the yellow-blue flame to the end of her cigarette. Mammy didn't like cigarette smoking, and neither did Ellen. It was going to make the room smell worse. Her aunt sucked in the smoke, dropped the lighter back into her bag, and blew a grayish blue cloud into the air. She looked at Ellen and smiled. "I think you can leave your socks on, darling. I'm not sure how clean the floor is."

The cigarette glowed brightly as she sucked it again, then blew more smoke towards the ceiling. It tickled Ellen's throat until she wanted to cough. Her aunt delicately picked something from her tongue. She did that a lot when she smoked, even though there seemed to be nothing there. Ellen put her clothes beside the suitcase and slipped the nightdress over her head.

"Would you like to sleep on the top bunk, dear, or this one?" Her aunt patted the pillow beside her. Ellen looked up to where a smoky haze floated close to the yellowed ceiling.

"Down here, please."

"All right." Her aunt stood, fastened the clasp on the old suitcase, and heaved it up onto the bunk over Brendan's. "Do you mind if I sit on the end of your bed until I've finished my cigarette?"

Ellen shook her head. Now that she was ready for bed, she wasn't sure if she should kneel beside it to say her prayers, like she did at home, or was it different when you were on a boat? Remembering what her aunt had said about the dirty floor, she decided to get into bed and say her prayers there.

Aunty Sheelagh tucked her in so tightly that Ellen was hardly able to move, so she just made a very small sign of the cross on her tummy under the covers before saying the prayers in her head. When she finished, she blessed herself again and turned to face the wall. After a while her aunt's weight lifted from the bottom of the bed.

"Goodnight, darling, sleep well." Her aunt was bent over her. She smelled the nasty mix of cigarettes and the perfume Aunty Sheelagh always squirted on herself. "We'll be in England when you wake up. Isn't that exciting?"

Ellen didn't answer her. After a while she heard the bunk over hers creak as her aunt climbed up onto it. But Ellen hadn't heard her getting undressed. Was she going to go to sleep in her clothes? She heard the snap of the cigarette case and the click of the lighter as another cigarette was lit.

She closed her eyes, but she didn't feel tired. She wished she was at home. It had sounded fun when her aunt and her Nan had asked if she would like to go and stay with her Aunty Sheelagh and Uncle Richard in Bristol, especially when everybody seemed to be so sad at home. Mammy was crying a lot, and Daddy hadn't been home for ages, and when she asked them no one would say when he *would* be coming home. Ellen felt her eyes tingling and bit her lip hard, but tears still leaked out, even though her eyes were closed, and they were making her pillow wet. She wished she had Mandy to snuggle into. She tried not to snuffle. She didn't want her aunt fussing over her. She hated fuss.

Bad News

Mr. Timmons sat at the dining table, his briefcase on the floor beside him. Beth sat opposite him. Her mother, as always these days, sat close by. Beth studied the elderly lawyer. *What a grey man*, she thought. His hair was grey, what was left of it, and his suit and tie were dark grey. Even his shirt was a paler shade of the same color. His hands and face also had the sickly, grayish tinge of people who rarely go out in sun, like nuns or night workers.

He shuffled through the papers in front of him and frowned.

"I'm afraid the information is not as good as I'd hoped, Mrs. Kelly. I do remember advising your husband on the benefits of making a will when he was signing the papers for the house. However …" he looked towards her mother with an expression of regret. "I have to assume he felt that, having survived the war and with being so young and healthy, it was something he could pursue at a later date." He looked back at Beth. "I have searched our papers and can find no trace of a will I'm afraid, my dear."

"But surely she'll inherit automatically, Mr. Timmons. She's his wife, after all. *I* did when my first husband died."

"That is not necessarily the case, Mrs. Fielding, not in Irish law. There are minors involved. As Mr. Kelly passed away intestate, Mrs. Kelly will, of course, inherit a portion of the estate." He smiled reassuringly at Beth, "but there is also a legal provision to be made for the children including…" he inclined his head slightly towards Beth's stomach, "the newest member of the family."

Beth frowned. "So what do you mean? What portion?"

The lawyer looked regretful. "That is very straightforward, Mrs. Kelly, and clearly covered under the inheritance laws, my dear." He fumbled in his bag, produced yet another document and handed it to her.

"So what does this mean, Mr. Timmons?"

"Of course we have to look at the mortgage payments, et cetera." He droned on as if he hadn't heard her. "There's a great deal of information we will have to get from yourself and the bank before we can be definitive as to the final sum."

"Have you no idea what she'll have? My daughter is considering selling the house and moving back to England. Do you mean she can't?"

Beth was about to protest. She hadn't said anything about moving or selling the house, but she didn't want to argue with her mother in front of the lawyer. She waited for his reply.

Mr. Timmons cleared his throat. "The Irish system is a little different to the English one, Mrs. Fielding. In the Republic of Ireland, in a situation where there is no will, inheritance is based on the welfare of the *entire* family, not just the widow or widower."

He sounded patronizing, so pompous Beth wanted to shake him. Why didn't he get to the point?

"But the children don't need the money. Their mother does," said Margaret.

"Yes, I fully understand your concern Mrs. Fielding, and I hasten to assure you that Mrs. Kelly will not be destitute. She will inherit one third of her husband's estate. Two thirds will then be kept in trust for the children until they reach their majority." He turned to Beth. "However, I am a little puzzled about one thing, Mrs. Kelly. You mentioned in your note to me that you thought your husband had a life insurance policy made out to you." His bushy, grey, eyebrows rose over the rim of the half-glasses.

Beth nodded. "I'm pretty sure he did. He took it out years ago. I can't remember much about it. He took it out in England. He asked his brother, Colm, to look after it when we moved here. I'll have to have another look in Michael's paperwork. Now that I think of it I don't remember seeing anything there."

"Good, excellent. The brother, you say? The insurance is held and paid regularly in England then, I assume?"

Beth nodded.

"That might explain why there is no record of it here." He turned to Beth's mother. "If your daughter is named as the sole beneficiary of that policy, which I'm sure she is, then that will certainly help her financial situation. Now ..." he sifted through his papers, selected one and pushed it across the table to Beth. "If you would be so good as to complete this form, my dear, husband's assets, bank accounts, insurance policies, that sort of thing, then I will do my best to expedite proceedings. I fully understand your anxiety to get things resolved as quickly as possible, especially with the coming happy event ..."

He hesitated as the two women looked at him blankly. His grey face even went a little pink.

"Ah, ... though I do, of course, understand that the circumstances are tragic." He fumbled with the remaining papers, tapped them into a uniform bundle and busied himself sliding them carefully back into his briefcase. When he had finished, he snapped it closed and stood.

"Well, I think that is all we can do today. I do appreciate the stress you must be under, Mrs. Kelly. Please don't hesitate to contact us with any queries you may have over the next few weeks."

Beth and Margaret stood too.

"Thank you, Mr. Timmons," Margaret extended her hand. "And I know my daughter appreciates you coming to the house."

He shook her hand. "My pleasure, Mrs. Fielding. I mean ... it was no problem." He turned to Beth. "Again, allow me to extend my deepest sympathy on your loss, Mrs. Kelly. It is a terrible business, terrible. Our thoughts and prayers are with you." He shook her hand. "I hope we can complete all the details of your husband's estate in good time." He smiled down at her. "Take things slowly, my dear. You have your children to care for, and particularly that little one." He again indicated her stomach. "They will be a great blessing to you."

Beth nodded. "Thank you, Mr. Timmons."

He moved toward the door. "However, I'm sure you appreciate that the sooner you can complete the paperwork and post it in to me, the quicker I can do my job, Mrs. Kelly?"

Margaret nodded. "Yes, of course. Do you have any idea how long it might take, once that's done, Mr. Timmons?" She opened the living room door, and followed him into the hall.

"I will pursue it as quickly as possible, but even with the best will in the world, Mrs. Fielding, these things take time. I suspect it will be several months before it's all done. However, in the interim, I'm sure we can temporarily release some funds from Mr. Kelly's bank account, so that Mrs. Kelly may have access to whatever immediate finances she might need." He shook his head and Beth thought she even heard him tut-tut. "A great pity it was not a joint account; it would certainly have simplified things."

Margaret handed him his overcoat. He shrugged it on and buttoned it closed as the two women watched. When he was ready Margaret opened the front door. He gave them a slight, formal bow, patted his grey trilby in place, and stepped out into the chill morning air.

Margaret closed the door behind him and turned to Beth, who still stood in the dining room doorway. "Come on, love, don't look so worried. We'll sort it out. Let's have a cup of tea and see if we can fill out all the answers to that paperwork." She led the way to the kitchen.

Beth followed her. "I felt like he was telling me off the whole time, or telling Michael off. *I* didn't know the children would get two thirds of everything over here." She said as she filled the kettle. "I'm sure Michael didn't either." She took two cups and saucers from the cupboard. "I wonder how much the insurance is worth. I never paid much attention when Michael told me about it." She looked at her mother and made a rueful face. "I remember that we laughed about it though, taking a policy out just when the war was over and we were safe."

Boat and Train

"Ellen, Ellen," Someone shook her shoulder gently. "Come on, darling, time to get up. We've arrived."

Ellen opened her eyes to see Aunty Sheelagh's face close to her own. Her aunty smelled horrible, of old cigarettes and too much of the nasty perfume.

Ellen couldn't think where she was for a moment. The ceiling behind her aunt's head seemed very low. It took her a few seconds before she remembered they were on a boat and that she was looking at the underneath of the top bed. Then she remembered the long night, the drub, drub, drub of the boat engine that made everything shake, and the rocking about that made her tummy feel funny. She remembered that sometime during the night her aunt was standing beside her in the dark near the wash basin. It sounded like she was being sick, though Ellen didn't open her eyes to look. It smelled like sick. It made Ellen feel sick too, but she'd swallowed hard lots of times, turned over, and pretended to be asleep. But then she must have really gone to sleep because now the light was on again and her aunt was wearing a different dress.

"Come on, sleepy head." Aunty Sheelagh kissed her forehead. "We don't want to miss the train do we? Brendan is already awake, aren't you, darling?"

Ellen looked to the other bunk where her brother lay, sheet and blankets still snuggled up to his chin. He was wide awake and staring at his sister, but he didn't answer their aunt's question.

"I'll get him dressed, if you can dress yourself. Is that all right, dear?"

Ellen nodded and struggled out of the narrow bunk.

"I've put out clean knicks and socks for you, but I think you can wear yesterday's dress, all right?"

Ellen nodded again. She sleepily took off her nightie, gathered her clothes from the bottom of the bed and dressed. Meanwhile Aunty Sheelagh got Brendan out of bed and dressed him. Ellen thought he was standing stiff on purpose, like he was trying to make it more difficult, but Aunty Sheelagh didn't say anything and did manage to get his clothes on him. When she was finished, she folded their nightclothes and yesterday's underwear, opened the battered suitcase, and tucked them inside. Before she could close the lid Ellen put out a hand to stop her.

"Can I have Mandy, please?"

Her aunt looked a bit cross.

"Your dolly? Oh, Ellen! It will only be another thing to carry, dear, and we have to go and get the train now. I need to be able to hold your hand. I don't want to lose you, do I? Why don't we leave her safe in the suitcase until we get home?"

"You can hold my other hand."

Aunty Sheelagh frowned and sighed as she tugged Mandy out of the suit-case. Ellen took her and quickly snuggled her close, saying sorry to her, inside her head, for leaving her locked in the suitcase all night. Out loud she said, "Thank you," to her aunt, but not very loud.

Sheelagh closed the lid and locked the catches. "All right, dear, now just make sure you keep hold of her."

"I will."

Ellen noticed her aunt had kept out their two toothbrushes. She watched as she opened a small, flat tin from her bag, rub both brushes into the hard pink stuff inside, and hand one to Brendan and one to her.

"Now, brush your teeth and then we'll see if we can get a porter to take these bags, shall we?"

"Mammy washes us before we get dressed," said Ellen, more awake now and examining the toothbrush.

"Oh, dear, I'm sorry, I forgot. You should have reminded me, Ellen. I'm not very good at looking after children yet, am I?"

She gave a little laugh, but Ellen didn't feel like laughing. She wished she was at home with Mammy and Daddy.

"We really don't have much time." Her aunt continued, "Perhaps I'll wash your faces and hands in a minute. Just brush your teeth for now. It's getting late."

The children silently exchanged brushes. Ellen began to clean her teeth. Brendan copied her. It tasted like medicine, and Ellen saw her brother make a face before he quickly spat out pink, bubbly stuff into the basin. He handed his brush back to Ellen.

Meanwhile, Aunty Sheelagh had taken a slim gold tube from her handbag, twisted it, and rubbed her lipstick onto her lips. She looked at herself in her compact mirror, then dropped her lipstick and compact back into her bag and frowned down at Brendan. "That's not much of a brushing is it, young man? You won't have those baby teeth for much longer if that's all you do."

"Mammy doesn't use that stuff," said Ellen rinsing both brushes under the dribble of tap water and handing them to her aunt.

"What does she use then, dear? I looked in your toilet bag, but I couldn't find anything. This is mine." She picked up the flat tin and tucked it into her own toilet bag along with the brushes.

"Just water."

"Ah, that explains it. Oh, well, never mind. You'll get used to the paste I'm sure. It makes your mouth taste nice and fresh doesn't it?"

Ellen didn't agree, but she didn't want to argue, so she just shrugged.

"Right then, let's get your coats on."

Ellen pointed to her brother who was clutching the front of his pants. "He wants to tinkle."

"Oh." The woman looked down at them. "Well, can you just give me a minute to find a porter, young man? Once they have taken the bags, I'll take you to the toilet."

Brendan was now fidgeting and hopping from one foot to the other.

"He can't," said Ellen.

"Oh, very well. You stay here, Ellen, will you? If a porter comes, tell him to wait, and I'll be back in a minute."

"I want to go too."

"Dear heaven! All right, come on then, the two of you. But we have to be quick."

Ellen laid Mandy carefully down on the bed. Their aunt hurried them out of the cabin and down the narrow passageway. It was busy with people hurrying everywhere and several cabin doors were open. Ellen saw other passengers packing bags and getting ready, like themselves, to leave the boat. White-jacketed porters carrying one, two, and even three suitcases darted between the passengers saying, "Excuse me, Sir, Ma'am," as they struggled towards the stairs. Other porters hurried, empty-handed, in the other direction, stopping at any open cabin doorway saying, "Porter?" Her aunt stopped one who tried to squeeze past her, loaded with bags, heading toward the stairs.

"Will you come back to cabin fifteen in about five minutes? I need two suitcases taken to the train."

"Yes, Ma'am." The porter nodded. "Cabin fifteen. Back in five minutes, Ma'am." He hitched a big, square suitcase under his arm, like he was trying to find a more comfortable position, and hurried up the passageway.

The toilets smelled even worse than the night before and Ellen told Brendan to hurry up before she went into her own cubicle. She was glad to get out and back to their cabin. Once there, her aunt wet a facecloth and gave their faces and hands a quick wipe. She dried them with the small white towel from beside the basin. The towel had a miniature picture of a boat in one corner. She'd only just put the towel back onto the rack when there was a knock on the door and the porter came in to take their suitcases. Her aunt quickly put on her coat and hat and stuck the long pin in it to keep it on, took her handbag from the top bunk, and gently pushed Brendan and Ellen out of the cabin in front of her. "Follow that man please, children, and don't get lost."

Ellen snatched Mandy from the bunk as she went, tucked the rag doll tightly under her arm. She followed the porter and the other passengers along the passageway, up the metal stairs, and out onto the deck. The stuffy, stale air inside the boat changed to an icy cold wind that took her breath away. It was still dark and Ellen saw faint flurries of snow swirling in the yellow pools of light on the dockside. She hugged Mandy even closer, and buried her face in the soft wool of the doll's hair as they walked down the gangplank onto the dimly lit quay.

They hurried along the dock, dodging crates, trolleys, porters, and other passengers and arrived in the dry, bleak, cold of the customs shed. Uniformed men waited behind battered wooden tables. They stamped their feet and rubbed their hands together, trying to keep warm. One of the men waved them past, and they followed the porter into the gloomy railway station, and along the cluttered platform. He stopped at an empty carriage, and Aunty Sheelagh helped them get up the big step and in. Ellen was glad to be out of the miserable, cold, snowy weather. The porter hefted their cases up onto the rope shelves over their seats. Aunty Sheelagh gave him some money, he touched his cap at her, banged the carriage door closed and left. Brendan took a seat beside the window, pressed his nose against it and watched the people. Aunty Sheelagh sat beside him, so Ellen took the seat opposite her brother. It faced the back of the train, but at least she could look out of the window too. She tried to read the big sign on the platform wall. She knew the letters, H-O-L-Y-H-E-A-D, but it was a big word and she wasn't very good at reading yet. When the platform was almost empty, except for porters, she saw a man in a uniform with a black cap wave a green flag and heard the loud blast of his whistle.

The train jerked forward and clouds of yellowy-grey smoke drifted past the window. It made the station look even darker and foggier. Even with the window closed she could smell the smoke. It was a bit like when Mammy lit the fire at home, smoky, and dusty, but this was oily as well.

* * *

Ellen thought the train was better than the boat. The carriage smelled nicer and there were comfortable seats instead of the bunks. It was getting light as they left the station and she watched the shadow of the train on houses, fields and factories as they went faster and faster. Everything seemed to be rushing past them, not them rushing past. Every now and then Brendan would point to a group of cows snuggled together to keep warm in a snowy field, or a horse, or once, a windmill. But he didn't say anything. Aunty Sheelagh didn't talk to them much either, just read the newspaper she'd bought. The three of them were rocked from side to side as the train moved, and it made Ellen feel sleepy.

After a while the train slowed into another station. It was huge, busy, and noisy. People hurried about everywhere. It was dirty too. Everything looked like it was covered in dirt, black and dusty; there were heaps of sacks and boxes piled on trolleys, and some that were just cluttering up the platforms, making the people almost bump into each other. Some trolleys were being pushed by porters, who looked dirty as well. Ellen looked up to the high glass ceiling. It was so dirty she could hardly see through, but there were lots of birds sitting on the beams up there. She'd never seen birds inside before.

One man in a cleaner uniform walked up and down calling, "Crewe, Crewe, all change at Crewe," very loudly. Aunty Sheelagh pulled at the thick leather strap that opened the window and called him over.

"Where are you going, Missus?"

"Bristol. Is the train in yet?"

He opened the door. "It is, Missus."

He helped Aunty Sheelagh, then Brendan and Ellen, down onto the platform and collected their bags from the rope rack. "Just follow me."

They set off, walking quickly. Aunty Sheelagh gripped each of them tightly by the hand as they half-walked, half-trotted beside her. Ellen stopped suddenly, almost tugging her aunt over.

"Mandy!"

Aunty Sheelagh stopped and turned. "Oh, Good Lord, child, I told you to keep hold of her. Where did you leave her?"

Ellen was afraid she was going to cry, "On the train," she bit her bottom lip hard. Mammy had told her to be a good girl, and now she'd made Aunty Sheelagh cross.

The porter put down the cases. "It's all right, Missus, don't worry, I'll get it, you wait right here." He smiled down at Ellen. "Your dolly is it, little 'un?"

Ellen nodded.

"Don't you cry, luv. I'll have her back in a blink." He hurried back down the length of the train, going the wrong way from the rest of the people, and peering into all of the carriage windows, looking for Mandy, as he went.

As they waited, Aunty Sheelagh lit a cigarette and tapped her foot impatiently, but then the porter came out from the crowd waving the doll over his head.

"You're very lucky, Ellen. You could have lost her," said her aunt, blowing a long line of smoke into the cold air. When the man got back to them her aunt thanked him and asked, "Are we all right for time?"

He looked up at the station clock. "We're fine, Missus, we've got fifteen minutes yet." He handed Ellen the doll. "And we couldn't have this little girl traveling without her dolly, could we?" He gave Ellen a wink, then turned and picked up the suitcases. Her aunt threw the cigarette on the stone floor and stepped and twisted her foot on it.

* * *

The second train was much like the first and they were soon sitting in the same places as before, waiting for the guard's whistle. Ellen hugged Mandy tight until the train began moving, then it rocked her gently to sleep.

The next thing she knew her aunt was shaking her awake.

"We're here, sweetheart, we're here. Let's see if Uncle Richard is waiting for us."

A New Home

No sooner had the train come to a stop than Aunty Sheelagh opened the carriage window, leaned out and looked up and down the platform. Then she waved and shouted, "Richard, Richard, here we are darling. Richard!"

She was waving so hard Ellen thought her hat might fall off. A tall man hurried forward, dodging between the waiting people, smiling and waving as he came. His long, dark overcoat, almost to the ground made him seem even taller. And he had a mustache. Suddenly, he and Aunty Sheelagh were kissing.

Ellen watched and wondered if it was prickly; her daddy didn't have a mustache.

When they stopped, the man laughed, tugged the door open, and helped Aunty Sheelagh down. "I missed you, my darling," he said and kissed her again before turning to Ellen and holding out his hands. "And you must be Ellen; can I help you down, young lady?"

Ellen took his hands, and jumped onto the platform. The man then turned to her brother. Brendan hadn't moved from his seat and was watching them through the window. The man ducked his head into the carriage. "So, you are the Brendan I have heard so much about. Come on, young man, out you get."

Brendan glanced past the man to where Ellen stood. She nodded and her brother let the stranger lift him out of the train.

"Good man. Now, I'll just get your bags and we'll be off."

* * *

Before he started the car, the tall man turned to them and handed Ellen and Brendan half a bar of chocolate each.

Aunty Sheelagh looked surprised. "Goodness, Richard that was thoughtful of you."

"Buying affection! Thank God rationing's over." They both laughed.

* * *

The car was grey and shiny and so big that two people could have fitted between Brendan and Ellen in the back seat, not like Daddy's car, which he called Betsy. That was quite a small car. The engine started first time, too. The man didn't have to wind it up at the front or get help to push it down the street.

Ellen spent the short journey peering out of the window at the streets and shops. Aunty Sheelagh didn't speak to them; she and the man were busy talking to each other in the front. They spoke quietly so that Ellen couldn't hear what they said, though she did see her aunt start to cry again at one time, like everyone had been doing in the house at home. Then the man said something about "for the children's sake" and Aunty Sheelagh blew her nose, nodded, and gave him a small smile.

Soon the car stopped outside a big shop. It had a deep, dark doorway with huge square windows sticking out on either side. The windows were full of all kinds of clothes, all folded neatly, and different colored shoes, fancy hats, and statues of ladies in beautiful dresses.

Aunty Sheelagh looked back at them. "Here we are, my darlings, home at last."

"You look after the children. I'll get the bags," said the man.

Her aunt helped them out of the car, and they followed her to a black door set to the right of the shop windows. She turned the key in the lock. "Mind yourselves children. Hold on to the rail, the stairs are a bit steep."

They followed her up the dark staircase, holding tight onto the rail. At the top was a wide hallway with a long, shiny black sideboard at the far end, a couch along one side, and a staircase opposite that led up to another floor. There was also a dark space in the other corner, and it looked like there were more stairs going down. It was a strange-looking house. Aunty Sheelagh threw her handbag, hat, and coat onto the couch, then turned to them.

"Now, my darlings, I'm sure you are quite exhausted. Let's take your coats off, shall we? And then I can show you your new home."

Ellen and her brother stood still as she unbuttoned and took off their coats. Ellen felt so tired she didn't have the energy to help. Aunty Sheelagh tossed them onto the couch beside her own, and that surprised Ellen. Mammy always made them hang their coats up. She looked over at her brother. His eyes were open very wide, he looked frightened, and she thought he was going to cry. But he didn't, he just stood and stared around him. Only a little light came into the hallway from a door with a window in the top. It smelled like old people, and it was a bit scary.

The man arrived up the stairs, carrying the suitcases. "Where shall I put these?"

Her aunt smiled at him. "Just leave them here for a minute, Richard, my love. Let's have a cup of tea and show them around first."

* * *

It was a strange place, Ellen thought. A house built on top of a shop. They followed Aunty Sheelagh into the room with the half-glass door. It was a big room. A fire burned in a small square fireplace that had yellow tiles around it. There was an armchair on each side of the fireplace and a big wireless on a shelf by one of the chairs.

"Oh, lovely, Richard, you lit a fire. I'm so cold. What a horrible bloody journey that is."

The man coughed and Aunty Sheelagh put her hands to her mouth, and looked down at Ellen. "Oh, dear, excuse me, Ellen. Aunty Sheelagh has to remember not to use words like that."

She went to stand in front of the fire. Ellen and Brendan stayed by the door and looked at the rest of the room. A dining table took up the space in the middle, with high-backed chairs tucked in around it. A large glass cabinet, full of blue and white china, filled one corner. Another long sideboard, like the one in the hall, stretched under a window and it had a fruit bowl and photographs on it. Outside the window all Ellen could see was a bumpy grey wall.

"Come all the way in then, children, and close the door. Let me show you the rest of your new home." She led them into a tiny kitchen with another window, set high, but still looking out at the same dark wall. She filled a kettle at the sink, put it on the gas stove, and lit the flame. "Right, well, this is the kitchen. Come along." She went back through the living room to the hall. The man was now sitting by the fire warming his hands. He smiled and winked at them as they passed. Out into the dark hallway, they crossed to a door at the bottom of the going up stairs. Aunty Sheelagh opened the door and Ellen stopped in surprise when she saw the huge room. She had never seen one this big, but it was very, very cold, even though there was carpet that went all the way to the edge. At home Brendan used the lino around the edges of the room as a road for his toy cars. There was no toy car road here. The carpet was green and when Ellen stepped on it, it felt as thick and soft as grass. On the other side of the room were two big windows with curtains that went all the way to the floor and all the way to the ceiling. In between them was a huge gold mirror. The furniture was covered in silky, gold material and there was even a gold light hanging from the ceiling. The fireplace at the far end had another gold-framed mirror over it and there was a shiny gold screen in front of the empty grate. Ellen thought it looked like a palace room.

"This is the sitting room. I don't suppose you'll be in here much. This is where Aunty Sheelagh and Uncle Richard have their friends." Aunty Sheelagh smiled down at them, patted Brendan's head, led them out of the room, and up the stairs. At the top there was a corridor with three doors; one by the top of the stairs, one in the middle, and one at the far end. Aunty Sheelagh pointed to the one by the stairs. "That's our bedroom," she said, but she didn't open it. Ellen thought it must be huge if it was the same size as the sitting room, but she didn't say anything. Aunty Sheelagh went on along the passageway to the second door. "This will be your bedroom," she said, opening the door. The room was dark. She clicked on the light switch, but it still wasn't very bright and the only other light came from a strange window in the ceiling. The walls had dark yellow wallpaper splotched with big, brown flowers. A yellowy jigsaw picture of fancy buildings and boats and water hung on one wall. There was a bed on either side of the room, both had green eiderdowns and yellow pillows.

"Now, isn't this cozy?" She smiled down at the children. Ellen and Brendan didn't say anything. She pointed to the jigsaw picture. "Your Daddy made that when he was about the same age as you, Ellen." Before Ellen could look at the picture more carefully, her aunt left the room. She switched off the light as she went. "And last, but not least, the bathroom and toilet," she said. They followed as she went to the end of the passage and opened the third door. It was another gloomy room with another of the strange ceiling windows. It was full of boxes, empty shelves, glass display cases, and two statues of ladies, like the ones in the shop window, except that these had no clothes on and one had no arms. They were on the floor beside her. Aunty Sheelagh didn't seem to notice them.

They walked through the store room to another, open, door. "And here it is. Your very own bathroom! We have one off our bedroom, but I think it's better if you have your own. As you can see, the bath is here and the toilet is through there," she pointed to the far end of the bathroom, "with a wash basin." *At least these rooms had real windows* thought Ellen, *though they only look out at the same bumpy grey wall.* But if she looked up she could just see a little bit of sky, over the top of the roof behind.

"Now, let's get back downstairs to the warm and see if that kettle has boiled, shall we?" She walked ahead of them and Brendan gripped Ellen's hand tightly as they passed the statues.

Adjustments

Ellen sipped her drink, watched and listened. Once her aunt had settled the two children at the table, with a cup of milky tea and a Marietta biscuit each, she seemed to forget about them. She *had* asked if they were hungry, but after the sandwiches they had on the train and the chocolate the man had given them in the car they didn't really want anything.

Ellen was cold. She wished she still had her coat on. There was no warm from the fire where she sat. The table was covered in a dark red, velvety cloth and had a thick gold fringe all the way round the edge. She ruffled it gently with her fingers. Aunty Sheelagh had put their cups and biscuit on big wooden mats with pictures of horses jumping over hedges and ridden by men wearing red coats and top hats. "Just in case you spill," she'd said, "so that you won't be worrying about staining the cloth, or marking the table."

Her aunt had taken her tea, and the man's, and sat with him by the fire. They drank their tea, smoked, and talked. It seemed to be mostly about a shop and Aunty Sheelagh was asking him all kinds of questions about stock, and takings, and factory orders. Ellen didn't understand most of it and soon got bored. Her attention wandered to the window looking out at the nasty grey wall. She wondered if there was a garden out there, and what they were going to do after they finished their tea. She looked across the table at Brendan who hadn't touched his tea, or biscuit, and just sat there, almost like he was asleep with his eyes open. Their cups and saucers were pretty, small, and white, with tiny pink and blue flowers painted on them. They looked so delicate that Ellen thought if the cups were empty you could almost see through them. At home they had thick cups with stripes on them and Mammy didn't put them in saucers because she said they'd broken too many. Mammy usually gave them milk too, not tea, and when the weather was cold she warmed it in the pan so that it was just right to drink. But this tea was all right.

Ellen was surprised by a clock chiming. It was the same music as the one on their mantelpiece clock at home. She looked around the room to see where it was. It was a strange-looking clock, high on top of the china cabinet and inside a tall glass dome. It was gold, with a ticker underneath that swung back and forth, and you could see all the moving bits that made it work. It didn't look a bit like their mantelpiece clock with its dark wooden case. Theirs was nicer, even though Aunty Sheelagh's was gold. But they sounded exactly the same.

Ellen got a sicky feeling in her tummy. She wished she was back at home. Her eyes suddenly got all cloudy with tears, and then they spilled over and dribbled down her face. They tasted salty at the corner of her mouth and fell onto her hands in her lap. The more she squeezed her eyes and tried to make the tears stop, the more they came. Her nose started to run and she sniffled.

Aunty Sheelagh looked up.

"Oh, my poor darling."

She quickly put her cup and saucer on the floor, threw her half-finished cigarette into the fire and hurried over. "Oh, Ellen, my poor, sweet thing, this must all be so strange to you. I am so sorry." She knelt and caught Ellen's two hands in her own. "Oh, dear, your poor hands are all wet. And you feel cold. I'm sure you're missing your mother, aren't you, sweetheart?"

Ellen nodded and the tears came even more.

Her aunt fumbled in her pocket, took out a lacy white handkerchief, and dabbed at Ellen's face. "Here you are, darling," she tucked it into Ellen's hand. "Blow your nose, and let's see what we can do to cheer you up, shall we?" She looked over at Brendan. He was watching them. "I know, how about we go shopping, and buy you some toys to play with, shall we? I'm afraid we don't have a toy box or anything suitable for little children here," she stood, "but we'll soon change that, won't we?" She looked across at the man. "You can keep an eye on the shop, can't you, darling, while I settle these little ones in, just for one more day?"

The man stood. "I suppose so. But I thought you'd be back and could do the close. I did say I'd join Harry for a bite of dinner in town. We want to start sorting out the summer fixtures. Cricket season will be on us before you know it, you know."

"Oh, I should be back in plenty of time for that," she said, glancing down at her watch. "It's only a quarter to four. I'll just go over to Peacocks. I'm sure we can pick up one or two little things over there to keep them happy for the moment." She turned back to the children. "Come on then, my loves, finish your drinks and we'll go and see what we can find."

Ellen did as she was told. Brendan slowly pushed his cup away.

"Don't you like tea, then?" asked Aunty Sheelagh. He gave a slight shake of his head. "Would you like something else instead? We don't have a lot of milk." She looked across at the man again. "Uncle Richard didn't think about that when he did the shopping."

"*I* didn't do it," the man laughed. "Can you imagine me in Winton's? No, I got Ivy to do it. She was glad to get out of the shop for a half hour."

Aunty Sheelagh frowned. "Mmmm, well, she knows nothing about children either. Dear heavens, Richard, a fifty year old spinster! You'd have been better sending Doris; at least she's had two of her own. Oh, well." She retrieved her own cup from the floor. "I'll get some more milk while I'm out."

Her aunt bundled them into their coats, and they headed back down the dark, scary, staircase, and out onto the busy street.

Mystery

The cold wind took Ellen's breath away. She tucked her chin down into the collar of her coat. Her breath made her collar wet, but she didn't care. She pushed her hands deep into her pockets to try and keep them warm. It was very cold, but there was no snow, not like when they were on the train. The street was like being back in the station too, with lots of people hurrying everywhere. But here, as well as people, it was cars, and bicycles, and horses and carts. It was all so noisy and busy compared to their road at home.

It was starting to get dark. The street lights were on, and so were the ones in the shops. Ellen felt confused. How long ago did they say goodbye to Mammy and Nanny Margaret and leave their house? She remembered it had been almost dark when they left the house too, but when was that? It seemed like ages ago. Was it yesterday or longer than that?

"Right then, hold my hands, you two, we have to cross over the road."

Ellen and her brother did as they were told. Ellen was terrified. Aunty Sheelagh dodged in and out of the traffic tugging them both with her. Ellen nearly stepped in some horse poo and was glad when they arrived safely on the other side of the road and she was able to loosen the tight grip on her aunt's hand. They hurried along the street, past clothes shops, shoe shops, and a chemist, past a shop with lots of lampshades in the window, and past a shop with books piled high on a table near the doorway. They finally stopped outside a huge, brightly-lit store with two large glass doors and a man in a red uniform standing in front. He seemed to know their aunt and smiled at her as he opened one of the doors. He touched his cap as they went in.

It was lovely and warm inside. Wood-floored passageways lined with clutter stretched away on either side of them, and another stretched away in front. Everywhere the counters and shelves were stacked with all sorts of things, pots and pans, mops and buckets, handbags, hats, gloves and scarves, pictures and mirrors, vases and lamps. Ellen even saw toy windmills on sticks in a tub by the register.

"Sheelagh, Sheelagh," a fat lady with lots of dark curly hair was calling from a far corner of the shop. She lifted up a flap in the counter and hurried towards them. "Oh, my poor dear, how are you? How was it?" She threw her arms around Aunty Sheelagh and hugged her tight. Ellen and Brendan waited. Finally, the lady let go of their aunt and looked down at them. "Oh, dear heaven, are these his children?" She bent and drew both of them to her, squashing Ellen so that she was afraid she wouldn't be able to breathe. The lady began to cry saying, "Such beautiful children, you poor, poor things."

"Betty," Aunty Sheelagh leaned forward and whispered in the lady's ear, "They don't know."

Ellen heard.

The lady let go of them and stood up. Ellen was glad to be able to take a deep breath.

"What? What do you mean? Why on earth not, Sheelagh?"

Her aunt tugged the woman to one side. Ellen pretended she was staring around at the shop, but she knew they were talking about a secret, and she listened. Aunty Sheelagh shook her head and spoke very quietly. "Their mother decided not to tell them, just for the time being."

"But how can they not know?" The lady was whispering as well now.

Their aunt shrugged. "It's what Beth wants. She says they're too young to understand. Anyway, I said I'd bring them over here for a while to give her a break. The baby is due in a couple of months."

Ellen wondered why they were whispering, and what they were whispering about. What didn't Mammy want them to know? With all the strange things that had been happening at home she had tried hard to listen and understand, but she hadn't. There was a big secret, and everyone was unhappy. All she knew, really, was that she and Brendan had to come to stay with Aunty Sheelagh on holiday, and that her aunt and Nanny Margaret had promised it would be fun. She also knew her Mammy had asked her to be a good girl, and that her Daddy hadn't come home from work to say goodbye before they left. But why was everyone so sad?

The woman stared at Brendan. "Dear God, he's the image of his father. Look at his eyes, just like his daddy's. Lord, Sheelagh, I remember when he worked in your father's shop. Such a good-looking young man." She sniffled and Ellen saw that Aunty Sheelagh looked as if she might cry too. The woman took a deep breath. "Well, what can I do for you, Sheelagh, what can I get for you?"

"We don't have any toys in the house, Betty. I need to get them something to keep them amused until I can sort myself out."

"Leave it to me." The lady held out her hands, "Come on, little ones, let's see what we can find." Ellen looked up at her aunt, who nodded. She took the stranger's hand. It was soft, and warm. Brendan took the other one and the lady led them towards the back of the shop where a giant teddy bear dangled from the ceiling.

When they got near the bear Ellen saw lots and lots of other toys on the shelves. The lady let go of their hands. "Right then, off you go, both of you, have a look around and see if there is anything you would like." She patted them on their backs and gave them both a gentle push. "Go on, off you go. I'll be back in a minute."

Brendan waited for a moment longer, then walked to a low shelf full of toy cars and trucks. Ellen waited and watched the lady go back to Aunty Sheelagh before she too went to explore the shelves. She went to the ones that had all kinds of doll's things; clothes, toy cooking sets, and doll's house furniture. She looked back at the two women. The lady was putting her arm around her aunt, who seemed to be crying. Again! Ellen sighed, watched as the lady patted her aunt's shoulder, and led her to a darker corner of the shop. Ellen turned back to the doll's shelves. She saw a large, pink box. On it was a picture of a teddy bear and three dolls sitting around a table. On the table was a tiny tea service with a teapot, milk jug, sugar bowl and cups and saucers. Ellen smiled to herself. Mandy would like to have a tea party like that, she thought. They could have small pieces of rhubarb to dip in the sugar bowl and eat, like Mammy let them do at home. Ellen only had a pretend tea-set, with egg cups and jam jar lids for plates. She carefully turned the box. On the other side was a picture of a little girl pretending to pour tea into the cups. She was smiling.

"Hello, are you the little Kelly girl?"

Ellen jumped and turned. Another lady had arrived and was standing just behind her. No, she wasn't a lady. She looked like Kitty, who minded them sometimes when Mammy and Daddy went to the pictures. The girl had wavy hair, just like Kitty, but her two front teeth had a space in the middle and Kitty's teeth didn't.

"Is that what you want then?" The girl nodded toward the box. Ellen quickly drew her hands back.

"No, it's all right, you can have it."

The girl had a funny accent, difficult to understand, and Ellen wasn't sure if she had heard her properly.

"Mrs. Bradley says you can pick any toy, and your little brother can too. Is that him?" The girl pointed to Brendan.

Ellen nodded and watched as her brother pushed a brightly colored toy tractor along the edge of the shelf and made spluttery engine noises. There was a farmer sitting in the tractor's driving seat wearing a straw hat, and he wobbled about as the tractor moved.

The girl took the box off the shelf. "It's a lovely tea set. Real china, it is, and it's got a tray as well. Your dollies could have a really nice tea party with this, couldn't they? Have you got a special dolly?"

Ellen nodded again.

"What's her name?"

"Mandy."

"That's a pretty name. Right then, let's go and see what your brother wants and we'll wrap them up for you, shall we?"

Ellen looked back to where her aunt and the lady stood.

"It's all right, little 'un, you're allowed, honest. That's your Aunty isn't it?" The girl pointed to the two women. "Well, that other lady is Mrs. Bradley, and she owns Peacocks Bazaar, and she said you could have whatever toy you wanted." She held out her hand to Ellen. "So, if you are happy enough with this," She indicated the pink box, "let's go and see what your brother picked."

Brendan seemed as confused as his sister when the girl asked if he wanted to keep the tractor.

"It's a crazy tractor, look," she explained as she knelt and showed him how it wound up. She put it on the floor and it raced around in all different directions, the driver wobbled like he was going to fall out, and waved his arms around. As it came toward him, Brendan dodged out of its way and smiled.

The tractor slowed down, the girl picked it up, and they watched as the turning key slowly came to a stop. "That's settled then, is it?' Brendan looked up at her, but he still didn't seem to understand. The girl spoke very slowly, "Do you want to take this home with you, little fella?"

He, like his sister, nodded.

"Good, come on then." With the tractor in one hand and the box under the other arm the girl led the children to the front of the shop. Aunty Sheelagh was now smiling at them, though her nose was red and her eyes were all shiny.

"Oh, my goodness! Look what you have." She turned to the lady.

"Thank you so much, Betty, it's so kind of you. Say "thank you" to Mrs. Bradley, children."

Ellen did as she was told but her brother just kept watching the girl as she walked away to the counter with the tractor. He watched as she wrapped both toys in brown wrapping paper, tied them with string, and came back to hand each of them a parcel. Each one had a loop of string to use as a handle.

The lady bent to hug them again and Ellen smelled face power, lipstick, and perfume a bit like Aunty Sheelagh's. "Mind yourselves, little ones, and come back and visit me again won't you? Your Aunty will bring you." She stood. "Please do, Sheelagh, they are so sweet, poor little dotes."

"Goodbye kids," called the girl, who was now standing behind the counter. "Have fun with your toys." She waved and Ellen and Brendan waved back before their aunt caught hold of their hands and they went back out into the cold evening and the traffic.

First Night

Ellen looked up at the window in the ceiling. She could see two very tiny, sparkly stars in the sky, but they didn't give much light. When they were getting into bed Ellen asked Aunty Sheelagh to leave the door open, but her aunt had smiled and said she thought it would be cozier with the door closed. Ellen didn't like the dark.

She rolled over on her side and tried to look around the bedroom again. If she stared hard for a long time she could just see the square shape of her Daddy's jigsaw picture on the wall over Brendan's bed, but she couldn't see the boats in it or anything. She could hear her brother breathing, slowly, with little snores, so she knew he was asleep.

She was still angry with him.

Ellen hugged Mandy close, turned to face the wall, and snuggled further under the bed covers and eiderdown. She squeezed her eyes tight closed and tried to pretend that the door was open and the light in the hall was on like at home so that she wasn't afraid. She tried to think of nice things, like her Mammy told her to when she couldn't sleep, but she couldn't think of anything nice. Even the tea set was spoiled.

* * *

When they got home and unpacked, it had been beautiful, even nicer than it looked on the box. The cups had tiny flowers painted on them, just like Aunty Sheelagh's. Her aunt told them they could play quietly with the toys until she came back upstairs to make the tea. "I have to go down to close the shop. I won't be long," she explained. "Uncle Richard has gone out, but you are perfectly safe up here. Just don't go near the fire, will you?"

Ellen had shaken her head and watched as her aunt left, closing the half-glass door behind her, then she had gone back to playing with the tea set. She put the four tiny cups in their saucers and set them in a circle in the corner beside the china cabinet. She propped Mandy against the wall and pretended to pour milk and tea into each cup, then spoon in sugar.

She heard Brendan winding his tractor yet again. Ever since he opened his parcel he had wound the tractor, watch it skitter back and forth under the table and between the legs of the dining chairs, picked it up when it stopped, wound it, and let it go again. The noise was annoying, but Ellen tried to ignore it.

The accident happened in an instant. The tractor suddenly veered towards Ellen's corner, and before either of them could stop it, it crashed head-on into one of the cups and saucers. The little cup flew sideways and hit the corner of the china cabinet. The cup shattered, Ellen let out a squeal, and Brendan ran to snatch up his toy. As he did so he stood on the upturned saucer, and Ellen heard the crunch of broken china.

For a horrified moment all that could be heard was the whirring of the clockwork tractor in Brendan's hands. Then Ellen lashed out at her brother.

"You broke it. You broke the cup, and you stood on the saucer. You're an idiot. I'm telling Mammy. You're so stupid," she screamed at him. "Stupid and mean! I hate you, hate you," she tried to pummel at his head and shoulders, but Brendan ducked and dodged out of her way. Finally, in her fury, Ellen snatched at his toy and, with all her strength, threw it across the room. Her brother let out a yell, and began to cry. Ellen turned her back on him. She was crying too, angry at him, and unhappy at her broken tea set. She bent to collect the broken shards of china, sobbing as she did so.

A door banged and there were rapid footsteps on the stairs. The room door flew open and their aunt stood in the doorway, breathless.

"What happened? What did you do? What was that noise?"

They both stopped crying and stared up at their aunt. Her face was red, an angry face.

"Ellen! Tell me. What happened, why are you crying? Why is Brendan crying? Oh, no, how did that happen?" She saw the shards of china in Ellen's hand.

She knelt on the floor beside Ellen and gently took the broken pieces. "Oh, dear, what a pity, be careful, darling, you'll cut yourself. Those pieces are sharp. How on earth did this happen?"

Ellen looked across at Brendan who stood stiff and still, close to the sideboard, hugging the tractor to his chest.

"Brendan! Did you do this?" Aunty Sheelagh stood.

He stared at her, his eyes wide, but he said nothing. Their aunt went over to him. When she got close, Ellen thought she looked like an angry giant towering over him. "Did you break Ellen's tea set, Brendan?" Her voice was different to one they had heard her use before, it was quiet and scary. Ellen was suddenly afraid of her. Brendan looked scared too. Neither of them said anything. Suddenly Aunty Sheelagh pointed to the splintered notch of wood at the lower edge of the sideboard. "Oh, good God, how did this happen?"

It was Brendan's turn to look towards Ellen.

"Dear heaven, I've only been gone for a couple of minutes. I asked you to be good. I said I wouldn't be long. Look at that!" She pointed again to the damaged furniture. "I am *very* cross with both of you. You have been *very* naughty."

She looked from one child to the other, then sighed. "Look, I *have* to go back downstairs. You are to sit in those chairs," she pointed to the two armchairs on either side of the fireplace. "Touch nothing, and stay quiet until I get back. Do you understand?"

Both of them nodded and moved towards the chairs.

"I am *extremely* disappointed in both of you. You had two beautiful new toys to play with and yet I couldn't leave you alone for five minutes before you're fighting and breaking things. Your mother would be so disappointed in you. It sounded like a pitched battle up here. Heaven knows what the customers, or the staff, think." She watched as they settled into the chairs. "I'll be back soon. We'll talk about this then."

She left, closing the door hard, behind her. Ellen and Brendan sat in silence until she came back.

When she did she didn't actually mention the fight again, but they were all very quiet for the rest of the evening. She gave them their tea, scrambled eggs on toast, and they ate in silence. Soon afterwards she took them upstairs, bathed them and put them to bed.

* * *

Ellen had been lying in the dark ever since. She hated Aunty Sheelagh. She wanted to go home. She didn't want to be on holiday.

And this was only their first night in this strange house.

A Message

Beth rinsed the breakfast dishes and stacked them on the draining board. Every sound, the clink of china on china, the rattle of the cutlery, echoed in the too-quiet house. She hadn't slept well. She wondered if the children had arrived in Bristol yet, and how their journey had been. Should she have let them go? She hoped they hadn't been ill. She clearly remembered her own first boat crossing of the Irish Sea, and how violently ill she had been. But then, she'd been pregnant with Ellen.

She dried the dishes and decided she would take a walk down to the phone box later, call Sheelagh, and find out if they had arrived safely. If only they had a telephone in the house. She and Michael had talked about it a few times, but in the end he'd only laughed and asked her who they knew that they would want to call, who had a telephone, except for Sheelagh, of course. She needed one for the shop. Funny, just a few days before the accident, Beth had finally talked Michael into getting one, convincing him it would be handy for calling the doctor if the children were sick, or so that Michael could let her know if he was delayed on a flight somewhere, and especially if she needed to call an ambulance when this next baby decided it was time.

That *did* convince him. They both remembered the panic when Brendan almost arrived the night she sat waiting in the car outside the house, her bag beside her, and Michael tried frantically to crank the temperamental engine into life. It had been a close thing. When Beth reminded him of *that*, Michael had promised to fill out the application forms on his next day off.

"It's that or a new car, I suppose," he'd laughed. "I think the telephone's cheaper."

She dropped the dried cutlery into the drawer and pushed it closed. Michael! He was in almost every thought, every action.

If they'd had a telephone perhaps the airport people would have called her when the accident happened. Then she wouldn't have had to find out from that reporter, standing on the doorstep, asking her for a photograph of Michael. Of course he hadn't realized that she didn't know, and he'd been very kind after he had told her what happened and she'd started crying. He'd helped her back into the sitting room and gone to fetch Oonagh from next door. But he'd still asked for the photograph again before Oonagh shouted at him and pushed him out of the house.

Beth wondered where the newspaper got the picture in the end, because they did, and it was on the front page of all the papers the next day.

"Beth, Beth, where are you?"

"Here, Mum, in the kitchen."

"The post has arrived." Margaret came in from the hall holding a large handful of letters. "Look at all these; I can't believe so many people are writing to you. I suppose they're more Mass cards and letters of sympathy." She rifled through them. "Oh, look. Here's one from Germany." She handed it to her daughter.

Beth eased herself carefully into a chair and rested a hand on her stomach. The baby was kicking under her ribs and her back ached. She opened the envelope and read. She read the letter twice.

"What is it Beth; you've gone as white as a sheet?"

"This woman says it's a message, from Michael."

"What?"

"She says her son was a pilot, in the war." She looked at the envelope again. "On the German side, I suppose. She says he died just before the end." Beth looked at her mother. "She says he's been in touch with her, and asked her to pass on a message from Michael."

"Oh, Beth, that's terrible. What a horrible thing to say. Give me that," she held out her hand. "You don't need to read nasty stuff like that."

Beth held the pages a little closer. "No, it's not horrible. She's trying to be nice, I think. She says Michael says he's sorry, and he hopes I'm all right, and the new baby. He says I am not to worry about him. He's all right."

"Beth, that's just nonsense, you know it is. Give it to me, it will only upset you."

Beth shook her head. "It sounds like Michael, even though her English is not very good. The bit about Michael sounds like him. That's just the kind of thing he would say."

Margaret sat. "May I read it?"

"I don't want you to tear it up or anything."

"I won't."

She handed her mother the two, neatly written pages.

They sat in silence while Margaret read. She, too, read it for a second time. "Oh, my goodness." She shook her head. "I wonder how she knew the address," she looked over at her daughter, still shaking her head, "and about the baby." She frowned and scanned the two pages yet again, "I don't know, Beth. I find it hard to trust anything like this. But she doesn't seem to be looking for anything from you." She paused. "She seems to be very genuine about what she writes. It's *all* hard to believe. Not so long ago we were fighting and killing and hating each other, and then she can write this?" She pointed to the bottom of the second page and read aloud.

"May God bless you and keep you safe."

She folded the pages, tucked them back into their envelope and gently laid it down on the table.

The two women sat for a while, staring at it, then Margaret abruptly stood. "Oh, dear, come on, this won't do." She smiled down at Beth. "I think maybe we can read the rest of these letters later. What do you think? Now then, I'll make a cup of tea, and *you* go and powder your nose. The children are gone, and it's time we started sorting things out here, especially if you're coming back to Bristol with me."

Beth nodded but remained in her seat while her mother busied herself making tea. She had finally agreed that going back to Bristol was the best idea. Her mother was right, her family was there, and she would need all the help she could get. Mr. Timmons, the lawyer, had reviewed more of their paperwork and said that she probably wouldn't have an awful lot of money. He had made enquiries and discovered that the airline had no insurance on Michael. However, they had explained, as far as preliminary investigations showed, they were not liable in any event; bad weather had caused the accident. It was an Act of God. Un-insurable. They did say that of course they would give his widow Captain Kelly's final month's salary plus an 'ad hoc' allowance to cover incidental expenses, like any possible funeral, but that was where their involvement ended.

The bank manager had been even more gloomy, and explained that very little had been paid off their mortgage, that the children were indeed entitled to two thirds of whatever there was, which would be put in trust for them until their majority, and that there would be precious little left for Beth.

Every time she thought about the future, she got so frightened. The baby roiled in her stomach and she would rest her hands there, trying to reassure it. Him! She couldn't even get a job ... certainly not while she was pregnant, and how could she go out to work afterwards, with three small children to care for? No, it seemed Beth's only hope was Michael's insurance money, but everyone said that would take a while. She *had* to move to Bristol. She *had* to put the house up for sale to pay off the mortgage. She had no choice but to go and live with her mother, at least until the baby was born and her finances were clearer. Sheelagh promised to talk to Colm as soon as she got back to Bristol. He would know how much the insurance was worth, and how she should claim it. That was her lifeline. God bless Michael for taking it out, even though they couldn't really afford it.

"Here you are, love." Margaret startled Beth out of her reverie. Her mother put the cup of tea in front of her. "And I've put some extra sugar in, to give you a bit of energy. Now, what are we going to do today?"

"Thanks Mum." Beth sipped at her tea. "I want to call Sheelagh and see if they arrived safely."

Margaret looked at her watch. "They're hardly off the boat yet, darling. Remember, Sheelagh said she would take a cabin so the children could sleep through the night? They'll get the morning train. They won't be in Bristol 'til late this afternoon. So ... in the meantime why don't get we get busy and tackle some of the cupboards and drawers, clear them out, you need to get your mind off things a bit. We can call Sheelagh this evening, after tea. They should be home by then."

"But the phone's in the office; the shop will be closed. They won't hear it."

"Oh, yes, of course. Well, we'll just have to wait until tomorrow. You know they'll be fine anyway, Beth, love. Sheelagh was so excited about having them. I suspect she'd really like to have children of her own."

"Mmm. Ellen and Brendan might change her mind." Beth smiled. "All right then. Cupboards and drawers it is." She tapped the pile of letters still on the table. "But I'll finish reading these first. And I think I'll keep this one," she said, taking up the German woman's letter, and setting it to one side.

Sorting

Beth sat on the edge of the bed and stared at the battered shoebox. A thick rubber band kept the broken lid in place. The box had been tucked in the back corner of the wardrobe for as long as she could remember. Michael had put it there when they first unpacked. When she'd asked him about it he'd laughed and shrugged and said, "It's just some of my old junk. I'll throw it away some time." But he hadn't. She'd never looked inside, hadn't even opened it when Mr. Timmons asked her to go through any paperwork Michael might have. She just knew the contents of this box would be different, personal, and if Michael had wanted her to know about it, or see it, he would have shown it to her. Anyway, he said it was junk. Beth tugged the box across the eiderdown towards her. Her heart beat a little faster. It felt like she was spying on Michael; this was his private stuff. But she wasn't spying! She had to sort everything before the move. She took a deep breath. She had to open it.

As she eased the rubber band to one end it broke apart, brittle with age, and the lid rose slightly from the pressure of the contents. She jumped and looked towards the bedroom door, as if the band had made a loud enough noise it might attract her mother's attention downstairs. But the door was closed and she could still hear her mother puttering in the kitchen, where she'd left her sorting the children's toys before boxing them up. Beth pushed the lid gently aside with her finger; there was a slight musty smell, like the one from old books in libraries.

The yellowing pile of paperwork inside was topped by what looked like a thin school book, grubby and grease-stained. It had clearly been rolled into a tube at some time. She lifted it out, smoothed it flat, and saw it was an atlas with a picture of a world globe on the front cover. Opening the first page she saw in one corner an inked inscription, faded and brown. 'To Michael. Christmas 1938.' It wasn't signed, but Beth knew who it was from. She knew Mr. Porter,

Aunty Wyn's brother, had given it to him. Michael told her about it when they were courting. She knew he'd carried it with him all through the war, even taken it to Africa with him when he went there to do his flight training. Beth looked from the grimy, dog-eared book to the engagement ring on her finger. Michael had bought it in Africa, a tiny diamond, in a fragile, thin gold band. He'd said that one day he would buy her a better one, 'when they were rich,' but she insisted she thought it was a perfect size. And it was. She kissed the ring, paused for a moment, then returned to the atlas. She flipped slowly through the pages. Some countries had been shaded in with pencil and there were circles around several places in Rhodesia, but they didn't seem to be around towns. She closed the book, laid it on the bed and gently rested her hand on it.

It was a while before Beth looked back at the box. The next item was a small, folded, cream card, a thin ribbon tied around the fold. She smiled, remembering. It was the menu from the hotel in Devon where they'd spent their honeymoon. Well, the three days leave that had been their honeymoon. She remembered they had to give the receptionist their ration books when they arrived, but they got a fresh boiled egg, each, for breakfast the next morning, and rations couldn't buy those. The owner of the hotel told them that she still kept a couple of chickens, and it was the least she could do, Michael being in the air force, and they being on their honeymoon.

Beth took out the menu and laid it beside the atlas, her attention now caught by a much-creased, sepia photograph tucked upright at the side of the box. It was a picture of an old lady and a little boy. She looked closer, Aunty Wyn and Michael, taken in their back yard by the look of it. Michael was in his cassock and surplus, his altar boy clothes. He looked so handsome, even then. Beth smiled again, brought the photograph to her lips and kissed it softly.

Aunty Wyn. Poor old lady! They had tried to talk to her a few times after the wedding, but she closed the door in their faces. She'd refused all help from Beth and Michael too, returning letters unopened. Michael tried to visit the old lady on his own, before he left for Ireland. By that time her brother had placed her in a home for elderly, indigent women. He'd said it was because her eyesight had failed and she couldn't live on her own anymore. Michael said it was more likely because she couldn't earn enough with her sewing to pay her brother his rent money.

Aunty Wyn had died two years after they moved to Ireland. It was Sheelagh who told them. Poor old lady, so lonely, so bitter. Sheelagh said there were only five people at the funeral.

Beth took out another photograph, it was of Michael in khaki shorts and shirt and wearing a forage cap. That must have been when he was in Africa. Beth had never seen this picture before. And it was funny to see him in shorts. In England, and in Ireland, men just rolled up their trousers if they were paddling at the beach. Michael's knees looked knobbly though she never remembered noticing that before. She glanced back at the menu. They hadn't been able to paddle when they were on their honeymoon, because of the rolls of barbed wire along all the beaches, put there in case of a German invasion.

She put the photographs to one side. Next was a large bundle of letters, tied together with a piece of string. She picked open the knot and saw they were the letters she had written to Michael during the war. Beth didn't know he'd kept them. She put them beside the photographs; she didn't want to read them, not yet anyway. She was surprised to find a letter to Michael from her mother, thanking him for all his help and support after Beth's father and brother had been killed in the bombing raid. Beth vividly remembered that day.

At the very bottom of the box there was a small colored picture of Saint Patrick, in his blue bishop's vestments, wearing his bishop's miter, holding a gold crosier and with one hand, the other on his heart and his bare foot on a snake. She turned the picture over and read: '*To Michael, on the occasion of your First Holy Communion. May God always hold you in the palm of his hand. Best wishes, Sister Thomas.*' Beth stroked her finger over the words. Sister Thomas, one of his junior school teachers. She'd always been nice to him; Michael had mentioned her a few times.

Beth gathered these few, small, personal mementoes of Michael's life. Sad, there was so little. She put them gently back in the box and replaced the lid. She had a collection of rubber bands in the kitchen drawer; she'd get a new one. And she would make sure this box went in her suitcase. She didn't want to lose it during the move.

Preparing

Now that Beth had finally agreed to the move to Bristol, Margaret began planning in earnest. Bless Bill that as soon as they heard the terrible news, he'd suggested she should bring Beth and the children back home with her. He'd no children of his own, but, even before their marriage, he'd taken to Margaret's children, and grandchildren, as if they were his own. They liked him too. He was kind, and loving, and he surely filled the huge emptiness she'd felt after her Tom, and poor George, had been killed.

Who would have thought that she would ever marry again? "Especially," as Evelyn insisted on pointing out, "with the shortage of men after the war."

Evelyn would be glad Beth was coming home too; she was close to her sister.

Margaret took up a handful of children's building blocks and examined them. There were tiny teeth marks on one or two corners and some of the alphabet letters were scratched and faded, but Brendan might still get some fun out of them. The new baby, too, in time. She put them with the small collection of 'keep' toys on one side of the kitchen table. There was a larger pile on the other side; broken cars, threadbare teddy bears, and any number of chewed, torn, and ragged story books. She would get the children new story books in Bristol. That would be easy. As she sorted through the cluttered remnants of the toy box, her thoughts again went to her new husband. New! She smiled to herself; silly really, it had been three years since she re-married. But it still felt new.

Margaret sat, and took a battered tin kaleidoscope from the box. She raised it to her eye, twisted the far end, and watched the multi-colored tinsel and beads tumble and twist into sparkling, ever-changing patterns. *I do miss him. It will be good to go home, there's too much sadness here. This family has had more than their share of sadness.* She stood and added the kaleidoscope to the 'keep' pile. *Yes, for sure, the sooner we get things packed up and ready for the move the better.*

The toy box was almost empty.

Margaret had arranged for three different removal companies to come and give them quotes over the next few days, but in the meantime she couldn't sit still, just waiting; she needed to do something. That's why she was sorting the toys. It was better to keep busy, *and* to keep Beth busy too. The sooner, the better, she said to herself, yet again. They had to be in Bristol long before the baby was due. What if it decided to arrive early? Perfectly possible, after everything Beth had been through, though the doctor said she was holding up remarkably well.

She took out the last few building blocks and added them to the 'take' pile, then stopped and listened. The house was very quiet; Beth was very quiet. She'd said she was going to sort stuff in her bedroom. Maybe she just wanted to be by herself. Margaret shook her head and sighed. It just wasn't fair, none of it.

She went out into the hall and called up the stairs. "How are you doing, Beth? Are you all right, love? Do you need a hand?"

There was silence for a few seconds before Beth replied. "No, I'm fine, still sorting."

Margaret went back into the kitchen. She scooped the 'keep' toys into the now-emptied toy box; there was plenty of space left, they could fill it with the children's clothes later. She gathered an armful of the rejected, battered toys and took them to the back door. She struggled to open it, then tossed the discards into the dustbin with a clatter. She looked up. It was cold, and the sky was a bright, clear blue. At least there would be no more rain, or snow, tonight. Margaret shivered and slipped back inside. Someone was knocking on the front door and she hurried to answer it.

Help

"Good day to you, Missus. I'm sure you'll not be remembering us." The young man indicated a second man standing behind him. "We attended the funeral service, but we didn't like to bother herself, what with the day that was in it, and all. A terrible thing, Missus, a terrible thing."

Margaret didn't recognize either of the young men, though she did recognize the whiff of alcohol.

"Donal Murphy's the name, Missus, and this is my brother, Sean. Paddy would have been with us, but he has a new job and his boss was not too keen on giving him the time off."

He noticed Margaret's puzzled stare.

"He's the oldest. Well, he is now, since poor Frankie died, God rest him."

Margaret still had a firm grip on the door. She had begun to close it when Donal put his hand out to stop her, and explained.

"That would be Frank Murphy, Missus. He trained with Michael, Lord rest his soul. They flew together. They were friends."

Margaret released the door. Her hands flew to her face. "Frank? Frank Murphy? The one who was supposed to be Michael's best man?"

"The very one, Missus. The mammy sent us over to see if there was anything we could do for the young widow. She said we should leave a decent bit of time, that ye'd have all kinds of people coming around, and things to do. She said to wait a bit, 'til things settled down, then we were to come around and ask if we could help." He thrust a large, brightly colored biscuit tin towards Margaret. "She made a cake. And she said to tell you it has three eggs in it."

Margaret smiled and stood back. "Come in, come in, I'm so sorry. I didn't know who you were. We've had newspaper people and all sorts knocking on the door."

"I quite understand, Missus." Donal and his brother snatched their caps from their heads as they stepped into the hall. Donal was still holding the tin.

Margaret indicated the front room. "Please, go in, take a seat. I'll call my daughter."

Donal held up his fist, still clutching the cap. "We don't want to intrude, Missus. If she's busy, or resting, we can call again. The mammy would have come herself, but it's the terrible arthritis she has now, in her knees especially. Getting about is a bit of a struggle. But she sends her deepest condolences. Heartbroken she was when she heard. Michael came over to the house a few times after they moved here; told her stories about Frankie and himself during the war. She was very grateful to him for that. She knew what a good friend he was to our Frankie. Indeed, a great friend, if you don't mind my saying so, Ma'am."

Donal, who finally seemed to have run out of steam, thrust his cap into his jacket pocket and stood looking at Margaret.

"She thought he was a lovely lad too." He added, again offering her the tin.

Margaret took it and nodded. "Thank you." She edged behind them to close the front door. "Please, go on inside. I'll get Beth."

The two brothers did as they were asked. Margaret hurried upstairs and knocked on Beth's door. "Beth, love, you have visitors, Frank Murphy's brothers. I've put them in the front room. I'm going to put the kettle on."

"Thanks Mum."

Beth's voice sounded muffled, like she was crying again.

"I'll be down in a minute. I'll just tidy myself a bit first."

"All right, love." Margaret returned to the kitchen, busied herself filling the kettle, rinsing the pot, and soon heard Beth come downstairs. Margaret cut thin slices of Mrs. Murphy's cake and arranged them on a plate. As she waited for the kettle to boil she heard the murmur of voices from the front room. Beth sounded pleased to see the two young men. She heard her laughing. How long had it been since she heard her daughter laugh? Margaret finished making the tea, loaded the tray, and carried it through.

"Here we are." She put it down on the coffee table and began to pour. "Mrs. Murphy, Frank's mother, sent you this cake, Beth."

"Donal and Sean have just been telling me about Michael's visit to Southern Ireland, Mum, during the war. I didn't realize he could have been arrested, and interned. He never mentioned that bit when he told me about it."

"Sure Frankie would have minded him, Mrs. Kelly, Ma'am. No danger of him gettin' locked up with our Frankie along." Sean reached to take the offered tea.

"Mmmm. Well, I'm certainly glad he didn't get into trouble." As soon as she said it Margaret knew she sounded disapproving, critical. She felt her face warm.

Beth looked up at her mother, a little surprised. "I mean, I know he was visiting his family, but getting arrested ..." Margaret felt flustered and decided a change of topic would be best. She turned to the older brother.

"So, Donal, what is it you do in Dublin?"

"I work in Graingers Bar and Lounge, Ma'am, near the Five Lamps. And a grand job it is too. I work late, but it means I can be around in the mornings, to help the Ma. You know, get her a bit of breakfast, that sort of thing, before I go out to work."

"And what about your brothers?" Maybe that was why she could smell the drink, she thought, he worked in a bar. "What about you, Sean?' She poured the tea and handed a cup to Beth.

"I work on the docks, Missus, in the coal yard. Dirty work, but it meant we never went without coal, right through the war. We were always warm. Still are."

"And your brother ... Paddy, is it?"

"Well, like we said Missus. He just started a new job; working for a removal company."

"Really?" Beth had been sitting quietly during her mother's questioning, but she leaned forward now, her face alight. "We're looking for a removal company, aren't we, Mum?"

"We certainly are. Is his company a reputable one?"

Sean frowned and Donal looked surprised.

"Oh, dear, I do seem to be putting my foot in it. I'm sorry. I didn't mean to sound rude. It's just I'm concerned for my daughter. I really need to be sure her things are taken care of. They may need to go into storage for a while … does your brother's company do that?"

"I don't really know, Ma'am, but how about we mention this to Paddy tonight. He can talk to his boss and then maybe they could come over and talk to you. Does that sound like a plan?"

Beth leaned forward and touched his hand. "That would be wonderful, Sean. I would be much happier if I knew the people who were looking after the packing and moving."

"Right so, consider it done. I'll get the brother to come over tomorrow evening." He turned to Margaret, "If that is all right with yourself, Ma'am?"

"Thank you Sean, that would be perfect." Margaret smiled, "Now, would you like a slice of your mother's cake?"

The brother returned her smile and the visit continued with talk of Dublin, their mother, and how things had improved since the end of the war. There was no more talk of Frank, or Michael, or the impending move. Margaret was grateful for the diversion from talk of death, and loss, and problems. She thought Beth probably was too.

* * *

True to the brother's promise Paddy and his new boss, a bluff, middle-aged man called Eamon Rafferty, arrived soon after tea the following evening. Paddy had clearly explained the circumstances, and connection, to his employer. Mr. Rafferty sympathized with Beth's loss, told her he would be honored to do the work, and assured her he would make sure his charges were less than his competitors.

Despite not having an actual figure, and even though the other companies had not yet submitted quotes, Beth thanked him and said she would certainly be using his firm.

All that was needed now was for a date to be set.

First Night

Brendan was crying, very quietly. That must have been what woke her. Ellen opened her eyes, it was very dark. She saw a square in the ceiling and stars. She got a frightened feeling in her tummy, where was she? She sat up and made her eyes open really wide. Was she dreaming? Mammy hadn't left the door open, or the light on like she usually did, and the bed smelled different. She must be dreaming. She stretched her hand out to find Mandy and pulled the doll close. She heard Brendan's muffled crying again.

"Brendan? What's wrong Brendan?"

"I need to tinkle."

Her eyes were getting used to the darkness. She could see the shadow of her brother's bed. He was huddled, sitting up, in the corner. Then she remembered. She remembered the boat journey, their arrival in the strange house over a shop, Aunty Sheelagh ... and the broken tea set. And she was cross with Brendan again. But he was crying, and Mammy had told her to mind her brother.

"All right, do you want me to take you?"

"Yes, please."

She put Mandy down, and struggled out of the bedclothes. The floor was cold on her bare feet. She pulled back the covers of Brendan's bed and helped him clamber out too. Arms outstretched she found the door, then turned to her brother.

"Stop crying, Bren, we don't want to wake them. I'll take you. Hold my hand, come on."

He grabbed at her hand and held onto it, very tightly.

"Ouch, stop squeezing."

She fumbled around the door with her free hand, found the knob and turned it slowly, carefully, but it still made a loud click as it opened and she froze into stillness, waiting to hear if it had disturbed her aunt.

Nothing.

Ellen slowly pulled the door open and, tugging her brother behind her, felt her way along the dark corridor towards the bathroom, pushed open the storeroom door and peered in. There was another ceiling window in this room. The faint, bluish moon glow let her see more clearly. It shone on the boxes and shelves. It also outlined the shop mannequins she had seen earlier; they startled her. Ellen jumped back, bumped into her brother and stepped on his foot. He whimpered, then stopped almost immediately when she shushed him. Ellen had never felt her heart beating this fast. It almost hurt. They were statues, she told herself, they were only statues. She turned to Brendan and whispered.

"Close your eyes, Brendan. It's dark so you can't see anyway, just close your eyes and I will lead you, just keep hold of my hand. I'll tell you when we get to the toilet. Are they closed?"

She thought he nodded his head. She tugged him into the room and pushed the door almost closed behind them, her brother was snuffling again. She was afraid he would start crying more loudly.

"Don't cry, Bren, hold my hand, nearly there."

Ellen led him slowly across the room, careful to avoid the statues and the boxes, aiming for the far corner where she knew the bathroom door was. They were almost there when she heard his foot kick something; she turned, just as he must have opened his eyes. She saw the hand on the floor at the same time as he screamed.

A door opened, a light went on and she heard Aunty Sheelagh's voice.

"Oh, my God, what's happened, where are you?"

The storeroom door opened and her aunt was standing in the doorway. She was a dark shadow against the hall light, but Ellen could see she was wearing a nightie you could see through. Her aunt must have turned on the light switch. The brightness blinded Ellen for a moment. Her aunt was struggling into a dressing gown, but it was almost as see through as the nightie. Ellen was embarrassed. She turned back to her brother who was still screaming. When she looked down she saw the hand was now in a puddle of pee. She looked back at her aunt.

Aunty Sheelagh was tying the cord of her dressing gown "Oh, good heavens, what happened? Why are you both in here? Oh, lord, Brendan! Have you wet yourself?"

His screams had changed to sobs. He glanced up at his aunt then bowed his head and nodded. The man appeared beside her aunt.

"What the hell's wrong?"

He was only wearing pajama bottoms and his hair was all sticking out and untidy, not smooth and shiny like it was in the day. He didn't have any hair on his chest, not like Daddy.

"He's wet himself," said her aunt.

"Good grief. Well, he's all yours, my love." He turned and left.

"What happened, Ellen? Why didn't you call me? Why are you both wandering about in the dark?"

Ellen didn't want to look at her, so she kept her eyes on the brown and yellow floor covering with all the tiny cracks in it. "He was crying. He wanted to go to the toilet. I didn't want to wake you."

"Well, I'm awake now." Her aunt sighed. "All right, you go back to bed. I'll look after your brother."

Brendan immediately reached out and grabbed Ellen's hand again, squeezing even harder than before. Ellen looked up at her aunt.

"All right, both of you, come on. Let's get into the bathroom and clean him up."

* * *

It took Ellen a long time to get back to sleep, her feet were cold. She wanted to go home. She wanted to snuggle into bed with Mammy and Daddy, and make everything better. She hugged Mandy tight. Why did they have to be here?

Visitors

"Good morning, my little sleepy heads; just listen to that rain."
Ellen heard the drumming sound. She squinted her eyes a little bit open. She could just see Aunty Sheelagh, standing beside her bed, but it still seemed quite dark. She opened her eyes a bit more and she saw the ceiling window behind Aunty Sheelagh's head, and the rain twisting and blurring the sky and the clouds outside. Then she opened her eyes all the way and she could see the horrible wallpaper, the jigsaw picture, and her brother's bed. Then she remembered the night.

Her aunt sat down beside her. "I thought you'd probably be tired this morning, so I let you sleep in." She was dressed nicely, in a pretty blue dress, and her curly hair was all shiny and neat, and she didn't even have her perfume on. But she still smelled of cigarettes.

"I've already opened the shop, *and* I've been talking to your mother. She says to give you both a big hug and a kiss and to tell you she misses you."

"Where is she?" Ellen struggled upright. "Can I talk to her?"

"She's not here, silly; you know that, Ellen. She's still in Dublin. She telephoned. She will be here soon, though."

"Can I talk to her on the telephone then?" Ellen repeated.

"Well, not right now, dear. Your Mummy was calling from a phone box. She will be back home by now. And our telephone is downstairs. We can't have you going down there in your nightdress, can we? What would people think? Perhaps later, when you're up and dressed and you've had your breakfast we can think of something."

Brendan kicked back his bed covers and sat up, rubbing his eyes. "I want Mammy."

"Yes, I know you do, sweetheart, but mummy is a bit busy now. She'll be here soon."

Brendan stared at his aunt and frowned.

"Come along then, you two. Let's get you washed and dressed, then we'll go downstairs. Maybe you can come down and see my shop later on."

When breakfast was finished, their aunt led them to the other stairs Ellen had seen yesterday. Her aunt flicked on a light switch. "I'd better go first; the stairs are a bit steep. Mind your step, won't you? And hold tight onto the banister."

When she got to the bottom she opened a door and Ellen and Brendan followed her out into a huge shop, almost as big as Peacocks Bazaar. The passageways had glass cabinets filled with all kinds of ladies' things. At the ends of the cabinets were lady statues, like the ones upstairs, except that these statues had clothes on. They had big eyes, painted blue, and dark red lipstick, but their hair was hard and the same pink color as their skin. Far over on one side of the shop Ellen saw a wide mirror, almost as big as the wall itself, with all sorts of hats on stands, on a wide shelf in front. The hats were every color you could think of. Some of them had flowers on, others had ribbon and lace, and one, very beautiful white one, looked like it was all made of feathers. A lady was trying on an ugly purple hat with green flowers and smiling at herself in the mirror as she turned this way and that.

"Come on, children."

Aunty Sheelagh took their hands and led them to a giant desk. It was so high Ellen could barely see over the top. It was cluttered with piles of big books, stacks of paper, jars full of pens and pencils, a mound of envelopes, and a few shiny, metal tubes with holes in. Her aunt took them behind the desk where there were two ladies sitting on high stools. One was fat, old, with white hair, like Ellen's teacher, Miss Carmody. The other lady was much thinner with brown hair and she didn't have many lines on her face.

"Ivy, this is my niece, Ellen," The thin lady smiled down at them. "And this young man is Brendan." Ivy had thick glasses on and they made her eyes look very big. "This is Miss Taylor, children. Say hello."

But before Ellen could speak, she was startled by a whooshing noise. Miss Taylor quickly turned back to her desk, reached out to a pipe that came down from the ceiling, and took out another of the metal tubes. She twisted it and tipped out money and a piece of paper onto the desk. Ellen watched fascinated as she counted the money, then she scribbled on the paper and slammed it onto a metal spike. She put some pennies into the tube, twisted it, and pushed it back into the pipe. Another whooshing sound, and it was gone.

It all happened so quickly, Ellen was amazed. She cast a sideways glance at her brother and saw that he too had watched. Now he stared at the pipes that crisscrossed the ceiling to see where the container went.

"Children. Children!"

Her aunt was speaking to them again, and the old, fat lady was smiling at them.

"This is Mrs. Wall."

Even though the lady was smiling, she was also dabbing at her eyes. Another crying person, thought Ellen. Everyone seemed to cry when they met them.

"Hello, my little angels. How are you?"

The lady struggled down from her high stool, and Ellen caught a glimpse of a pink silk and lace under slip.

"You know, little man," she said to Brendan, "I knew your daddy, but it was a long time ago. He worked in this shop, so he did, when he was a young boy," she bent to Brendan. "He was a lovely young man. Looked a lot like you he did." She sighed and dabbed at her eyes again. "So sad."

"Doris!" said Aunty Sheelagh sharply. Mrs. Wall looked up and Ellen saw her aunt shake her head, stiffly, just a tiny bit.

"Oh, I'm sorry, Mrs. Hudson." The lady fumble in her pocket, "wait a bit, I think I may have something you children might like." She pulled out a crumpled paper bag, opened the top and offered it to them. "Do you like toffees? I'm sure you do, all my grandchildren like toffees; go on, my dears, take one, one each, I'm sure your aunty won't mind."

Ellen looked at Aunty Sheelagh who smiled and nodded, so she took two of the paper-wrapped sweets. "Thank you," she said, gave one to her brother, then unwrapped hers and put it in her mouth. It was sweet and chewy. It stuck in her teeth.

"You're welcome. Well, I have to get back to work; it was so nice to meet you. I'm sure I will see you again." The woman tucked the bag back into her pocket. She was struggling back onto her high stool when someone called, "Sheelagh! Are they here? Where are they?"

Their aunt gave Ellen and Brendan a little push out from behind the desk. Ellen saw a lady, hurrying towards them. The shop was quiet and the woman's shoes made a loud clatter on the wooden floor, her coat flapped open as she ran, and her long curly brown hair was all untidy from running.

"Oh! My goodness."

The lady raced past the last two glass cabinets, her arms open wide. She went on her knees caught both children in a big hug and nearly knocked them over. "Oh! Heavens! Look at you!" she squeezed them both, tight, and kissed them and was sort of laughing and sort of crying. "I came as soon as I heard you'd arrived." She put her hand on Brendan's hair. "Just like your Daddy's. How are you little ones? Did you like the boat journey? Was it nice on the train? Is your Aunty Sheelagh looking after you all right?" She glanced up at their aunt, "Sorry, Sheelagh, I know you are. How are they doing? How's Beth? How's Mum doing?" She looked back at Ellen and Brendan, and hugged them again, then she let go and sat back on her heels. "Oh, I'm sorry, look at you, you poor dears, you look so frightened. I'm sorry." She put her hand in her lap. "I'm Evelyn, your Aunty Evelyn, your Mummy's sister. Do you remember me? I was in your house after ..." She stopped herself, changed what she was going to say. " ... from when I was in your house a little while ago?"

Ellen wasn't sure that she did. There had been so many people.

"Don't worry, darling, it doesn't matter. I remember you, you're Ellen, right?" Ellen nodded.

The lady turned to Brendan, "And you are little Brendan."

He stared up at her, and poked at a piece of toffee stuck in his front tooth.

"I am so glad to see you both again."

She stood up, but put a hand on each of their shoulders and tugged them close as she spoke to their aunt. "How *was* the journey, Sheelagh? How are they taking it all?"

Ellen watched the two grown-ups. She saw Aunty Sheelagh's lips go tight again as she shook her head quickly.

There was a secret! Ellen knew there was a secret. Why wouldn't they tell her? Why did everyone cry? Was it something about Mammy? Was she sick? Was that why her tummy was getting all big, and why Brendan and her were sent away?

"Look, I have to dash to work," said Evelyn, "I'm late as it is, but I just had to come and say "hello". Can we take them at the weekend, Sheelagh? I know Mum's not at home, but Paul is dying to meet them again, and Bill of course, and Maggie, and especially her girls. Paul will pick them up, if that's all right with you? I expect you'll need a little break by then."

"That would be wonderful, Ev. I'm not very good at this looking after children business yet, and this is only my second day. It seemed easy when I watched Beth and your mother do it." She nodded her head towards Brendan. "We had a little accident last night and by the time I cleaned everyone and everything up I don't think anyone got much sleep."

Brendan slid his finger out of his mouth and stared down at the floor.

The lady ruffled his hair again. "A lot of strange things are happening to you, little lad, aren't they? Not to worry, we'll look after you. Won't we, Aunty Sheelagh?"

"We will." Her aunt's voice went quieter. "I was speaking to Beth, Ev. She's agreed to move over here. Your mother is going to stay and organize it all, and Beth wants me to get in touch with Colm about Michael's life insurance policy. If you could take the children on Sunday, I'll see if I can sort that out then."

"Fine. We'll collect them after lunch?"

Her aunt nodded, "We'll be ready, won't we children?"

Ellen was still not too sure who all the people were that the two women were talking about, but she nodded. She felt Brendan slip his hand into hers, and hold it tight.

"Great! OK then. That's terrific, I'll tell the others. Right," the lady tied her coat belt, "I'm off. See you on Sunday, you two. We're all so glad you're here. Do you like ice-cream?"

Brendan looked up. "What about chocolate cake?" he gave a slight nod. "Good, I thought you might. So do I." She kissed them both, gave them a hug, and turned to go.

"Thanks a million, Sheelagh, for doing this," she said over her shoulder. "See you on Sunday, you two," she called as she hurried out of the shop as fast as she had come in.

Settling In

Mammy did telephone later on, and Aunty Sheelagh brought them down to the office and sat them on the desk so that the wire could reach. Ellen and Brendan both asked Mammy if they could go home, but she said she would be coming to them soon, and they were to be good for Aunty Sheelagh and Uncle Richard. She said she loved them very much, but when Ellen said she wanted to talk to her Daddy, Mammy was quiet for a long time and then she asked to talk to Aunty Sheelagh. And that was all.

She didn't telephone again. Aunty Sheelagh explained that it cost a lot of money to make a telephone call from such a long way, and would they like her to write a nice letter to Mammy instead. Ellen said no. She decided if Mammy didn't care about them, then she didn't care either, even though she was lonely. And she was bored. It would have been nice to have someone to talk to. Brendan hardly talked at all; except for the few times he said he wanted Mammy or Daddy. He did stay close to her all the time and Ellen didn't like it when he did that, it made her fidgety. She wished Mandy could talk. She missed her school friends, she missed her toys and her books, and she missed having her own bedroom. Most of all she missed Mammy and Daddy.

As the days went on, Aunty Sheelagh sometimes seemed to be angry with her, though she didn't shout or anything. She just looked frowny and cross. If Ellen cried or said she wanted to go home, or pushed Brendan away when he was too near her, Aunty told her he was her brother and that she should love him, or she would give Ellen a hug, but sometimes she would sigh and tell Ellen she was doing her best and that her Mammy would be here soon. She bought them comics and books. Ellen wasn't very good at reading yet but she could make the sounds of most of the letters. Aunty Sheelagh read them a bedtime story before they went to bed every night, *and* she made sure that Brendan went to the toilet before she tucked him into bed. After the first night she tidied up the statues and put all the broken arms and legs in a cardboard box so that Brendan wouldn't see them and be scared. Even Uncle Richard tried to be nice. He didn't talk to them very much, but he did smile at them a lot and even read them a story one night when Aunty Sheelagh had to work late in the shop. They were also taken to Peacocks Bazaar for more toys, and they listened to Story Time and Children's Hour on the wireless. But Ellen still wanted to go home.

On Sunday morning Aunty Sheelagh took them to Mass. Uncle Richard didn't come with them. Aunty Sheelagh said he went to a different church. When they got home her aunt cooked the lunch and she and Uncle Richard talked a lot to each other when they ate, but not to Ellen or Brendan.

Aunty Sheelagh said she had to go and talk to someone called Colm and then Uncle Richard said something Ellen didn't understand and it made Aunty Sheelagh cross, and she said "He's my brother, Richard, and Beth needs to know about the life insurance."

Uncle Richard made a snorting noise and said, "Well, I hope he doesn't let you down. Always dances to his own tune, does your brother. Hasn't even bothered to help his folks out, since the old man's business went bust, has he?"

Ellen felt nervous; she had never heard grown-ups get cross with each other like this.

"Look, I'll deal with Colm, I might have to go over there; so could you go over the books for me. I think we're finally in the black, and making money. The shop's doing well."

"Can't believe it with all the stuff you got rid of."

"Let's not go over that again. It was old-fashioned. It needed modernizing. Haberdashery wasn't enough to keep the business going, and anyway I'm better with women's fashion stuff. It's working. You can see that yourself, Richard."

"Your father wouldn't have like what you've done."

"Yes, well, it's my business now." Aunty Sheelagh looked cross. She turned to Ellen and pushed the empty sauce boat toward her. "Give me a hand will you, dear?" She collected all the dirty plates and knives and forks. "We agreed on the changes, Richard. So let me do it." She took up the dishes and went into the kitchen. Ellen followed her. Her aunt banged the things down beside the sink, took the sauce boat from Ellen, put it beside the dishes, and went back to the sitting room. "Paul will be here for the children in a minute, then I can go over to Colm's flat. He never answers his phone. I've tried a couple of times. I'll be back here in time for tea."

The front door buzzer went three times.

"That will be him now. Come on, Ellen dear, and you, Brendan, let's get your coats on. Uncle Paul is here."

She bustled them into their hats and coats and down the front stairs. Halfway down Ellen stopped and turned to her aunt.

"Can I bring Mandy?"

Aunty Sheelagh shook her head. "We can't keep your uncle waiting dear, and I have to go out myself. Maybe next time."

On the pavement outside a tall man stood waiting, stamping his feet and blowing into his hands to keep warm. Even though it was Sunday he wasn't wearing his best clothes, only a bright-colored jumper and a blue shirt, and trousers that looked like there were lots of things in the pockets.

"Hi, Paul. Good to see you."

"And you, Sheelagh. Well, hello you two, how are you? I'm Paul, Uncle Paul, your Mum's brother. Do you remember me? I have been in your house a few times." He bent to Brendan, "The first time I met you, you were a tiny baby, and now you are such a big boy." He turned to Ellen, "and you are more beautiful every time I meet you, young lady."

Ellen felt her face get warm, but she stretched to stand a bit taller and look more grown up. This new uncle had a nice smile. She smiled back at him. His eyes were the same color blue as his shirt, like the bluest crayon in her pencil box. They were smiley eyes too. Ellen liked him. She wasn't so sad about leaving Mandy behind.

"Come on then. Let's get you both into the car before we freeze. What time do you want them back, Sheelagh?"

"Bedtime is about seven, but you could keep them a little bit longer, if you like."

"Sounds good. Bye. See you later. Follow me, little people." He walked off down the road and Ellen and Brendan hurried to keep up. There were lots of cars parked along the street, but he stopped at a bright red, shiny one with a low black roof that looked like it was made out of material.

"Not really made for more than one passenger, but I'm sure you two can squeeze into one seat can't you?"

Daddy always made them sit in the back when they went out in the car. Ellen was excited to snuggle in beside her brother in the front seat. There was no back seat anyway; the inside of the car was very small.

"Wave to your aunt," said Uncle Paul as he started the engine and wiggled the stick in the middle. There was a loud roaring sound, and Ellen felt herself pushed back into the seat as the car drove off down the road. It felt scary, but fun. They were near the ground and going very fast.

They drove past a long line of shops, turned into a very wide street, on a hill, with buses lined up at the sides of the road, and cars parked in a line up the middle.

"Your dad walked this way to work every day," he shouted over the noise of the car. Ellen stretched to see out of the front window. At the top of the hill they turned into a smaller road, with trees on either side. With each sharp turn Brendan gripped Ellen's arm and she held on more tightly to the edge of the seat. Uncle Paul smiled down at them. "You all right, kids?"

Ellen nodded and tried to smile up at him, but she was really very scared.

"We're nearly there," he said as he turned into another road where all the houses were joined together and looked the same except some were painted different colors. He stopped outside a yellow house with a green porch, and a green gate, and beeped the horn. Before he could climb out and open their door, Ellen saw the Aunty Evelyn that came to the shop waving out of a front downstairs window. Her hair looked tidier than the other day; she had an orange scarf tied around it so it didn't fall over her face this time. Uncle Paul helped them out of the car, the front door of the house opened, and suddenly a lot of people were crowded there, looking at them. Ellen was a little bit afraid. There was Aunty Evelyn, and a big man with no hair and a shiny head, and another lady carrying a baby. Ellen thought she had met the lady before, in her house, when everyone was crying. She remembered the nice smell she had, like flowers. There were two girls standing there too, staring at her. They looked a bit older than Ellen.

Aunty Evelyn ran down the path to them as Uncle Paul opened the gate.

"Hello you two, welcome, come on in. We've been waiting for you." She took their hands and hurried them up the path. Stopping at the porch she pointed to the lady with the baby. "Now, remember Aunty Maggie? Another of your mummy's sister's, like me, and here are your cousins, Georgie and Susie."

The bigger girl smiled at her and said hello; the younger one just stared. "And that's baby Thomas," said Aunty Evelyn. The lady holding the baby smiled at them, but Ellen thought she looked like she might cry as well.

"And this is Grandpa Bill."

The man with no hair put out his hand. Ellen took it. "Hello, Miss Ellen, so nice to meet you." He shook her hand, then turned to Brendan, "How do you do, young man, welcome." He stood back, "Come on in out of the cold all of you. We've a nice fire lit in the front room," he said.

They all crowded into the hall and Evelyn helped them out of their coats. "In you go," she said, "follow the girls."

The room was small and cozy, warmer than Aunty Sheelagh's house. There was a big fire and there were lots more easy chairs than in Aunty Sheelagh's. There was a squishy brown couch in front of the fire, and two big armchairs on either side of it. There were two more chairs beside a small table under the window.

Everybody started talking at once, and then they all laughed.

"You see, we all want to talk to you," said Aunty Evelyn. "Come and sit on the couch with me and we'll try and take it in turns. Go on, Bill, you go first."

The man was laughing too. "I just wanted to know how your Grandma Margaret is. Did she remember to send me her love or anything?"

"No, I don't think so," said Ellen, trying to remember. It seemed so long ago, but she didn't think her Grandma had given her any message.

He laughed again, "Humph! Fine thing, she's forgotten me already." But he was still laughing so Ellen didn't think he was really cross.

"You know she hasn't forgotten you," said the lady with the baby, "She must have written you at least six letters since she left."

Aunty Evelyn asked them if they liked it on the boat and then said, "Would you like something to eat children? We have cake and ice-cream, like I promised,".

"No thank you," said Ellen. She still felt full after lunch.

"What about you, Brendan?" Her brother gave a quick glance sideways at Ellen, then shook his head.

After a while the other lady said to the girls, "Why don't you show them some of your toys. The poor things must be overwhelmed with all these new faces."

The big girl nodded and held out her hand to Ellen. "All right, come on then."

Ellen scrambled out of the sofa. The other girl whispered, loudly, "but she talks funny, Mummy. I don't know what she's saying."

"Sshh, Susie, that's very rude. Ellen has an Irish accent, that's all. She probably thinks you have a funny accent too. Now off you go and play?"

The girl pulled a face, but her mother frowned and gave her a little push towards the door. Ellen followed them and Brendan hurried after her.

* * *

Georgie seemed very nice and asked Ellen lots of questions about what kind of house they had in Ireland and what dolls and toys she had. Ellen told her about Mandy and about the tea service and how Brendan had broken some of it.

"She still speaks funny," said Susie.

"Mummy told you why, Susie, don't be mean. She's just from Ireland, like Uncle Michael," said Georgie.

Ellen thought they were the ones with the funny way of talking, but she didn't say that.

Later, after they had played with the toys, when they were sitting down to tea, the grown-ups told stories about when Mammy was a little girl, like Ellen, and Uncle Paul told them about going to school with their daddy and how they had been best friends. It went a bit quiet after that and Aunty Evelyn asked if they wanted more ice-cream and cake.

It was a strange afternoon, because Ellen didn't really know these people, but they were her Mammy's brother and sisters and they were being very nice to her and Brendan, except for the Susie one, who just kept staring at her and didn't let Ellen hold her dolly or play with any of her toys.

* * *

Brendan was looking all sleepy on the couch by the time Uncle Paul said it was time to go home, back to Aunty Sheelagh's. Ellen didn't want to go. The house over the shop seemed dark and cold compared to this one, but she let them help her into her coat. Everyone kissed them goodbye and said they would see them again soon, then she and her brother squeezed back into the car, the "Red Devil" Uncle Paul called it, for the journey home.

When they arrived outside the shop he parked the car, helped them out and they walked to the door. When Aunty Sheelagh opened it he followed them upstairs. Ellen was glad he did. She hoped he would stay; he was nice, and funny, he'd told them lots of jokes at tea time and in the car. Now, as they took off their coats, he talked quietly to Aunty Sheelagh. Brendan climbed up onto one of the dining chairs and rested his head on the table. Aunty Sheelagh saw him, stopped talking, and put her hand on Uncle Paul's arm.

"Oh, look, Paul, I have to get them to bed. The poor little fellow's exhausted."

"I'll get going then, Sheelagh. We'll have to talk about this again."

When he bent to say goodbye, Ellen began to cry.

"Hey, no need for tears. I don't live too far away. You'll see me again."

She couldn't stop crying. Aunty Sheelagh sighed, knelt, and put her arm around Ellen's shoulders. "Would you like Uncle Paul to stay until I get you into bed, sweetheart? Maybe he could read you your story tonight?"

He smiled at Ellen. "Would you like that?"

"Yes, please," she said, trying to stop crying.

Brendan fell asleep as soon as they tucked him into bed. Paul sat on Ellen's bed, and began reading to her, but she couldn't stop crying so he put down the book, and smoothed her hair back from her face.

"Why so sad, little one? Are you missing your mother?"

Ellen nodded through her sobs. "And my daddy," she said.

He was quiet for a while, just smoothing her hair with his hand, then he took a deep breath. "Ellen, I want to say something to you, and I want you to be a very big brave girl when I do. Can you do that?"

She nodded again. Was he going to tell her the secret? Was he going to explain why everyone was crying all the time?

Empty

Beth sat perched on the edge of one of the packing cases. The house was quiet. The removal men had gone for lunch, and her mother was at the shops. She looked around the room. The whole house was almost empty. The furniture had already been wrapped in sheets and loaded into the van; these few packing cases were the only things left. Paddy Murphy had been true to his word, and his new boss couldn't have been kinder. He promised Beth the furniture, and all of the household goods would be carefully stored in his depot until she needed them. She had hesitated at this, not wanting to incur more expense, though she couldn't imagine what else she could do with it all until she had a new home of her own. *If* she ever had a new home of her own!

"Don't worry about it, Missus. There'll be no storage charges, not for the first three months anyway."

"No, no! I know that's not right," Beth protested.

But he was adamant. She noticed that Paddy had been quick to leave the room when this conversation began and she suspected the Murphy brothers knew more about this arrangement than they would admit. Paddy denied all knowledge of it when she confronted him later, and the boss continued to insist it was. "No charge, Missus, it's all taken care of, just 'til you get on your feet. Give you time to have the babbie and decide where you want it all sent."

But where, she thought, where was she going to go, once the baby was born? What was she going to do?

The baby kicked at her ribs, hard, and she put her hand on her stomach to quiet him. She pushed herself up off the packing case, wandered out into the hallway, and glanced towards the front door. More letters jammed the letterbox. She sighed. Would they ever stop? Her mother was very good; she read them first and only gave her those she thought Beth would have to answer herself. But Beth didn't want to write any more letters. What could she say? Thank you for your sympathy? Thank you for the Mass cards? Thank you for your offers of help?

'BUT YOU CAN'T HELP ME,' she wanted to shout. 'HE'S GONE, I'M ON MY OWN. I DON'T KNOW WHAT TO DO, AND I MISS HIM SO MUCH I WANT TO DIE TOO!'

She leaned against the wall.

"Michael! MICHAEL! Where are you? Help me ...please help me."

She was still for a while, then looked again towards the front door, remembering the first day.

The key rattled in the lock, Beth's mother pushed open the door and stopped in surprise. "Hello darling, what are you doing standing there?" she tugged the bundle of letters out of the letterbox. "There are still a couple of chairs in the kitchen you know. I have some fresh bread, and some ham. Come on, I'll make us a sandwich."

Beth slowly drew her thoughts back to the present, glanced back at the front door. Yes, she still liked the color blue.

She smiled at her mother, and nodded. "I'll make the tea; the lads will be back soon."

Lost

Sheelagh had pressed on the doorbell for the third time, but Colm still did not answer. She was sure she had the right address, though Colm moved home so often it was sometimes difficult to keep up. She turned away in disgust. Richard was right; her brother *was* a waste of time. He never answered his phone, and he rarely called 'round to see them. He hadn't gone to the memorial service, and she didn't even hear from him when she wrote from Dublin saying she was bringing the children over. She had decided to push the bell one last time, when the door opened. Colm squinted at her in the afternoon sunlight. He was still in pajamas and clutched his pants at the waist as if they were in danger of falling.

"Sheelagh! Good God, what's the matter? Is the whole damn town on fire? I thought it was the bloody police with all that racket."

She looked at her wristwatch. "Colm, it's four o'clock in the afternoon."

"That would be *Sunday* afternoon, right?" He ran his free hand through his mussed hair. "I don't know about you, Sheelagh, but I usually like to have a bit of fun on a Saturday night. And, if I'm not mistaken, even the good Lord rested on the seventh day?" He smiled at her. She didn't return his smile.

"I need to talk to you, Colm."

"Talk away, woman."

An elderly couple walked by. The old woman stared at Colm. He smiled and winked at her, then looked back at his sister. "So?"

Sheelagh lowered her voice. "Do you think I could come in? I'm not used to conducting my business in the middle of the street."

Colm glanced at the staircase behind him.

"Ah. Well …."

"Oh, for goodness' sake, Colm. I've no doubt your place is like a pig-pen, but I think I can put up with it for a few minutes."

He shrugged and stepped to one side. She brushed past him. The smell of stale drink and cigarettes was unmistakable. She hurried up the stairs. He closed the front door and followed her.

Arriving at the landing she scanned the four doors.

"At the back, second on the right," he called.

She pushed open the door. The room was larger than she'd expected, deep-carpeted, the furniture surprisingly elegant. On the far side of the room a small, period dining table and chairs were framed in the recess of a dramatically-curtained bay window. The window looked onto a small park that sloped up behind the building, its tufted winter grass bordered with a twiggy, shrub hedge.

Sheelagh had never seen this apartment before; they usually met at a restaurant somewhere for lunch, or dinner, and then only on the rare occasions when she was able to catch up with him. She knew he'd lived in various places in Clifton over the last few years, a very stylish part of the city and she often wondered how he could afford it, but she was impressed now at the basic elegance of the room, though it was just as shambolic as she had expected. Clothes were strewn over the gilt-edged chairs and the floor. An ashtray, full to overflowing, empty whiskey tumblers, wine glasses, and discarded bottles littered a low coffee table.

"Who was it, my darling?"

The woman's voice came from a slightly open door to Sheelagh's left. She turned sharply to her brother who was now standing at the entrance to the apartment. He smiled, shrugged, and called out, "Just my sister, sweetheart. Better make sure you're decent before you come out here."

The door opened wider and a tousle-haired blonde woman, wearing a man's dressing gown that was too large for her, appeared from the darkened room beyond.

"Naughty boy! I'm always decent, sweetie?" It was an American accent, a drawl. The woman cinched the thick cord tighter at her waist, pouted her lips in a kiss to Colm, and walked towards Sheelagh, hand outstretched. "Hi, honey, I'm Margot. Your brother is full of surprises. A sister!"

Sheelagh cast another hasty glance at her brother before shaking hands.

"Sheelagh," she said abruptly.

Colm rubbed his hands together, as if he were cold. "Right, well, that's got the introductions over." Sheelagh thought he might at least look just a little embarrassed. "Now, Margot, darling, would you be a love and rustle up a pot of tea. My mouth is as dry as dust, and I'm sure my sister could do with a cup, couldn't you, Sis?"

The woman arched an eyebrow, her forehead creased in a frown "If you will excuse me, darling, I'm not sure I should be entertaining your sister, quite in this fashion." she indicated the dressing gown. "I think perhaps I'll go get bathed and dressed, if you don't mind." Her voice was soft, almost husky. She smiled at Sheelagh and winked. "Slip into something less comfortable, don't you know."

Sheelagh was horrified at the brazenness of the woman. And she *was* a woman. Old enough to know better! She could even be older than Colm.

"Off you go then, my love. Little sister wants to talk to me for a minute anyway. The tea can wait."

He scooped up a pile of discarded clothing from an armchair, and indicated that Sheelagh should sit. The woman reached forward. "Ah, I would have been looking for those." She tugged two silk stockings from the jumble of clothes, then smiled at Sheelagh. "Do excuse me for a while, won't you, sweetie, so embarrassing!" She turned and walked without haste, toward what Sheelagh assumed was a bedroom, the stockings, like delicate transparent streamers, trailing along the carpet behind her. She didn't think the woman was the slightest bit embarrassed.

Colm watched Margot's departure for a moment, then dropped the remaining clothing on the floor. He cleared another pile from a chair opposite. "Wonderful woman! American you know, a widow." He lowered his voice. "Loaded!" He scrambled amongst the debris on the coffee table, found a slim, silver cigarette case and removed the last cigarette from it. "You don't smoke, do you sis?" he asked, tucking the cigarette into the corner of his mouth without waiting for a reply. He fumbled through the mess on the table for a lighter, and finally sank back into the chair as he blew out his first stream of smoke.

"So, what can I do for you?"

"Colm, you do know about Michael, don't you?"

"Of course I do, Sheelagh. Very sad, ironic really, when you think he survived all the way through the war. Got your message too late, couldn't make it. Tried."

"Did you even write to Beth?"

"I meant to. Really!" He shrugged, "But what for? What could I say? Never was very good at writing, and I can't imagine it would make her feel any better."

"Colm, he was your brother. She's his wife! I have his children back at the shop. Don't you care about anyone except yourself?"

He sat forward. "Ah, now, come on, Sis, let's not get all worked up. Of course I care. I care about Margot, don't I? And I said it was very sad. What else can I do? What do you want me to do? Mind the kids?"

"Oh, don't be so damn stupid." She looked around the room, and impatiently waved her hand. "You can't even mind yourself."

He gave a short laugh. "Come on now, it's just a little untidy, nothing a good cleaning lady won't fix. I think it's quite a nice little place, myself."

"You could at least write her a letter of sympathy."

He raised his hand in a gesture to silence her, "All right, all right, I'll write her a letter, though nobody wrote me one. He was my brother you know."

Sheelagh glared at him.

"Sorry, sorry. I know, yours too." He sucked deeply on his cigarette, and blew out another stream of smoke before continuing. "So, what *did* you want me for, not just to make me write a letter, I hope?"

"No," Sheelagh was perched on the edge of her chair. She wanted to be finished with this conversation, and be gone before that woman came back. "Beth wanted me to ask you about Michael's insurance policy."

Colm frowned at her. "His what?'

"His life insurance policy. Beth says Michael left it with you. She says she thinks he was sending you the money, to keep up the payments."

Colm was quiet for a moment. He stubbed out the remains of his cigarette in the overflowing ashtray, knocked ash and cigarette butts onto the table. He leaned back into his chair, clasped his hands, praying fashion, in front of his mouth, and closed his eyes.

"Insurance … Insurance … Oh, yes, I remember." He opened his eyes and sat forward. "Right, I'll have to look that out. Yes, of course. Probably in my paperwork. I'll look it out in the morning." He nodded his head towards the now closed bedroom door. "Probably not a good time to do it right now." He smiled again at Sheelagh.

"But I thought you had to pay in so much a month. That's why Michael left it with you, because it had to be collected every month?"

"Yes, I know, … but I had to come to a different arrangement with the fellow. I was hardly ever here when he called."

"Colm, don't lie to me. You do have that policy, don't you?"

"Of course I do." His voice now had a hard edge to it.

"Beth is banking on it. It's almost all she'll have. Michael didn't leave a will."

Colm made a quiet tut-tutting noise. "Didn't he now, careless fellow."

Sheelagh took a deep breath, her anger about to erupt, but before she could speak he waved his hands at her.

"Relax, relax, of course I have it. It just slipped my mind. Still a bit sleepy-headed you know. Wasn't expecting visitors." He stood. "Look Sheelagh, leave it with me, will you? I'll dig the paperwork out in the morning. Another day isn't going to make much difference, is it?"

It was clear the conversation was at an end. Sheelagh stood too. She was not convinced he was telling the truth, but her brother was smiling at her. And he couldn't be lying; he surely knew he would be found out if he did. No, he wouldn't lie, not about this.

"I'll call you tomorrow, promise." He walked with her to the door and opened it. "Stop looking so worried." He put a hand on her elbow and squeezed it reassuringly. "I will have it tomorrow." He released her elbow. "Make sure the outside door downstairs is closed properly will you? Sometimes it sticks a bit." He gave her a soft kiss on the cheek, his stubble scratching her skin. "Always nice to see you, Sheelagh. We'll have to have dinner again soon. It's been a while since we did that, hasn't it."

She found herself standing on the landing. "Call me tomorrow" she said.

Colm nodded and continued to smile at her as he stepped back and slowly closed the apartment door.

Excitement

Sheelagh cut the top off Brendan's boiled egg. "Perfect," she said and buttered his toast. "Your Mummy will be here tomorrow. Isn't that nice news?" She cut the toast into narrow fingers. "Here you are, darling. Now, look, you can dip these little soldiers in your egg. Is that what Mummy calls them? Does she do this?"

The boy looked at her blankly. She dunked the toast into the soft yolk of the egg, held the sliver of toast towards him. He obediently opened his mouth.

"Here? She's coming here?" Ellen dropped her spoon and looked up at her Aunt. "Really?"

Sheelagh smiled at her niece's excitement. "Of course 'really,' my darling. You don't think I'd tease you about something like that?"

"Can we see her?"

"Eat your breakfast, Ellen; give Brendan a good example." She said as she put toast fingers on Ellen's plate.

"Yes, but can we?" The little girl pleaded.

"Of course you can, but probably not tomorrow morning. She will be coming on the boat and train, just like we did. I expect she'll be very tired after her journey. Remember how tired you were?"

Ellen nodded.

"Grandma Margaret is coming with her, and I expect they'll go straight to Grandma's house. I'm sure we can go over, after she's had a little rest."

As they spoke Brendan dipped a piece of toast deep into his egg. The china egg-cup was shaped like a chicken, carrying the egg on its back. He watched as the yolk ran slowly over its wing, then glanced nervously up at his aunt as if fearful she'd noticed.

She had, but she smiled reassuringly at him, "That's all right, baby, just mop it up with your toast," she said and turned back to Ellen."Perhaps we can go over to Grandma's after tea?"

"Will Mammy be sleeping here, then?"

Sheelagh was not at all sure what the arrangements would be; she had no idea what Beth's mother intended; they hadn't talked about this part of Margaret's plan before she left Dublin. She was beginning to admit to herself that she found looking after the children much harder than she'd expected, even though they'd been with her only a short time. Did Margaret want to have Beth and the children living with her until the baby was born, she wondered, or did she want Sheelagh to keep the children until after Beth had the baby and decided what she wanted to do. After all, Margaret's house wasn't that big, only three bedrooms. Did she have enough room to take Beth and the children? But if she didn't take them, then they would be with Sheelagh for at least five or six more weeks, until the baby was born!

She didn't think she could last that long. They should be with their mother anyway; they were clearly missing her very much, only natural after all.

"Eat your breakfast, there's a good girl. We won't know for sure until I hear from your grandmother, or your Uncle Paul. They'll tell us when they know."

"But who is minding Daddy?"

"What?" the question startled Sheelagh. "What do you mean, Ellen?"

"Uncle Paul said Daddy wasn't very well and it might be a while before we could see him."

"He said *what*?" Sheelagh sank into the chair beside the little girl. What on earth was Paul playing at? He knew very well that Beth wanted to tell the children herself, when she was ready, though heaven knows it didn't seem right not to have told them by now. "When did he say that, sweetheart?" *Good heavens, he might at least have mentioned what he'd said. Now what was she supposed to do, or say?*

"When he was reading me the story in bed and I was crying and he said why was I crying and I said it was because I wanted Daddy. Then he told me the secret. He told me why *everybody* was crying. He said it was because Daddy was in an accident and he wasn't very well, and me and Brendan had to be very brave, and that Mammy would be coming to see us soon, and she would be able to tell us how Daddy was." Ellen took a deep breath. She gave Sheelagh a puzzled look. "But who will mind Daddy if Mammy comes to see us. Is she coming to take us home?"

Sheelagh stared at the child for a moment, then pushed her chair away from the table, stood, and hurried into the kitchen.

Dammit, Paul, she thought, what am I supposed to say? She thudded her fist on the worktop. Dammit, Michael, why? She leaned her head against the cabinet door and pressed her handkerchief to her mouth. She couldn't let the children hear her crying. She'd tried so hard to be strong for Beth, and then for the children. She didn't want to cry. It didn't help anyone. Her father had always told her that tears were for babies; that only weak people cried. 'Sniveling' he called it. She wasn't going to snivel. She wasn't weak. But still her tears came.

Sheelagh felt a hand on her shoulder, and spun round. Richard. She hadn't heard him come in.

"What on earth has happened? Are you all right, old girl? Did the children do something wrong? They seem to be eating their breakfast all right."

Sheelagh shook her head, and then leaned into his shoulder and burst into tears again. "Oh, Richard, I can't do it! I don't think I'm any good at looking after them. I don't think I can cope." She glanced up at him, "And to think I wanted children of my own!" She leaned into his shoulder again. "And now Paul has told them that Michael is sick, and Beth's arriving tomorrow, and I don't know what I'm going to say to her." She looked up at her husband, "And *I* miss Michael, too, even though nobody thinks I do."

He put his arms around her, patted her shoulder. "Come on, old girl, this isn't like you. I know it's been hard, but you've been doing very well." He made hushing noises. "You don't want them to see you all upset, do you?" he fumbled in his pocket, and drew out a neatly folded linen handkerchief with a finely embroidered R visible in one corner. "Here you are, blow your nose, and wipe your eyes. You're doing fine, Sheelagh, really you are." He watched as she dabbed at her eyes and nose. "And I'm sure caring for someone else's children isn't a bit like looking after your own." He continued reassuringly. "You'll be a wonderful mother. I know you will."

Sheelagh tried to control her tears, and smile. "Sorry, didn't mean to do all that."

Richard dropped his arm from her shoulder. "Good, right then, glad you're feeling better. Don't like to see you upset, old girl; you're our rock you know. We all rely on you."

She nodded and returned his handkerchief. "I know, sorry," She reached for his hand, and smiled up at him. "Did you mean that about having our own children? Do you really think I'll make a good mother?"

He squeezed her hand, briefly, then released it, "Of course you will, darling. We just have to get the business on a good footing first."

He looked awkward, like he always did when she mentioned having children. She was about to press the subject, assure him the business *was* on a good footing, that they could start a family any time they wished, but he spoke again, before she could, and his tone had sharpened. "And what the hell do you mean he told them Michael was sick?"

"Apparently Paul did, when he was putting them to bed. At least he told Ellen. Now I don't know *what* to say to them. Beth is going to blame me." She was crying again. "And she's arriving tomorrow."

"Stupid, irresponsible bastard."

Sheelagh looked toward the sitting room, "Shhhhh, Richard, the children!" She struggled to get her tears under control. Richard remained silent. Eventually she took a steadying breath. She shook her head. "No, to be fair I don't think he was trying to cause problems. He was just trying to comfort Ellen." She saw her husband's face darken, his frown deepen, and hurried on, trying to prevent one of his angry outbursts. "You don't understand, Richard; you're not with them very much, you've been looking after the shop, but Ellen is always asking about her father. I suppose Paul just felt cornered. I know I have, more than once. It was stupid of Beth not to tell them, before we left Dublin."

"You're damn right there, and then expecting *you* to pick up the mess and deal with it! I didn't think all this was a very clever idea, right from the start. They should have stayed with their mother, far better for all concerned."

Sheelagh stopped crying, startled by the vehemence of her husband's reaction. "But you said it was a good idea for them to come back with me?" She frowned, put her hand on his arm. "I called you, and asked you, and you said it was a good idea."

Richard shrugged off her hand and stepped away. "Well, you were upset. I missed you. Thought you might feel you had to stay over there if I'd said no." He stiffened. "It's been damned hard work running the business on my own, you know. I couldn't get out at all while you were away."

"But you had Doris; she would have kept an eye on things if you needed to do something, go somewhere, or Ivy."

"Oh, yes, right, of course I could! And then have you down on my head telling me I was letting everything go to rack and ruin."

Sheelagh darted a quick glance toward the sitting room, "Richard, please, the children! You know I trust you."

"So you say. But no matter what you say, it's *your* business." Richard jabbed his finger angrily in her direction "That's the point? It was your father's, and now it's *yours*. It's still Porter's isn't it? *Emporium* and *Haberdashery* may have gone but not Porter's. Oh no! I don't see 'Hudson' Fashions up there, do I?"

"You never said you wanted your name up there. It's always been known as Porter's. I just thought I should keep ..."

"No, you didn't, Sheelagh, you didn't think. You didn't think at all. And it's *our* name, not just mine. No, I'm just the help, not even the *hired* help; I came free, along with the marriage contract. What was it? Love, honor, and obey? ... Obey? ... I thought it was *you* who said that, not me!"

Sheelagh stepped towards him, tried to grasp his hand, to calm him, but he snatched it away and quickly turned to leave, calling over his shoulder, "you go back to your precious kids. Don't worry about me, I'm fine. I'll get some lunch in the club, *if* you can spare me from my shop-minding role."

Sheelagh stood, motionless, stunned, as he left the kitchen. Where had all that come from? What had she said? The living room door slammed with such force she thought she was going to hear the glass smash. It didn't. Instead it was very, very, quiet. She dabbed at her eyes, brushed away the remains of her tears, and gave her hair a quick pat into place. She squared her shoulders, and returned to the dining room. The children had stopped eating. They stared at her, eyes wide.

Leaving

Beth and her mother stood at the front door looking back into the house that had been Beth's home for the last seven years. It was time to go, even though the taxi man had assured them they could take all the time they wanted, that there was no rush, that he would be in the car when they were ready.

Friends and neighbors had been calling all afternoon, wishing her well, hugging, promising to write, to keep in touch. Beth was hardly aware of them. All she knew was that it was time to go. She looked up the stairs to the half-landing and the bathroom. The door was closed.

Please Michael, open the door, look down at me, smile your beautiful, sad smile. Tell me I've been dreaming.

Beth held her breath, just for a brief moment, willing it to be so, then sighed and turned.

Margaret put her arms around her daughter and hugged her gently. "Are you ready, dear?"

Beth nodded.

"It's going to be all right. I promise. This time tomorrow you'll be with Ellen and Brendan. You'll be home again, with your family. Everything will be all right."

Beth wanted to push her mother away, wanted to shout at her, NO! It will *never* be all right, and *this* is my home. Michael and I chose this house; *this* is where we wanted to live. We chose to come here, to live in *Ireland*. I don't want to leave our family home. I don't want to leave at all. I feel like I'm leaving him, too.

They stepped into the porch and Margaret closed the front door behind them. She led Beth down the path, her arm still around her daughter's waist. Suddenly Beth stopped. She pulled herself free of her mother's arm, and turned back to the house. Slowly raising her hand to her lips she kissed her finger and blew the kiss softly toward the front bedroom window, *their* bedroom, then, reluctantly, she turned once more and faced the small knot of friends and neighbors waiting patiently at the gate.

There were no more words, nothing more to be said. The taxi-driver hurried round to the back passenger door and opened it. The bags were already loaded. As she climbed into the car Beth heard her mother thanking people for their help. She laboriously eased herself over to the far side of the car so that her mother could climb in beside her.

While she waited Beth stared up at the tall, graceful, birch tree in the garden opposite. She'd always liked it, but now its bare silver-white bark seemed extra bright against the dull gray of the evening sky.

"Please, let's just go," she whispered to herself.

Finally her mother joined her; the driver took his seat and started the engine. The small crowd raised their hands in a silent goodbye, and the car moved away from the curb.

"Dun Laoghaire, you say?"

Margaret nodded at the driver's reflection in his rear view mirror, then leaned back into the seat with a sigh. "We're on our way, Beth." She reached for her daughter's hand and held it tightly in her own. "We're on our way."

Beth nodded, but said nothing as they drove to the end of the road. The taxi driver stopped, waiting for a gap in the traffic onto the busy Whitehall Road. Beth glanced over at the chemist shop on the corner. She'd weighed Ellen, and Brendan, there every week, on the baby scales, just as the nurse had told her to. The Chemist, Mr. Nelligan, had always been so nice to her. He and Mrs. Nelligan. She was a retired nurse, and worked in the shop alongside her husband. She'd given Beth all kinds of helpful advice when Ellen was newborn and Beth was terrified she was doing everything wrong. Beth remembered when Brendan had fallen in the garden and bumped his head on the concrete path. Michael had scooped the child up and run all the way to the shop almost before the child had time to let out his first, full-throated yell of pain and shock. Mr. Nelligan had said he was fine, just his first bump and there would be many more before he was grown. He'd put a cold compress on it, "just in case, to keep the swelling down," and told them, "Just keep an eye on him for the next hour or two." Beth smiled at the memory. Michael was even worse than her when it came to worrying about the children, every sniffle and cough, cut or bruise, involved a quick visit to the Nelligan's, "just in case."

Now she'd have to look after the children by herself, *and* this new little one, she thought, as she felt a sharp kick in her side. She gently pressed at what felt like a tiny foot. I hope I can do it, little one, she said to herself and gripped tight to her mother's hand for reassurance.

* * *

Margaret had arranged for a cabin on the boat. An attendant showed them to their berth and said that there was food available in the restaurant until half past eight. Beth said she wasn't hungry. When Margaret tried to press her, Beth snapped at her for fussing, then quickly apologized. She knew her mother didn't mean to irritate her, but she was tired of being fussed over, advised, and yes, maybe even nagged! She wanted time to herself, to think, to rest.

"That's all right, Beth, I understand." Her mother said, soothingly, "You must be exhausted, you poor dear. Let's get you settled in here and perhaps I'll go and get something for myself. You wouldn't mind if I left you on your own for a bit, would you? It's going to be a long night. Maybe I can bring you back a sandwich? In case you feel hungry later."

Beth shrugged. She didn't feel hungry. She didn't feel anything, except perhaps very, very tired.

"All right then, dear." Her mother helped her off with her coat and pulled back the bed covers. "Why don't you lie down? Get some rest."

Beth kicked off her shoes and lay back on the bunk, grateful to stop, to do nothing. Margaret pulled the bed covers over her, tucked her in. She kissed Beth's cheek, as she had when they were small.

"Goodnight, love."

Beth closed her eyes.

"I won't be too long," said Margaret. "You're sure you'll be all right?"

Beth nodded. Her mother's voice seemed to come from a long way away. She heard the cabin door open and click closed.

She slept.

Dreaming

Someone was knocking on a door. Beth, her mind fogged with sleep, couldn't think where she was. She struggled to wake. A man called, "First breakfast, first breakfast." She felt the solid pounding of heavy machinery somewhere close by, but she couldn't think what it was. She didn't care, she was tired, she didn't want to wake. She rolled onto her back, her eyes still tight closed and, as she did so, her hands rested on her swollen stomach. *Then* she remembered … and smiled.

She was on a boat! The machinery she could hear was the ship's engine, and the gentle rocking was the sea. This is how a baby must feel in a cradle, so comfortable, so soothing. Beth kept her eyes closed, enjoyed the cozy warmth of the bunk, the steady throb of the engine, the rocking. She was going to Ireland, going to join Michael.

Through her sleepy, waking, haze she began to remember the strange dream she'd had, that the baby had already been born, that they had called her Ellen. She cupped her belly with her hands. No, it was only a dream, she was still pregnant. She smiled again, reassured. It was a strange dream, though, very strange. She'd actually dreamed they had two children, Ellen, and Brendan, a little boy that Michael had named after his father. She felt the child inside her move. It was snuggling into a more comfortable position, she thought, just as she had. And she would be with Michael soon. He said he would be at the pier when the boat docked.

So why had the dream made her feel so sad, so upset? She tried to remember. It was something to do with Michael. But then, she was always worrying about Michael, especially now that he was going to be flying again.

Then she remembered the part of the dream about the accident, and the funeral.

Beth instantly opened her eyes. Now she was truly awake. Her mother was sitting on the opposite bunk, watching her.

It wasn't a dream. She wasn't *going* to Dublin. She was *leaving*.

"Good morning, sleepy head. It seemed such a shame to wake you. You looked so peaceful and happy. It must have been a nice dream. You were smiling."

Beth closed her eyes again. No! She didn't want to wake up, wanted to stay asleep. She *never* wanted to wake up. She squeezed her eyes tight shut, heard her mother moving around the small cabin. *Please let this be the dream.* But she had two children. She was going to them. She had to wake up, had to open her eyes.

Her mother was dressing. She glanced down at Beth, stopped buttoning her dress, and smiled her gentle, kind, smile. "I'm so glad you slept well. You didn't even wake when I came in last night."

Beth pushed the covers back and struggled to sit up. Her mother helped her.

"I think we're coming into the harbor." Margaret looked at her watch. "We can stay on board for an hour or so after we dock, but how about we get you dressed and go and have something to eat now? Then we can get the first train. We could be in Bristol a bit earlier."

Beth shook her head, trying to clear it, trying to wake properly, to clear it of the confusion of the then, and the now. She so vividly remembered her last boat journey, when she'd traveled *to* Ireland, pregnant with Ellen. And now here she was, pregnant again, and on a boat again. She looked around, wondered for a moment if it was the same boat.

"Are you all right, darling?"

Beth nodded. "Yes, just a little muddle-headed."

"That's because you had such a good sleep. You'll feel better in a minute. Here, let me help you get dressed."

Beth eased her legs over the side of the bunk. Margaret helped her, lifted Beth's crumpled dress up over her head, put it to one side, and took a neatly folded one from her daughter's suitcase. Beth obediently raised her arms and Margaret dropped the lavender-scented dress over her head.

"Here, let me help you with your shoes." She knelt in front of her daughter. "I remember when I was expecting you children, there would come a time when I thought I'd never see my feet again. Your father always helped me put my shoes on then, when I couldn't bend over any more." She tapped Beth's feet and stood. "There you are, dear."

"Thanks, Mum. My mouth tastes awful."

"Why don't you brush your teeth? Splash some water on your face." Her mother indicated the tiny wash basin. "I'm nearly finished." Margaret took a comb from her handbag and ran it through her hair, squinting to see her reflection in the tiny, yellow-speckled mirror fixed over the basin. "Then we can go and eat."

"I'm not hungry."

"You didn't eat last night, dear, and that baby needs nourishment, even if you don't. If you just have some tea and toast ..."

Beth stood. She felt light-headed and the smell of diesel was now making her feel ill. She stumbled slightly. Margaret quickly turned from the mirror and steadied her. "Careful, Beth. You look very pale, dear. Do you want to sit down again for a minute?"

"No. I'm fine, just a little dizzy. I think I want to get out of the cabin though. It feels very stuffy in here all of a sudden."

Margaret dropped the comb into her bag, snapped it closed, and hurried to open the cabin door. "Come on then, dear. Let's get you up on deck. A breath of fresh air and you'll be fine."

Holding the handrail, they walked the narrow corridor to the companionway, their footsteps echoing off the metal-plated walls. Margaret's hand on her daughter's elbow steadied Beth against the uneven rocking of the boat. As they climbed the iron stairway Beth felt the cold, damp, morning air gust down to them from the open door above. She heard the screams and shrieks of seagulls and saw them wheeling and squawking overhead.

Once she and her mother were on deck Beth went to the ship's rail. They were indeed coming into the harbor. Broad-shouldered men in navy overalls waited on the quayside, ready to catch the heavy ropes thrown from the crewmen standing, ropes in hand, at the lower rails. She glanced up at the circling gulls again, and took a deep breath of the cold, salt-laden air.

Her mother squeezed her hand. "Does that feel better?"

She nodded, took another deep breath, then turned to her mother. "All right." She made an effort to smile, to reassure her mother, "I think I will try some of that tea and toast now, Mum. Maybe it will settle my stomach."

Margaret nodded and they made their way to the boat's restaurant.

It was as a crew member opened the door for them, that Beth felt the sharp pain in her side. She gasped, bent double, folding her arms tightly across her stomach. The crewman stepped forward as Margaret quickly wrapped her arms around her daughter.

"What's wrong, dear?"

"Just the baby kicking me again, I think."

"Stay still for a minute. It will probably go."

The crewman looked concerned. "Is she all right, Ma'am? Can I do anything?"

Margaret shook her head, "No, thank you, just give us a moment would you?"

"Certainly, Ma'am." He returned to his post inside the restaurant entrance.

When the pain lessened, and Beth could relax a little, she eased herself upright, holding firm to her mother's arm for support. She saw the crewman watching them through a window. She gave him a slight nod and he pushed open the doors again.

A young man in a starched-stiff, white, high-collared jacket waited inside, menu in hand.

"May I show you to a table, ladies?"

"Are you all right now, Beth?"

"I'm fine."

"Can you walk all right?"

"I'm sure I can. Just go slowly will you, Mum?"

She wasn't going to tell her mother. She didn't want to worry her any more than she was worried already, but Beth was frightened. This pain didn't feel like any she'd had before, not like the baby kicking.

"All right darling, take your time."

As the steward arrived at their table, the pain came again.

Waiting

Ellen had been awake since before it got light. She watched through the ceiling window as the sky changed from black, to dark blue, to a lighter and lighter color. The stars faded at the same time, until she couldn't see them anymore. Aunty Sheelagh had told Brendan and herself to stay in bed in the mornings, until she was ready to take them downstairs and look after them. Ellen got bored waiting, especially when she knew her aunt and uncle were up already, but she waited, as she had been told. She was a bit afraid of Uncle Richard since he had shouted at Aunty Sheelagh and slammed the door yesterday. While she waited she usually played with Mandy, told her stories. This morning she whispered to the rag doll about all the things they would do when Mammy came and they went back home.

She heard water noises in the bathroom next door, then her aunt and uncle going downstairs, and the loud noises when her uncle turned on the wireless. Uncle Richard liked listening to the news, and the sport, and all the talking programs, though Aunty Sheelagh liked the music. It was always the first thing he did in the living room, but then he and Aunty Sheelagh nearly always talked as well so that Ellen wondered why they bothered with the wireless. But they weren't talking this morning, and there were only the wireless voices.

Ellen crept to the bathroom, then back to her bed. Her tummy was making gurgling noises; she was hungry. She had just decided to go downstairs anyway, when she heard Aunty Sheelagh coming up the stairs. As she pushed open the bedroom door Ellen pushed Mandy to one side.

"Is Mammy here?"

"I don't know, Ellen, it's too early. They may be on the train by now, but they won't be here for a few hours yet. Come on, let's get you both washed and dressed so that we are ready when she does arrive."

Ellen clambered out of bed, hurried over to her brother's and shook him. "Come on, Bren. Mammy's coming today."

He struggled to sit up and scrambled out of his bed.

"Hurry, Brendan, we have to be ready," said Ellen, and held out her hand.

He took it, sleepily, and she tugged her brother, stumbling, out of the bedroom, followed by their aunt. He almost tripped over his drooping pajama pants and Ellen sighed with impatience.

"Hold them up, Brendan," she snapped, and continued to tow him in the direction of the bathroom.

Ellen tried to be extra quick brushing her teeth and washing her hands and face, not even waiting for the water to get warm like she usually did. She usually hated washing in cold water. As she rubbed her face dry she chivvied her brother to be quicker. "Come on Brendan, don't be such a slowcoach. We have to be ready for Mammy."

Her aunt laughed. She combed and braided Ellen's hair. "Give him a minute, Miss Impatience. I keep telling you, Ellen, we have plenty of time. Your mother won't be here for ages yet."

Ellen was not to be deterred. Once her hair was done she hurried back to their bedroom. By the time her brother and aunt arrived she had already picked out what she would wear. Her yellow dress with the tiny blue birds on the collar and cuffs was her favorite, and she knew it was her mother's favorite too. She wanted to wear it especially for her. Aunty Sheelagh agreed.

"When will we know they've arrived?" she asked as her aunt helped Brendan get dressed.

"Ellen, please stop asking so many questions. I don't know, darling. As soon as I do I'll tell you. Be patient. How about if I telephone Grandpa Bill after you've had your breakfast and see if he knows when the train gets into Bristol, all right?"

Ellen nodded, but she didn't know how she was going to stay still long enough to have breakfast. She was so excited; it was even more exciting than birthdays, and she loved birthdays. Mammy was coming, and they were all going home to mind Daddy.

"Now remember, I told you," her aunt continued. "I expect they'll be tired. She'll probably want a little rest before she comes over here. You understand it might even be after tea?"

Ellen didn't think her Mammy would want a rest. She'd come here as quickly as she could. Ellen knew she would. But she didn't say that.

When they got downstairs Uncle Richard was in his chair by the fireplace, but there was no fire and the room was cold. She wished she'd put on a cardigan like her aunt suggested. Her uncle was reading the newspaper and didn't say "good morning". The man on the wireless was talking about the weather. Ellen peeked around the edge of the paper; she wanted to show him her dress. He looked grumpy. Aunty Sheelagh sat them at the table and went to the kitchen to make breakfast.

Ellen said, "Mammy's coming today."

Her uncle didn't say anything.

"And then we're going home to mind Daddy."

He carefully folded the paper and looked at her, but he didn't smile. "Who told you that?"

"Uncle Paul."

He stood, dropped the paper on the chair behind him and said. "Tell your aunt I've gone down to open the shop."

He didn't bang the door today, not like yesterday, but Ellen thought he was still cross

"Will you two have bread and butter and jam this morning?" asked Aunty Sheelagh as she brought the teapot and a jug of milk from the kitchen.

"Yes, please," said Ellen as Brendan nodded his head. "Uncle Richard says to say he has gone down to open the shop. Can I come down with you when you make the telephone call to Grandpa Bill?"

Her aunt didn't really look like she was listening; she looked like she was thinking a lot, but she said no, anyway, and they'd have to wait up here and be good and not get into any mischief.

When she mentioned mischief Ellen knew she was probably talking about the face powder Brendan had spilled on the dressing table and floor in their aunt and uncle's bedroom when Ellen and himself had gone exploring one morning when Aunty Sheelagh was busy in the shop. Or she might have been talking about when she found them in the front room looking down at the traffic in the street below. She said she'd told them they weren't allowed in the front room, it was for grown-ups only. But it was boring in the back room all the time, even with the toys. And looking out of the window wasn't mischief anyway.

It must have been the face powder. And that was Brendan, not her.

"Brendan spilled the face powder. I told him not to touch it."

"Don't tell tales, Ellen, it's not nice."

"But it was him, and I didn't do anything."

"And don't answer back," said her aunt sharply.

Ellen squeezed her lips together. Mammy was coming and she was going to tell her how cross Aunty Sheelagh was, as well as Uncle Richard, and then she would take them home even more quickly.

"All right …, look, if you promise to sit quiet, I'll go and call your grandfather, though I *know* they can't have arrived yet. Will you stop asking me then?"

Ellen nodded.

"Touch nothing while I'm gone. Do you hear me, Brendan?"

Brendan looked up at his aunt, his face and hands smeared with the raspberry jam.

"Wipe his fingers and face when he's finished please, Ellen. I'll be back in a moment. Don't touch the teapot either, it's hot!"

What!

Bill said Margaret telephoned from Holyhead, and that they were going to catch the first train, with a change at Crewe. They should arrive by early afternoon. He promised to call as soon as they got home.

Sheelagh thanked him. It was going to be a long morning. Staring down into the shop she noticed the large roll of brown wrapping paper by the service desk. Perhaps they could do some drawing and coloring as a present for Beth for when she arrived. It might keep them entertained. Armed with a large sheet, she went back upstairs.

*   *   *

"Sheelagh? Bad news, I'm afraid. They're taking Beth to the hospital, the Royal Infirmary; seems there's complications."

"What? Oh, no! What happened? When? How serious is it, Ev?"

"We don't know yet. Mum is with her, of course, and Bill's going to drive me there in a minute. Paul's going to stay here at the house, in case Mum rings for anything while we're on our way."

"Can I do anything?"

"Not at the moment. Look, I have to go, Sheelagh. Bill's waiting. I'll call you later. I promise."

"But what ... yes, of course, thanks, Ev. Give her my love, won't you?"

"I will."

The line went dead. Sheelagh put down the receiver.

"Are you all right, Mrs. Hudson?"

She nodded as she sank back in her chair.

"Will I get Mr. Hudson? You look a bit pale. He's just checking the cash drawer."

"No, no I'm fine, Doris, thank you. I just need to think for a minute."

What was she going to tell the children? *How* could she tell them after everything they had been through already? And they were both so excited.

Sheelagh looked over her shoulder. Richard was indeed at the cash desk, transferring money into the bank bag. Probably checking to see if the business really was still making money! He usually left most of the other work to her, ordering, designing, planning. Said she was much more used to it than he was. He glanced up and she immediately turned away.

He seemed to be so moody since she had come back. He sat up there in the office all day, when he wasn't at the club, trying to look busy, keeping an eye on the activity in the shop. Her thoughts returned to the children. She picked up the telephone and dialed the Howard house. Funny, she thought, as she dialed, it must be over three years since Margaret re-married, yet everyone still called it the Howard house.

Paul answered on the first ring.

"Paul. Sorry to call back so quickly."

"That's all right, Sheelagh; I'm just sitting here watching the phone. But if you want to talk to Ev or Bill, you've missed them. They've gone already. Or will I do?"

"No, that's all right, I can talk to you. I was so stunned to hear about Beth, I just needed time to gather my thoughts. Now I've started to think about the children. What am I going to tell them, Paul? How long do you think they are going to keep her in the hospital?"

"I have no idea," he said "I don't think anyone does at this stage. We have to wait to hear what they say. I don't know what Ev told you. She's pretty upset, as you can imagine. Mum said Beth started to feel unwell even before they got off the boat. They caught the early train, trying to get back here quicker. Mum said she got worse on the way down. Apparently Beth collapsed on the platform, just as they were getting off the train in Temple Meads. Mum said the ambulance was there very quickly. We're all worried about Beth, of course, but we're worried about the baby too."

"Do you have *any* idea how long it will be before they know?" Sheelagh pleaded.

"Sorry, no, I don't, Sheelagh. Mum was calling from the station-master's office; said to meet her at the hospital. She was going in the ambulance. It was a very quick phone call, while the ambulance men were helping Beth. I can't imagine they're even there yet. I'm sure she'll let us know as soon as she has any news."

"But I have to go upstairs and tell the children something. What can I say?"

There was a brief pause.

"Would you like me to come over, give you a hand?"

"Oh, Paul, would you?"

It would be a relief to have someone else here, to help when they were told.

Then Sheelagh remembered what Paul had said to Ellen about Michael. "And, Paul, what on earth were you thinking of, telling Ellen her father was sick?"

"Ah, yes, I meant to get back to you about that. I'm sorry, Sheelagh. The poor kid just seemed so confused and unhappy. She kept asking questions. I knew Beth didn't want us to tell them he was ….." he paused.

Sheelagh knew he was struggling to say the awful word aloud. Dead. She heard him take a breath,

Paul continued, " … didn't want us to tell them he had died. But I had to say something. Bloody stupid, I know."

"Well, it's certainly going to create more confusion," Sheelagh snapped, then stopped. She didn't want to start an argument with him, especially not now. She needed support with the children, and she didn't think Richard was going to be any help. "Anyway … Yes, please. I would really appreciate it if you came over, Paul."

"I'm on my way. I'll leave a message at the hospital. Mum can call me there, at the shop. That will be all right won't it?"

"Yes, of course."

"Fine, I'll be about fifteen minutes."

"Thanks, Paul. Use our front door would you, not the shop?"

Paul agreed and hung up.

Sheelagh replaced the handset on the receiver. She remained motionless for a moment before she stood, ran her fingers through her hair, then patted it back into place. She went down into the shop. She couldn't see Richard but she saw the concerned face of her cashier.

"Everything all right Miss Sheelagh?"

"I have to go back upstairs to the children, Doris. You can cope down here, can't you?" She glanced around the shop as she spoke. She could only see two customers, both in the handbag department. "We're not busy anyway."

Doris nodded, "We'll be fine, Miss Sheelagh. You go right ahead. Minding those children is far more important, poor little waifs. We can look after the shop. And Mr. Hudson is always around somewhere if we need him."

Sheelagh felt disinclined to comment on Richard's help. He hadn't spoken to her since he stormed out yesterday morning, sulking like a baby. He'd come home after she went to bed, and he'd reeked of whisky. Communications had been decidedly frosty this morning too. She would tell him about Beth later. To hell with him and his moods right now!

* * *

When she got back upstairs the living room door was open. It was very quiet. Ellen and Brendan were no longer at the table. Dammit, surely they hadn't got into mischief again, and after she'd told them to stay put! She crossed to the kitchen. They were not there. She hurried to the sitting room. No sign of them there either. She went to the foot of the stairs and called.

"Brendan? Ellen? Are you up there?"

She heard footsteps running through the stock room, then out onto the upstairs landing. Ellen called as she came, "Is she here? Has she arrived? Come on Brendan, Mammy's here."

"What are you doing up there? Didn't I tell you to behave while I was gone?" Sheelagh snapped.

Ellen arrived at the top of the stairs. She stopped and stared down at her aunt. Her lower lip began to tremble, her face crumple. "Brendan wanted to go to the toilet. Where's Mammy?"

Sheelagh bowed her head, "I'm sorry, Ellen. I didn't mean to sound cross." She took a steadying breath, then looked back up. "All right, sweetheart. No, your mother isn't here yet. But don't leave Brendan there on his own; you know he gets frightened. Go back and fetch him, will you? Bring him down when he's finished. There's a good girl. I'll wait here."

Ellen heaved a huge sigh, reluctantly turned and disappeared from view. Sheelagh heard her walk back along the landing and through the stockroom, shouting for her brother as she went.

"Brendan, Mammy's coming soon. Come on. Hurry up. Dry your hands on your shirt, it'll be fine."

Before long the two children appeared back at the top of the stairs.

Ellen stared at her aunt. "Is she coming now?"

Sheelagh was becoming exasperated with the child, but she felt guilty, too. She didn't want to snap at her, or answer her, and she didn't want to lie; she understood how Paul had felt so trapped.

"Come on downstairs, both of you. "

They arrived at the bottom of the stairs, Ellen still watching her aunt closely.

Sheelagh tried to give her niece a reassuring smile. "Come on, why don't we all go and sit down. I'll make a fresh pot of tea, and then we'll talk."

The little girl stared up at her, her face somber. It was clear to Sheelagh that the child knew something was wrong.

"Can I go back up and get Mandy first, please?"

Sheelagh gave Ellen a quick hug. "Yes, of course you can, darling." She kissed the top of the child's head. "We'll wait right here for you, won't we, Brendan?"

When Ellen returned she was clutching the doll tight to her chest. All her excitement was gone.

The poor little mite, thought Sheelagh. Dear Heaven, Beth, I hope you're going to be all right.

Decisions

As soon as she heard the doorbell Sheelagh hurried downstairs to let Paul in, avoiding the shop. She wasn't ready to talk to her husband yet, at least not until she spoke with Paul and had a better idea of how Beth was; *and* whether the children might have to stay for longer than she had expected.

"Thanks for coming, Paul. No more news, I suppose?"

"No, I left a message and came as soon as I put down the phone. They'll call here when they know anything."

"We do have to tell them, don't we? The children, I mean. We can't keep any more secrets from them."

"No, I agree, Sheelagh. I think we have to."

"I'm guessing Ellen knows something is going on anyway. She's clutching onto her doll for dear life, and she's not talking at all, no more questions about her mother, or when she'll be here. Poor little thing, she looks so upset."

They reached the hallway. Sheelagh lowered her voice.

"Paul, if I have to keep them here for longer than expected, I need to talk to you."

"All right, but let's get this over with first."

Paul followed her in.

As soon as the door opened Ellen turned to them. Brendan continued sipping on his cup of milk.

"Hello, Ellen, nice to see you again," Paul gave her pigtail a gentle tug, then playfully poked the doll in the tummy. "You too. Mandy, isn't it?"

Ellen gave her uncle a faint smile.

He turned to the little boy. "Hello, Big Man," he said, putting his hand on Brendan's shoulder; the child only glanced at him briefly before looking back to the table.

"Wow, look at those chocolate biscuits. Are they all for me?"

Brendan gave him a concerned look, but then saw his uncle's grin, grinned back, and shook his head.

"May I take one of them please, Aunty Sheelagh?" said Paul, winking at his nephew.

"Of course. We put them there for when Uncle Paul arrived didn't we?"

Brendan nodded.

Paul leaned over, took two biscuits and made a big pretense of secretly handing one to the boy. Brendan took it. Paul offered the other one to Ellen, but she shook her head.

"Can I pour you a cup of tea, Paul?"

"Yes, please, Sheelagh." He pulled out the chair beside Ellen. "You don't mind if I sit here do you?"

Ellen looked up at him and shook her head.

Sheelagh sat at the other side of the table. "Ummm, Paul, will you ..... or should I ..."

Paul indicated he would tell them and Sheelagh sat back, relieved.

"Right then, you two." he said, "I have a bit of news for you, but I don't want you to get all upset until I finish explaining, all right?"

They both nodded.

"Your Mummy is not feeling too well at the moment."

"Is she coming here?" asked Ellen.

"Let me finish explaining first, if you would Ellen. Then you can ask me all the questions you want, is that all right?"

Ellen nodded.

"You know she was coming here on the boat and train? Well," he continued, "Grandma Margaret was with her and Grandma Margaret decided it would be a good idea to take your Mummy to the doctor because she wasn't feeling very well on the boat. Just to make sure she was all right."

"*Then* is she coming here?"

"Ellen *please* ..." said Sheelagh. Paul held up his hand.

"It's all right, Sheelagh, I'll look after it. Just let me finish first, Ellen. The doctor she is going to see is in the hospital, and it might be that he thinks she needs a rest. He might want her to stay in the hospital for a little while."

Sheelagh saw tears well in the little girl's eyes. "She's not coming, is she?" she said with a whimper.

Paul put his arm around her and gently lifted her onto his lap. "Don't cry, little lady. It will only be for a short time, I'm sure. She's just very tired and she needs a rest, and it will be nice for the doctors to mind her, won't it? You don't want your Mummy to be sick, do you?"

Ellen shook her head; she was sobbing now.

"Here, would you like my handkerchief to wipe your tears?"

She held out her hand. He fumbled in his pocket; took out a crumpled blue and white handkerchief. "It's clean," he said, "it's just that I'm a bachelor you see, Ellen. I don't have a wife, and I don't know how to iron very well."

She took it and scrubbed at her face.

"Perhaps one day you could come over and do some ironing for me? Do you know how to iron?"

Ellen shook her head. "I'm only six." She said through her snuffles.

"Six? And here I thought you were nearly twelve!"

A faint grin broke through her tears. "No, not yet."

"Well, Ellen, I would like it very much if you were nearly twelve, because then you'd be big enough to understand about Mummy. So how about we pretend you are nearly twelve, just for now, shall we?"

She looked worried. "But I still can't iron."

Her uncle laughed. "No, that's all right. I'll manage with crumpled hankies for the moment. I would just like you to be big and brave and understand that as soon as Mummy is better you will see her. Can you do that for me?"

Ellen nodded. She was no longer crying.

"Good girl, thank you. And in the meantime will you help Aunty Sheelagh to mind Brendan. Just until Mummy is better, then you can be six again. What do you think?"

Ellen nodded again.

"Terrific," he said.

Sheelagh leaned towards them, more at ease now. "Paul, I had an idea about that. Ellen might like it too." She smiled at him, and the little girl on his lap. "I know the children are very bored here. Especially when they really can't go outside, you know we don't have a garden. Daddy built the storeroom out the back long before we lived here. Well, I wondered if I could get them into school, now just until we know ..." her voice trailed off.

Ellen frowned, and looked up at her uncle for his response.

"Goodness, Sheelagh, what a great idea." He bent his head to his niece. "What would you think about that, Ellen? That might be a bit more fun than being up here all the time, mightn't it?"

Sheelagh could see the mix of emotions on Ellen's face. The child continued to look up at her uncle, as if considering the suggestion. She finally gave a tiny nod.

"You could make new friends, play games, all kinds of things," he continued and Ellen mirrored his smile.

Paul looked over at Sheelagh. "That really *is* a good idea, Sheelagh. Do you think you can find somewhere to take them?"

"I can try. We did talk about it, in Dublin, but I had thought to wait and let Beth decide ... but ... They're going to need schools in the long run, so why not now?"

Paul nodded. "But where?"

"Well, I was going to talk to Beth about this first too, but I don't suppose she's in a position to think about schools right now. I thought I'd like to send Ellen to my old school. I'd pay, of course."

"That's very generous of you, Sheelagh, that's an expensive school."

"My contribution, under the circumstances."

"But what about young Brendan here? That's an all-girls school isn't it?"

They both looked towards the little boy. He had finished eating the biscuit and sat, oblivious to the conversation, sucking his thumb, his face and hands covered in chocolate.

"I believe Saint Nick's has a new kindergarten attached to their junior school, and Sister Thomas is the headmistress now. Brendan might be a little young, but you know she thought an awful lot of Michael, so she might be prepared to take in his son. We could talk to her. I could."

The door opened and Richard stepped into the room.

"Well this is cozy. .... What the hell are you doing here, Paul? I would have thought you'd caused enough trouble for the time being, ignoring your sister's wishes, lying, putting my wife in one hell of a spot."

Sheelagh stood. "Richard," she said sharply, "not in front of the children."

Her husband ignored her and continued to address Paul. "Your mother is on the phone, from the hospital," he turned to Sheelagh, "and thank you for letting me know what was going on. Sounded like a bloody fool, I did, not knowing what the hell she was talking about."

Paul moved Ellen onto her own chair. "Sheelagh's right, old man. No need to use that kind of language in front of the little ones."

Richard ignored the comment. "She's waiting on the phone, to speak to you, though I said I didn't think you were here. Clearly she knew better."

He turned and left. Paul followed him. "I'll be back in a minute, Sheelagh. Will you stay with them?"

She nodded. The children watched as she sat back at the table. She rested her head in her hands, hiding her face. In a moment she felt Ellen's hand on her arm.

""Don't cry, Aunty Sheelagh. Please don't cry."

All Change

By the time Paul returned from speaking with his mother on the phone, Sheelagh had recovered herself, and was telling Ellen about how much she had enjoyed attending Sacred Heart, the kindness of the nuns, the friendships she'd made. Brendan was busy licking the chocolate from another biscuit.

Paul stood in the doorway. "How would you children like to do me a favor?"

Ellen turned toward him. "What?" she said warily.

"Well, I would like to talk to Aunty Sheelagh about a plan I have for the weekend. But I need to see if she approves first. So, can I ask you to play up in your bedroom, just for a few minutes? Then, if she approves, I'll tell you."

"But what if she doesn't approve?"

"Then I will have to think of another one, won't I? I'll call you very soon; just give us a minute on our own, would you?"

Ellen considered for a moment, her face a study of earnest concentration. Paul hoped she wouldn't ask more of her questions, just this once. She looked just like her father when she was serious like this, despite her blue eyes which were so like her Aunty Sheelagh's, not like Michael's brown eyes Beth always mentioned. Lord, but he missed his friend. They hadn't seen that much of each other since Michael and Beth moved to Ireland, but they'd been best friends for so long, almost since their first day at school. Even back then, even when it was simple spelling or sums questions from Sister Thomas, Michael always considered very carefully before he gave an answer. Just like his daughter was doing now.

Eventually she answered, with a question. "Is it a nice plan?"

"I think so."

"All right. Come on, Brendan."

"Would you wipe his hands when you get him up there?" Paul added as Brendan scrambled down from his chair.

Ellen sighed, but nodded, and they left. Paul closed the door behind them, his smile faded.

Sheelagh watched him. "So … is it bad news?"

"No, no, Mother and baby are both fine, for the moment. The doctor says it's hardly surprising this has happened after all she's been through. He says her blood pressure is up, and the baby's heartbeat is a bit rapid too. What with one thing and another he's advised complete bed rest."

"Where? At home?"

"No, not with everything she's been through, and the advanced state of her pregnancy. He wants her to stay in the hospital, to keep an eye on them both. So, for the moment she is in the Matthew Dimmock Ward."

"For how long?"

"Until the baby is born."

"Oh, no! Paul. That could be weeks from now."

"I know."

He waited. She was clearly upset. Only to be expected under the circumstances, he thought, trying to run the business, care for the children, as well as mourning her brother. Richard didn't seem to be helping much either. "I think your idea of finding schools now is a good one, Sheelagh. It will give you a break during the week, and I'm sure Mum can take them at weekends, or Maggie. Evelyn and I will help too."

"Uncle Paul!"

He opened the door. Ellen peered through the rails at the top of the stairs.

"Yes, Ellen?"

"His hands are clean. Can we come down yet?"

"Just two more minutes, Ellen. You can sit there and wait if you like."

Ellen nodded and Paul closed the door again.

"We're not going to tell them how long Beth might be in the hospital, are we Paul?"

"No. Not yet, anyway."

"So, what surprise have you got for them?"

152

"I thought I might take them to the zoo at the weekend; if that's all right with you. Keep them busy for a few hours. And out of your hair!"

"Oh, that's a great idea. And I'll try and organize the schools in the meantime."

"Good. Anyway, just wanted to catch you up on Beth. I think we can call them back down now, don't you?"

"Of course. Just one other thing, Paul. Can they go and see her? You know that's the first thing she's going to ask."

"Mum didn't say. I'm going into the hospital later. I'll ask them myself."

"When are we going to tell them about her staying in?"

"Why don't we wait? Just say she is staying there for a day or two, until we know more."

"Fine, I hope Ellen accepts that."

"Will I call them down now?"

"Yes, of course. And thanks again, Paul. You're a great support."

He opened the door to see both children sitting at the top of the stairs, waiting patiently.

"Come on, then," he smiled, "Aunty Sheelagh has said 'yes'."

"Yes to what?" said Ellen hurrying down the stairs, leaving her brother to come down more cautiously, gripping tight to the banister. "What's going to happen? Are we going to see Mammy?"

"No, not today, Ellen. The doctor wants her to rest today, in the hospital. Maybe tomorrow, we'll see. But the surprise I have is nearly as nice."

She reached a step close to the bottom, where she could look him straight in the eyes.

"What?"

"How would you like to go for a ride on an elephant?"

Her eyes opened wide. "A real one?"

"Yes, a real one."

"Really?" she was smiling now.

"And a camel, if you're very good."

"I will be." She jumped down the last three steps. "And Brendan too?"

"Of course... 'and Brendan'."

"Now?"

Paul laughed, picked her up and swung her in a circle. "You have more questions, Ellen Kelly, than anyone I know." He lowered her to her feet. It was so nice to see her happy and excited. "No, not now, I have to go to work. How about Saturday? Will that be soon enough for you?"

"Is that far away? Where is the elephant? ... and the camel?"

"In the zoo. We're going to Bristol Zoo." He turned to Sheelagh. "Right then, Aunty Sheelagh, I have to go now. I think you should ration young Ellen here to five questions a day. What do you think?"

Sheelagh smiled. "I think that's a wonderful idea, Uncle Paul."

"Why?" asked Ellen, and the two grown-ups laughed.

"I'll call you later, Sheelagh. Goodbye for now, Ellen. Do you think I could have a goodbye kiss? "

She nodded, he picked her up, and she kissed him on his nose.

"Does the elephant bite?"

"He doesn't. And I do declare that must be your five questions for today." He lowered her once more and bent to Brendan. "Goodbye, young man. I'll see you on Saturday, all right?"

The little boy nodded. Paul took the child's two small hands in his own. "And I hope to see a smile on that serious young face of yours then. Do you think you can do that, little man?"

Brendan nodded, but still did not smile.

"I'll see myself out, Sheelagh. I won't go through the shop, if that's all right with you? I'll call you later."

"Thanks again, Paul."

"The least I could do. 'Bye, Ellen, 'bye, Brendan."

"'Bye," said Ellen.

They watched as he descended the side stairs to the front door.

New Plans

Beth punched the bedclothes with her fist. "I can't stay here until the baby's born, Mum. What about Ellen and Brendan? I have too much to do. I have to decide where we're going to live, find a house."

"Beth, will you please relax. You're in the best place. You heard what the doctor said. You don't want to harm this baby, do you?'

"No, of course I don't, Mum, but I can take it easy at home."

"He said bed rest, Beth, you know he did. And they can look after you far better here than I could. You know I'd take you home if I thought it was a good idea. Just lie back, and try to relax. Ellen and Brendan are fine. You know Sheelagh will take good care of them, and you're in no fit state to be deciding where you're going to live until after that little one is born. We'll have plenty of time to talk about it then."

"But I only have three months to get all the furniture out of storage."

"Beth, stop it. They said they wouldn't charge you for three months, and very kind of them it was too, though I suspect those Murphy boys may have paid that. Your furniture can stay there as long as necessary. Now will you please stop making problems where there are none?"

Beth lay back onto the stiff-starched, hospital pillows. Maybe it *would* be nice not to have to worry for a while. Just to stop, take some time to think before she made any more decisions. She closed her eyes. She was so weary. She should give the baby some rest too; the poor thing was tumbling and turning in her tummy again. He must be almost as upset and confused as I am, she thought, and smiled.

"Well now, that's a welcome sight."

She opened her eyes to see Paul standing at the foot of the bed.

"Hello, Sis. Sorry to see you in here, but nice to see a smile. What were you thinking about?"

"Just about the baby."

"Good, glad to hear it." He kissed his mother, "Hi Mum, nice to have you back." Paul kissed Beth. "Sheelagh and the children send their love."

Beth sat forward eagerly. "Oh, Paul, how are they? Are they all right? Are they behaving themselves? How is Sheelagh coping?"

"Well, thank you, Paul," Margaret shook her head. "I'd just convinced her to relax a little."

He pulled a chair up beside his mother, and sat. "Sorry, Mum. Everything is fine, Beth, truly. I've just come from the shop; the children have a mountain of new toys. I think Sheelagh must have bought up the whole toy section of Peacocks Bazaar." He paused, glanced at his mother, then back at his sister. "There is one thing Sheelagh mentioned, that I said I'd talk to you about though."

Beth frowned, "What? Are they sick? What, Paul?"

"Will you relax, for the love of heaven? Relax! She wondered if you would mind her arranging schools for you, now that you might be here for a while. She thought they might like to meet other children, have a change of scenery from being cooped up over the shop. I think it's a great idea."

Beth leaned back against the pillows and sighed. "I haven't even thought that far ahead yet. I have no idea what schools, or where, or even where we're going to live. Nothing."

"Well, maybe you don't have to. It seems she has been giving it some thought. She says she'd like to send Ellen to her old school, the Sacred Heart."

"But that's a private school."

"She said she'd like to pay for it, for Michael's sake," he added hastily before she could argue.

"But it's a girls' school! That would leave Brendan on his own in Sheelagh's. He'd be so lonely."

"No, she's thought of that too. She said she'll try Saint Nick's."

"Your junior school?"

"Yes, and Michael's. She says Sister Thomas is the headmistress, and she always had a soft spot for Michael. Sheelagh says she'd talk to her, if you like. Even though she knows Brendan's a bit young. What do you think?"

Beth closed her eyes, but still felt tears coming, unbidden. Everyone was being so helpful, so kind, doing their best to help her. Maybe she truly could rest for a while, do what the doctor said. It would be nice to stop worrying, even if just for a short while. She brushed her tears away and smiled up at her brother.

"That sounds like a really nice idea, Paul. I know you and Michael thought the world of Sister Thomas too; she'd be kind to Brendan. If you're *sure* Sheelagh can afford to put Ellen in the Sacred Heart, just for the time being, until the baby is born, and until I can work things out. That would be wonderful."

"Consider it done. I'll telephone Sheelagh when I get home and tell her to go ahead." He took her hand. "Now, how are you? I haven't seen you since the funeral."

"I'm fine."

A nurse arrived at the bedside. "I'm sorry, I didn't see you come in, but Sister told me to tell you it's not really visiting time right now and the doctor said he'd like Mrs. Kelly to rest. You could come back this afternoon, perhaps, three until four? Evening visiting is from seven until half past eight."

Paul and his mother stood.

"I really should go home anyway, Beth." Margaret smoothed her daughter's hair. "I can still smell the boat and train on these clothes. I just wanted to see you settled in. And my poor Bill has been waiting outside for ages. Poor man, I've hardly spoken to him. And our bags are still in the car."

Beth felt a sudden panic. Her mother had been with her for weeks now, since ... She suddenly felt afraid. She didn't want to be on her own. She grabbed at her mother's hand.

"I won't be too long, darling," Margaret reassured her, "Just time enough to do some unpacking and freshen up. I'll fetch out one of your own nightgowns too, that hospital thing looks pretty old. I'll be back soon, I promise." She squeezed Beth's hand. "I'd like to see the family, *and* find out what state my house has got into since I left." She smiled, "I promise, Beth, I'll be back soon."

Beth nodded, relaxed a little. She released her grip on her mother's hand. "I know. Sorry. Thank you for everything, Mum. I couldn't have coped without you."

Margaret kissed her daughter's forehead, patted her hand one last time, and turned to her son. "Are you coming back to the house, Paul?"

"Yes, sure, I don't have a flight until this evening." He looked down at Beth. "I'll be back in as well, Beth, soon. Mind yourself, and do what the doctors tell you."

She smiled up at him. "I will, and thank Sheelagh, will you?"

He nodded and had turned to leave when she called him back.

"Paul."

"Yes?"

"If she's not too busy, could she bring the children in to see me?"

He smiled. "I'll say it to her."

Beth watched them walk the length of the ward, returned their wave as they opened the double doors, lay back, and rested her hands on her belly.

Come on baby, hurry up and arrive. I have a lot to do.

Meeting

Ellen was bored. Aunty Sheelagh and the nun had been talking for ages. They were doing it very quietly, so that she wasn't supposed to hear. She could, but she didn't understand most of it anyway, some of it was about money. From the side Ellen could only see the nun's nose; the rest of her face was hidden by the white bit that stuck out of the black veil. Her nose wiggled when she spoke. Every now and then the nun, Sister Laurence, looked straight at Ellen and Ellen thought it looked like the nun was peeping out through a tiny white door. Like Alice in her picture book, when Alice grew very big after eating the cake. Her face looked all squashed up when she smiled, or frowned.

Ellen's chair was not nice to sit on. The seat was very shiny and slippy. It was difficult to sit still, but the wooden arms stopped her from sliding off. Her legs didn't quite reach the floor. She held onto the arms, swung her legs backwards and forwards and started to hum. Aunty Sheelagh reached over and put her hand on Ellen's knees to keep her still. She stopped humming, sighed, and looked around the room again. It was dark with lots of books on shelves. One shelf was empty except for a big cross with Jesus on it. The walls over the books were dark yellow. So was the lace on the two windows, and they were so thick she could barely see through them to the playground outside. The floor was shiny, dark wood, with a red patterny rug in front of the desk.

"Well, Ellen."

The nun was talking to her, and frowning. Ellen could see all of her squished face; she decided she didn't like it. She had little lines around her lips and she looked like she could say nasty things; she was a little bit afraid of the nun.

"Do you think you would like to be in this school?"

Ellen looked at her aunt who gave a tiny, secret kind of nod, so Ellen nodded.

"Good. Would you like to see the class you would be in?"

She looked at her aunt, saw the secret sign, and nodded again. It would be better than sitting here any longer anyway, she thought.

They walked along the corridors, their shoes making clacking noises on the tiles, past doors with windows in so that you could see the classrooms inside, each with lots of girls at desks, and a teacher. But it was still quiet; you couldn't hear any noise from the classrooms, but she wasn't afraid. It was like her other school. Another nun swished past them in her long black nun clothes. The nun's clothes were a bit different.

They stopped at nearly the last door and Sister Laurence opened it. It was full of girls, like the other ones. They all turned and looked at her. It was like her classroom in her other school, the same kind of desks, blackboard, and holy pictures on the walls. A lady sat at a table at the front of the class. She looked up as they came in.

"Miss Singleton, I think we have a new student for you. This is Ellen Kelly. Ellen, this is your new teacher, Miss Singleton.

Aunty Sheelagh gently nudged Ellen forward, "Go and say 'hello', Ellen."

She went forward to the teacher's desk. She knew all the girls were still looking at her, but she didn't look back at them. She was looking at Miss Singleton's glasses; they were like the bottom of a drinking glass when it was empty. They made her eyes look tiny and a long way away. "Hello," she said.

The teacher smiled at her, then looked up at the nun who was now standing beside Ellen.

"Do you mean for next year, Sister Laurence?"

"No, no, Miss Singleton, we are making a little exception for young Ellen. She will be joining your class as soon as Mrs. Hudson here can get her a uniform. I didn't think we wanted her standing out, looking different, did we?" She bent her head to the teacher and said something very quietly.

The teacher looked at Ellen again, "Oh, really?" she said, and then she looked at Aunty Sheelagh and said, "I'm so sorry," but Ellen didn't know what for.

The grown-ups talked a bit longer. The teacher had told the girls to take out their copies and practice writing, and she told Ellen she could look around the classroom, which she did, glancing at the books on the shelves and the boxes of blocks with numbers on. One girl smiled at her, and she smiled back. Then Aunty Sheelagh was saying goodbye and they left the classroom.

"Well, what do you think, Ellen? Do you think you would like it here?" asked the nun, smiling down at her with her squashy face. Aunty Sheelagh was smiling too, and nodding. So Ellen nodded. The three of them walked back along the corridor. They stopped at the giant front door with the shiny gold letterbox and huge keyhole.

Aunty Sheelagh shook the nun's hand. "Thank you Sister Laurence, I do appreciate this. Say goodbye to Sister, Ellen, and say 'thank you'."

Ellen did as she was told.

The nun took a little step back. "Of course, I think we would have to do something about her accent. Very Irish! Never mind, Sheelagh dear. We'll get Miss Pollard to do some elocution with her. I'm sure you'll be happy if we can smooth that out a bit, won't you?"

Aunty Sheelagh started to say something, but then she stopped. Instead she just said goodbye again and they walked to the car.

When they had waved a last time and were driving away, Aunty Sheelagh said, "Well that was nice of Sister Laurence, wasn't it Ellen, to say she would take you? You'll love the school. I just know you will. I did."

"What's that word?"

"What word, darling?"

"Elly something."

Aunty Sheelagh frowned and beeped the car horn at somebody. "Oh, you mean elocution? It's sort of speaking lessons."

"But I can speak."

"Yes, I know darling, but it will just help you speak like all the other girls."

Ellen wasn't sure what her aunt meant. But it would be nice to make some friends until she went home, to her real friends.

Resolutions

Sheelagh stood in front of the desk. Their desk! Her desk! "Have you finished sulking, Richard? Because I need to talk to you."

He hadn't looked up when she'd come into the office, but she knew he'd seen her walking through the shop. The only thing open on the desk was the order book but she knew the orders had been completed for the month. He'd probably flipped it open when he saw her coming. He really was such a child sometimes.

He threw his pen onto the open pages of the book and looked up at her.

"I was *not* sulking, Sheelagh."

"Fine, if you say so." It wasn't worth getting into another spat, she thought; the only way to ease him out of these moods was to act as if nothing was wrong. She sat opposite him in the 'customer chair,' leaned forward, rested her hands on the desk. "Look, Richard, I know I've not been here much for the last few weeks, what with going over to Ireland, then bringing the children back, and then having to settle them in."

He leaned back in his chair, continued to look at her, his face expressionless.

"But I had a chat with Paul this morning," she said, "And what with Beth in hospital and us having the children for a while longer ...."

He raised his eyebrows, but still said nothing.

"I thought it might be an idea to try and get them into school. Beth was going to do it when she arrived, but now ...."

He reached into his pocket, pulled out his cigarette case, flicked it open, and took a cigarette. He held it upright and tapped it gently on the desk as Sheelagh continued. 'That's why I asked Doris to babysit Brendan. So I took Ellen to the Sacred Heart this morning and spoke to Sister Laurence and she said she'd be happy to take her."

Sheelagh waited, wished he would say something, show some interest, even act as if he cared, even if he didn't. Dammit, she was doing this for him, so the children would be out of the way for a bit.

"Then I went to Saint Nick's." she continued, "Sister Thomas, Michael's old teacher, is headmistress there now, and she said she'd take Brendan, even though he's a bit young, but she understood. She said she would be very happy to do it, actually."

Again she waited.

He took the lighter from the desk and leisurely lit his cigarette, inhaled deeply, exhaled, frowned. "How much is that going to cost?"

"Well, of course I haven't spoken to Beth about it yet, I'm going to go to the hospital tonight. But I thought I would offer to cover the cost of Ellen's schooling, at least for the moment." Her words came out in a rush.

He leaned forward, his frown deepening.

Sheelagh didn't want another confrontation, "Of course I was going to speak to you about it, too." she added hastily.

"Right, of course you were. But nonetheless you've already been to the school and arranged it?"

His voice had that hard edge that always made her nervous. Sheelagh felt her face color. "Just to enquire, it's not finalized; I have to get her a uniform. We would only need to pay for Ellen, Saint Nick's is free."

"I seem to remember your old man going on about how much your education cost him, so your old school is not cheap, I assume."

"We can afford it. I wish you'd stop worrying about money, Richard. We're doing fine."

"I see. Well, you're the boss." He closed the book and stood. "I suppose I should give you your desk back, unless you have to dash off upstairs to babysit?"

"Please don't start that again, Richard." She stood, her fists balled tight to her side, nails biting into her palms. She tried to keep her voice even, calm. "You know I'm doing my best. If you and Beth agree, the children could be starting school next Monday; things could get back to a bit more normal. Look, will you come and visit Beth with me this evening to talk about it?"

He shook his head. "I don't think so. I promised some people at the club I'd drop by." He stepped out from behind the desk. "Right now, I'm going to get a haircut."

"I'll see you at dinner?"

"Fine."

Sheelagh leaned forward to kiss him, but he ignored the gesture. He passed her, carefully avoiding contact as he did so.

She stood for a while after the door closed, then move to the seat behind the desk and sat down.

They had been married three years now and of course she was happy, but just sometimes Sheelagh wondered if it was worth all the arguments she'd had with her parents about Richard *before* the wedding, and the arguments with him *after* the wedding. She'd known, deep in her heart that Richard was probably her last chance at a husband; after all she was thirty when she met him and in serious danger of becoming an old maid like Aunty Wyn, and Sheelagh didn't know anyone who had liked her. She sighed. Her father had always seemed to chase off any potential suitor. Richard was the only one who had persevered. She'd been so excited about the engagement that she'd travelled to Ireland, to Doonbeg, to tell her sister in person.

Mary hadn't seemed too happy for her, especially when Sheelagh told her that Richard wasn't a Catholic, *and* that he was a British soldier. Sheelagh was sure Mary would have changed her mind if she had seen him in his uniform. She would have understood then.

Richard hadn't travelled to Ireland with her. He had said his commanding officer couldn't give him the time off, and anyway Ireland was no place for a British soldier. She'd told Mary how handsome he was; tall, with amazing, beautiful pebble-grey eyes and blond hair. Totally irresistible, all her friends said so, very distinguished, even if he was only a lieutenant. She told her sister she thought he looked just like Leslie Howard in 'Gone with the Wind.'

When they first met, Richard told her he was to be promoted to captain soon. It hadn't happened, even after they had been courting for a year. "So, I've applied for a discharge," he'd said. "Precious little to do, now that the war's over. And your father did say that you'd probably be very happy to have a man helping you in the shop, now that he was retiring."

Sheelagh was hurt that her father didn't think she could run the business well enough on her own. Still, it would be nice having her new husband close all the time.

At least that was what she'd thought.

Mary had been hard to persuade. "But Sheelagh, why would you want to marry outside of the Church?" she asked when Sheelagh broke the news that he was 'Church of England.' "Sure, there are plenty of Catholic lads would be delighted to have you, especially around here. I could ask Joe to make enquiries. Wouldn't it be grand if we could find a local lad? You could come home, Sheelagh, be back with your family. Pierce and Maeve would be thrilled too."

That last suggestion had really startled Sheelagh. They had been getting the tea ready in the back room of Mary's home. Mary's eldest daughter, Norah, was minding the shop out front, and the other three girls were in the back yard playing chase around the water pump. Joe was digging the vegetable plot at the top of the garden. Come back and live here? Sheelagh watched Joe shoo away chickens that were getting underfoot. It's a completely different world, she thought. She loved her sister dearly, and her brother Pierce, and both their families, but she could *never* imagine living in such a place. In fact she couldn't imagine living in Ireland at all. Everything was so dowdy. Not a single woman in the village wore nylon stockings, or make-up, not even Mary, though Sheelagh had tried.

This time when she'd arrived she'd brought Mary a special gift, an expensive compact and matching lipstick holder. It was solid brass, decorated with a beautiful star and tiger stripe design. As usual, it seemed she had chosen wrong. Mary didn't seem too pleased with her gift, though she hugged and thanked Sheelagh and pretended to admire it, but Sheelagh knew. She had tried to show her sister how to put on the lipstick, and had to admit to herself that it did look a bit strange on her sister's healthy country complexion, though she would never have said that to her sister. The girls had laughed and said their mother looked funny, but they were fascinated with the compact. It opened by a push button on the front. They had great fun opening and closing it, taking turns to peer in the tiny mirror, pat the powder on their noses, and play 'film stars'.

"Look at me, I'm Hedy Lamarr".

"I'm Ginger Rogers".

Sheelagh always brought her older sister nylon stockings too, and Mary always thanked her profusely, saying, "Bless you, Sheelagh; they are beautiful, altogether too fine for me". Then she would tuck them into a drawer saying, "I'll have to keep them for a special occasion". Sheelagh knew she never would use them, always preferring her awful thick, black, woolen ones.

No, she couldn't possibly live back here. It was always lovely to visit, but hard to believe she'd even lived here as a child. No, Bristol was fine, and now she had found Richard.

"I don't want anyone else, Mary. I want Richard."

"But will you not be excommunicated?" her sister fretted. "I'm sure Father O'Brien said marrying a Protestant was being untrue to your faith. Sure, couldn't you be excommunicated for that?"

Sheelagh tried not to smile at her sister's concern. "I don't think so, Mary. Anyway, Richard has promised to take religious instruction, and he's said we can get married in a Catholic Church."

"What does your father say? Is he not heartbroken, Sheelagh?"

Sheelagh had laughed at that, and hugged her sister. "No, Mary, he is not. Now will you stop worrying and congratulate me. I'm getting married."

Mary had relented, and wished Sheelagh well. But she didn't come to the wedding, even though Sheelagh sent her the money for the ticket. She said she couldn't leave Joe with the children.

* * *

Sheelagh stared down into the shop. They seemed to be busy. That was good, Richard was never happy when he saw the shop empty. He would harangue the staff as if it was their fault. She closed the order book. As she did so her glance caught her engagement ring with the deep blue sapphire stone, "To match your eyes" he'd said. She twisted it, and the thin gold band of her wedding ring.

The wedding had been beautiful, though small. While her father had spared no expense, several family members had replied to the invitations with one excuse or another saying they were unable to come. It was a 'mixed marriage', and that upset people on both sides. Even Jim Porter had not been as accepting as Sheelagh had told her sister. She and her father had had many heated arguments before he relented. When Sheelagh pointed out how disastrous it had been the time he'd tried to meddle in Michael and Beth's engagement he finally, grudgingly, agreed. She smiled as she remembered that rare time she'd bested her father in an argument.

Her smile faded as she recalled the conversation with Richard a few days before the wedding.

Over the six months of their engagement he had assured the priest, on several occasions, that he was prepared to convert, yet he always seemed to have an excuse for delaying the process. Eventually, as the time grew close he assured Father O'Brien he would take the necessary religious instruction as soon as his discharge was complete, which would be after the wedding. In the meantime he expressed his unreserved willingness to be part of a Catholic ceremony, with a full High Mass. He also promised the priest that, of course, any children would be brought up Catholic. Under pressure from both Sheelagh and Jim Porter, the priest had reluctantly agreed to postpone the conversion.

But three days before the wedding Richard had said something very different to Sheelagh. Even now, when she thought of it, she wondered if she should have reacted differently.

They'd been sitting in his car, smoking, talking about the big day. Sheelagh thanked him for being so good, and understanding, about their 'religion difference'.

"No problem, old girl, window dressing really, isn't it? It won't make any difference once we're married, will it?" he'd said.

Sheelagh wasn't sure she understood what he meant.

"But you will become a Catholic, once we're settled, once you're out of the army, won't you?"

"What on earth for? Aren't we fine as we are?"

Her stomach started to churn.

"But, you said you would. You told daddy you would. You told Father O'Brien you would."

"Well, what else could I do? I could see you were all getting worked up about it. Seemed like the best way to calm folk down."

"But you promised."

"Now, now, here you go again. Sheelagh, relax." He caught her hand, kissed it softly and smiled at her. "We love each other. We're getting married on Saturday, and we're going to live happily ever after. What does it matter what damn church it's in."

"But I'm a Catholic."

"And yet I still love you." He smiled and leaned forwards to kiss her, but she pulled back, tugged her hand away.

"It's not a laughing matter, Richard."

"And I'm not laughing," he said. His face had turned very serious, even dark. "Look, Sheelagh, I agreed to get married in your damn church for the sake of peace and quiet. For *your* sake, even though my family isn't a bit happy about me marrying a Catholic. Let that be an end to it. I'm doing what you wanted, and there it finishes."

They were both silent for a while. Sheelagh's thoughts were in chaos. He'd lied. The wedding was on Saturday, too late to call it off. She didn't want to call it off. She loved him. She wanted to marry him, have his children. She had a sick feeling in her stomach.

"What about the children?"

"What about *what* children?"

"*Our* children! Are we going to bring them up Catholic?"

"Oh, for goodness' sake, Sheelagh. We're not even married yet. We don't need to get into that now. Who says we even *need* to have children."

"But …"

"Let's just get the damn wedding over with first."

"But you agreed."

He looked at her, his face serious, hard; his grey eyes suddenly seemed icy cold. Sheelagh had never seen him like this before.

"Why don't we have this conversation after the wedding, eh?"

Sheelagh stared at him for a long time before she got out of the car. She didn't want to start crying. Not here, not now. "I'll see you tomorrow," she said, before turning and hurrying up to the house.

Any time she had tried to talk about having children since it had been the same, never a resolution, always deferring the discussion, and decision, until later. And now she was thirty four, it would soon be too late. She wanted children!

She stood, slid the order book into the drawer and left the office. She had to go upstairs.

Hospital

Sheelagh walked down the ward, scanning the beds and their occupants, looking for Beth. She wondered if all the women were pregnant. No! There would hardly be this many pregnant women all needing to be in hospital at one time, would there? There must be at least twenty beds in the ward.

She saw Beth, smiled, and waved. Getting closer she was shocked at her sister-in-law's appearance, so pale and exhausted-looking. Thinner too! How could that be? Even her 'baby bump' seemed to be smaller. Surely that was very bad this far in her pregnancy?

"My, but you gave us a fright, Beth." They hugged. "How are you? You look tired, you poor thing." She handed Beth the flowers.

"Oh, Sheelagh! Freesias! My favorites. Thank you." Beth buried her nose in the delicate, blooms. "They smell wonderful."

"I love them too. But it looks like I've been beaten to it."

Sheelagh helped Beth sit up, tucking the pillows at her back.

"I know," Beth leaned back and glanced at her bedside locker. "And I've only been here a few hours! The whole family came in this afternoon. Ev and Maggie brought the flowers and fruit. Paul brought the chocolates. Even Bill, bless his heart, brought in a box of pretty hankies." She gave Sheelagh a wan smile. "The nurse got pretty impatient with them all, said they could only visit two at a time." She shrugged. "But it was so nice to see them, even for a few minutes." She tried to ease herself into a more comfortable position. "Mum and Bill came in again this evening, but only for a short visit. They've just left. She must be exhausted, poor thing; she's been fantastic. I couldn't have done all the house stuff without her. You know it's up for sale, do you?"

Sheelagh nodded.

Beth put down the flowers and reached for Sheelagh's hand. "It's all happened so quickly. Hardly a month ago I could never have imagined any of this. I still can't believe it." They were both quiet. A nurse arrived at the end of the bed, unhooked Beth's chart, studied it, asked Beth how she was feeling, and took her pulse and temperature.

"Can I get you anything, Mrs. Kelly?"

Beth shook her head, the nurse left and she turned back to Sheelagh. "Anyway, I'm so glad you could come. How are the children? Are they behaving themselves? How are you managing? I know they can be a handful."

"They're fine. You know they are, Beth. Doris, our cashier, is minding them while I'm here. She's been a treasure. Six grandchildren of her own; she knows just what to do. She's become the perfect babysitter, and Ivy is used to doing the cash so she takes over there. It's *you* we have to worry about, not the children. They're fine, I promise."

Beth waved the comment aside, "I'm fine too. Really!" she insisted, "I wish I could convince them of that," she indicated two nurses chatting by the door. "I only agreed to stay in the first place 'cos the doctor said they wanted to check on the baby. Then they said we both needed for me to stay here and rest. But I've so much to do, Sheelagh. I *have* to get back to the children."

"You have to do what the doctors tell you right now, Beth. Everything else can wait." Sheelagh pulled a chair up beside the bed. "I hope Paul told you about the school idea. You didn't mind that I made enquiries before talking to you, did you?"

"Of course not, Sheelagh. It's one of the things I'd been worrying about, even before I left Ireland. I knew I'd need to find out about schools as soon as possible, at least for Ellen."

"I probably should have asked you first, ..."

"No, I'm so glad you did it, but ..." Beth sat forward in the bed. "Once I get organized I don't think I'll be able to afford the Sacred Heart, Sheelagh."

"Beth, relax, don't get yourself in a state about that." Sheelagh patted Beth's hand. "I told Paul I'm happy to pay for her schooling, for as long as necessary."

Beth tried to protest, but Sheelagh silenced her. "Please, Beth, this is as much for Michael as for you, so please?"

"Are you sure?"

"Absolutely."

"Truth to tell, I don't think I've much money at all, Sheelagh; at least not until the house is sold and the insurance comes in."

The insurance! Damn! What with going to the schools, and fighting with Richard, Sheelagh had forgotten about the insurance.

"I know you are really busy, Sheelagh, but have you spoken to Colm yet? Do you know if he has contacted the insurance company?"

Sheelagh wasn't sure what to say. She didn't want to say too much about her visit to Colm, about her brother's confusion when she mentioned the insurance policy, or about that horrible woman. "I did go over to his flat. I'd tried to get hold of him a couple of times before, but you know how he is, always out." she hesitated. "He was a bit busy when I went over, and the flat was in a bit of a mess. He said he just had to find the policy. You know what Colm can be like." Beth nodded. "But he promised he'd get hold of the insurance company, today. I'll make sure he sorts it out." The excuses sounded lame, even to Sheelagh, but Beth seemed to accept what she said. She'd have to contact Colm in the morning, without fail, see if he had found the paperwork, though she was very afraid, from the way he'd behaved, that there was a problem.

Anxious to change the subject, Sheelagh returned to the children, and schools. "I'm hoping they can both start next Monday. Ellen seemed to like the Sacred Heart, said it was like her school in Dublin, and Brendan will be with Sister Thomas, so you know he'll be fine. You just stop worrying about those two and concern yourself with young Master Kelly." She pointed toward Beth's stomach. "Are you still sure it's a little boy?"

Beth smiled at her sister-in-law. "Yes, I am."

They went on to talk about the hospital, about Beth's journey from Ireland and about how sad she was to leave. Sheelagh could see how tired her sister-in-law was becoming. "I'll go now, Beth, let you get some rest, after all that's why you're in here. I'll ask the nurse for a vase for those on the way out," she said, indicating the flowers. She kissed Beth. "I may not get in to you again for a couple of days, but please don't fret about anything. The children are fine." She squeezed Beth's hand, "And you will be too."

"Oh Sheelagh, would you bring them in with you next time? I so want to see them."

"Of course I will."

She spoke to the nurse, and left.

Now all she had to do was contact Colm, sort out the insurance. And make peace with her husband!

Trouble

When Sheelagh arrived home Doris was sitting by the fire in the living room, knitting, and listening to the wireless.

"Have the children been all right?"

"They were fine, Mrs. Hudson, pretty much put themselves to bed." She busied herself packing the knitting into her bag. "I just made sure they brushed their teeth. That Ellen is a very independent young lady. Even said she would get Brendan settled for me."

"I know, bless her, she tries to be so grown-up. Thank you for staying, Doris."

"My pleasure, Miss Sheelagh. We've all been so upset about poor Mr. Michael. It's nice to be able to do something. You know, I remember his first day working downstairs. Of course your father ran things then. I'm not sure you had even started work here." She gave Sheelagh a sad smile. "The poor lad had cut himself to ribbons shaving. His chin was covered in little bits of bloody paper." She shook her head, "Oh, well". She stood, and tugged on her coat. "I'll see you in the morning, then." As she buttoned it she studied Sheelagh's face. "You should try and get some rest yourself, Miss Sheelagh, if you don't mind my saying so. You look exhausted. Mr. Porter wouldn't like to see you like that." She paused. "Perhaps I could make you a cup of tea before I go?"

"No, I'm fine thank you, Doris, just a bit tired. I'll be fine."

Once the older woman left, Sheelagh sank gratefully into the armchair. Doris was right, she *was* exhausted; she should really go to bed, but first she wanted to patch things up with Richard. She would try and wait up for him.

* * *

"What the devil are you doing still here?"

Sheelagh hadn't heard him come in; she must have fallen asleep. She glanced at her watch; it was late. She tried to clear her head. "I wanted to talk to you, thought this might be a good time, no distractions from the shop, or the children."

He cast his eyes to heaven, took a deep breath as if to begin another argument.

"Can I make you a cup of tea?" She cut in before he could start lecturing.

"Fine," he said and dropped, a little unsteadily, into his armchair.

By the time she returned with the two cups of tea he was already dozing, jaw slack, mouth open and making the thick, guttural noise he made when he slept on his back. It always sounded like he was going to choke. But he never did. She touched his shoulder gently, his eyes snapped open and the noise stopped. He hauled himself upright in the chair and put his hand out for the tea. "I've already sugared it," she said, handing him the cup. She perched awkwardly on the arm of his chair, facing him.

"Careful!" he said, transferring his cup to the other hand and taking a sip.

She brushed a finger softly along the side of his face. "I'm sorry we've been fighting, Richard. I hate it when we fight."

"Me too," he said, but he remained distant, waiting for more, keeping detached. She could smell the brandy on his breath.

"I love you, Richard; I didn't mean to upset you."

"I know," he said, taking another sip. "However, you do seem to have perfected the knack!" She saw the flicker of a smile.

"Well, how about I try to un-perfect it?"

"That would be good." He rested the cup on the bookshelf beside him and turned back to her. "You don't seem to realize, Sheelagh. I only want what's best for both of us. I'm sorry, but I'm really not that concerned about your family, and Beth has enough people who can look out for her, and her children. I swear ever since they arrived you've gone all broody, not a bit like you. I thought you wanted to develop the business?"

She was about to respond, to explain how important her brothers and sister were to her. For so long she only knew her adoptive parents, and her brother

Michael, and Aunty Wyn, though she didn't even get to know *them* very well until she and Michael were almost grown up. And they were even more important now that she had lost Michael. And children were more important than a shop anyway. But she bit her lip and only said, "I'm doing it for Michael."

He sighed and nodded. "All right. So ... how is Beth?"

Peace had been made. Now to keep it.

"She looks very tired, poor thing. I'm sort of glad she's in hospital; she needs the rest. She was happy about the children starting school."

"Good." He took up his cup and sipped his tea.

"I'll start them next Monday, then we can relax a bit."

"That would be good."

"She did ask about Colm, and the insurance. I can't imagine how, but I'd completely forgotten he was to get back to me. I don't suppose he called while I was out?"

Richard shook his head.

"I'll have to try and contact him tomorrow. Once that's done we will *almost* be back to normal. Will I ask Doris to babysit again tomorrow night? We could go to the pictures? Or for a drink?"

"Fine. There's a new Marilyn Monroe film I wouldn't mind seeing."

"Oh, you and Miss Blonde Bombshell. I'm surprised you married me at all."

"I like your red hair just fine," he smiled, raised his face to her.

"Hey, not red, auburn!" she corrected as she bent and rested her forehead against his.

They did not hear the door open.

"Aunty Sheelagh?"

Richard let out a snort of exasperation and pulled away from his wife. "Oh, my G..."

"Richard!" Sheelagh warned, and turned to Ellen, standing in the doorway, sleepy-eyed, clutching her doll.

"Ellen, I thought you were in bed, asleep."

"Did you see Mammy?"

"I did, sweetheart. Why don't you go back and climb into bed and I'll come up in a minute and tell you all about it."

"All right."

The little girl left and Sheelagh turned to her husband. "Sorry." she said, taking his empty cup. "I won't be long," She kissed him again. "Look, why don't you go on up to bed? I'll be there in a minute. Promise," she whispered, "And no more interruptions."

He raised his eyebrows and smiled. "Well now, I think that might be the best offer I've had all day."

"I certainly hope it is!' she said in mock outrage. "Just give me a few minutes."

He stood; seemed a little unsteady on his feet, pulled her to him and held her close. She smelled the brandy more strongly now, and his cologne, and the brilliantine in his hair. She wished he didn't drink so much. His lips were close to her ear.

"I'll be ready," he whispered.

They kissed once more. She hoped he would remember to brush his teeth before he got into bed. "I'll be there as soon as I can," she said, gently extracting herself from his embrace.

He said he would rinse the cups before he went up.

Sheelagh climbed the stairs. She felt oh, so weary. Why was it always *her* who had to back down; *her* who had to make the peace? Sometimes Richard could be so damn stubborn and pedantic! And he seemed to be worse since she came back from Ireland.

She crept on tiptoe into the children's bedroom, careful not to wake Brendan. Ellen was sitting up, arms wrapped tight around her doll, waiting. She edged over in the bed to make room. Sheelagh sat beside her. Slowly and carefully she explained about Beth having to stay in the hospital, and that she sent her love. She said how happy Beth was that Ellen and Brendan were to start school, and went on to promise Ellen they would go shopping for her uniform in the morning. The child was disappointed about her mother remaining in the hospital longer, but seemed excited about the idea shopping for her new school uniform. Sheelagh was relieved; it would give the poor mite something to look forward to.

When she had finished Ellen only had one question.

"When can we go and see Mammy in the hospital?"

"I'm not sure, darling, but I promise to telephone tomorrow and ask. Maybe we can go tomorrow afternoon? I just have to talk to your Uncle Colm first."

And tonight I have to humor my husband, she thought as she tucked Ellen in.

"Goodnight, sweetheart, see you in the morning," she brushed Ellen's hair from her face, gave her pigtails an affectionate tug, blew the little girl a kiss, and left.

More Trouble

Sheelagh dialed the number, and waited. It was the American woman who answered. She didn't want to discuss family business with her. She didn't want to talk to her *at all,* if truth be told, but she resisted the impulse to hang up. She needed to talk to Colm.

"Oh,… hello. … Margot, isn't it? Could I speak to my brother, please?"

"Hi, sweetie. He's not here at the moment and you know how he is? I really have no idea when he will be back."

Sheelagh swallowed her irritation. "Well, he said he'd be contacting me, but he hasn't. Would you ask him to telephone me when you see him? …. You could tell him Beth is in hospital … Anyway, I need to speak to him as soon as possible."

The woman said she was sorry to hear about Beth, assured Sheelagh she would tell Colm when he came in. Sheelagh felt angry, even though she knew it wasn't the woman's fault that Colm wasn't available. But it was clear she was living there, in Colm's flat. And they weren't married. Typical of Colm!

She tried to be polite as she said "thank you" and hung up.

She tapped her pen irritably on the desk, tried to decide what to do next. Richard would look after the staff wage packets; he did that every week. She was getting behind with things in the shop. She needed to talk to the new young woman about the window display, it was far too cluttered and old-fashioned; she need to speak to the new store man about the stock inventory, he wasn't keeping it current. But she also had to get Ellen's uniform and pay her school fee. She would start there.

She wrote the cheque, put it in an envelope, along with a thank-you note to Sister Laurence, and tossed it into the out tray. Perhaps she should call the hospital next, see when would be a good time to bring the children in to see their mother; then at least Ellen would stop fretting. Brendan didn't seem to mind too much, though the poor little mite was still very quiet. Sheelagh was sure he'd been a lot more talkative in Dublin. Still, it was understandable; he must be missing his mother as much as Ellen was.

Sheelagh remembered the first day Colm, Michael and herself had arrived in England, remembered being ushered up the steps into the Sinclair house in the dark of an early evening, and the group of strangers standing around them in the grand living room; Colm's new parents, the Sinclairs, and her own parents-to-be, the Porters. There was another man there too. She struggled to recall who he was. He'd been on the boat and train with them too. She turned the long ago journey over and over in her head ... Uncle Liam! That's who it was! But who was he exactly, why was he there? Then it came to her. Of course! Aunty Bridgie's brother. How could she have forgotten him? Then she realized she had never seen him again after that day. Why not, she wondered.

"Oh, my goodness," Sheelagh closed her eyes, covered her face with her hands, as she realized with a shock how history was almost repeating itself! Colm, Michael and herself had been shipped to England with an uncle when their mother died. Now Ellen and Brendan had been brought to England when their father died, by her, their aunt.

Beth had mentioned that to her in Dublin, but she hadn't really thought about it. She had forgotten so much of that time in her life. Thinking for a while, trying to recollect dates, she was startled when she realized that she couldn't have been much older than Brendan when it happened. Now, here was Brendan, not talking. It was just what Michael had done, become silent, too frightened and traumatized to speak. She remembered all the adults crowding around, staring at them, trying to get him to talk. She had never remembered it all so clearly before. Why not? She had been so concerned about Ellen, she hadn't given too much thought to Brendan. Why hadn't she remembered? Her heart pounded, her head spun, as memories came tumbling back; the house in Bristol, her father calling Michael a fool, shouting at his wife that he didn't want a fool for a son. Soon afterward Michael had been sent to live with Aunty Wyn.

This time it had to be different. It had been years before Sheelagh understood what had happened to her mother, that her father was still alive. The children *had* to see their mother, *had* to know they had not been abandoned, that at least *she* would be coming back to them.

The window display, and store man, could wait.

She picked up the receiver, telephoned the hospital. The switchboard put her through to the ward.

"Sister Franklin speaking."

Sheelagh's hands were shaking, but she tried to sound calm, explained who she was, asked about Beth, then asked when she could bring in the children.

"How old are they Mrs. Hudson?"

When Sheelagh told her they were six and four, the nurse was adamant.

"I'm sorry, no children under twelve are allowed."

"But ..."

"I'm sorry, Mrs. Hudson. I do understand, but we cannot risk infection, either to our patients, or our visitors." Her tone was crisp, efficient. "Children, especially young children, are most susceptible to infection, but they also seem to carry more than would seem possible."

"But they *have* to see their mother." Sheelagh persisted. "You don't understand, *really* you don't. They *have* to know she is really there, that's she's coming back to them." She was close to tears.

"I understand your concerns, Mrs. Hudson, and I can hear that you are a little upset, but our prime responsibilities are to mother and baby."

"But it will upset her dreadfully if she can't see them. I thought she wasn't supposed to be upset. Won't that only make it worse for the baby?"

"I will make a point of speaking to Mrs. Kelly and explaining hospital policy. I'm sorry, Mrs. Hudson. I'm sure you understand."

Sheelagh didn't. She curtly thanked the nurse and, for the second time that morning, resisted the urge to slam down the receiver.

Damn, damn, damn.

"Oh, dear, what has you so glum, old girl?" Richard stepped into the office and closed the door behind him. "Can't have my little kitten all gloomy, now can we?" He was coming around the desk toward her. Sheelagh put up a hand to stop him.

"Not here, not now, Richard."

He stopped, hands up in front of him. "Understood, understood." He shrugged, backed away, and went to sit in the customer chair. "So, what's wrong? You look a bit shaken."

She didn't want to tell him all that she had remembered. They'd never really discussed that she was adopted, or how it had happened, and he'd never seemed curious enough to ask for details. He knew that she was, and just accepted her "Irish connections"; had actually said every family had skeletons in the closets.

She did tell him about the hospital, and about her conversation with Colm's girlfriend. "More like *lady* friend than *girl*friend, though," she said. "She looks older than him, and 'lady' certainly isn't the right word either, under the circumstances," she added.

"Oh, come on, Sheelagh, he's just sowing his wild oats. Always was a bit of a lad, that brother of yours, not a bit like Michael from all I hear."

"No, not a bit." She still had the image of that first night in her head. She could see the three of them surrounded by adults, Colm all chatter and confidence, and Michael looking so scared. No, not scared, terrified! Why had she never realized that before?

She didn't want to talk to her husband. She wanted to be left on her own for a while, have time to gather her thoughts. But she didn't want to have another argument either.

"And he's hardly still sowing his wild oats," she snapped, "He's older than me."

She definitely needed to get out of the office. "I have to go up and tell Ellen what the hospital said." She pushed her chair away from the desk. "That's not going to be much fun either."

"Oh, she'll be fine. Are we still going out tonight?"

Sheelagh stared at him. How could he be so selfish? He really doesn't care about those poor children! Would he be any different, she wondered, if they were his own?

Richard lit a cigarette. "What? What are you looking at me like that for?"

"May I ask you a question?"

"Of course you can, old girl, ask away."

"Promise you won't get cross?"

He blew an almost perfect smoke ring toward the ceiling. "Why on earth should I get cross?" He smiled. "So, ask."

"How would you feel if we didn't, ever, have children of our own?"

He sat up, paused for a moment, seemed to consider his reply. "To be perfectly honest, Sheelagh, I don't think I'd mind. If you're having second thoughts about this children thing, I would be quite happy to go along with you. Forget about it entirely, if you like. Seems to me they can more trouble than they're worth. Which is, I think, what you are discovering?" He paused, "Can you imagine what a baby would be like? We'd have no time at all for each other. You know, I think we'd be perfectly fine without them." He smiled and reached across the desk to pat her hand... "More time for us, and for expanding the business, *and* a lot more money in our pockets."

She pulled away from him and stood.

He looked up at her, puzzled. "What's wrong? That's what you meant, wasn't it? Don't tell me you're going to go all moody again."

She looked down at him, felt her anger rising. "No, I'm not going to go all moody." She took a deep breath, walked around the desk. "I'm going to speak to Ellen. Will you do the staff wage packets while I'm gone?"

"Sure."

He stood as she left.

She closed the door behind her and leaned against it. Damn, damn, damn. Damn you Michael; damn you Colm; damn you Richard. I hate you all.

Telling

Brendan knelt on a chair at the table, thumb firmly fixed in his mouth, aimlessly pushing a toy car through a twisting avenue of building blocks. Ellen sat on the floor in the corner, talking quietly to her doll.

Sheelagh went to Brendan, put her arms around him and hugged him tight. "I love you, Brendan," she said. "Did you know that I think you are the best little boy in all the world?"

The child struggled out of her embrace, stared up at her, his face showing his bewilderment. He sucked his thumb vigorously. Sheelagh realized that Ellen was also looking a little puzzled at the attention she was suddenly showing her brother.

All right, no point in trying to sugar the pill; she would just have to tell them.

"I need to talk to you both for a minute." Sheelagh sat beside Brendan. She tried to lift him onto her lap, but he resisted, so she let him remain in his own seat. Ellen came and stood in front of her. Sheelagh reached out for the girl's hands, but she put them behind her back.

"Ellen, I know I promised we could visit your mother today, but I've just spoken to the hospital and they've told me that children under twelve are not allowed to visit."

"But you promised."

"I know I did, and I'm very sorry about that, but I didn't know the rules."

"But Uncle Paul said I could pretend I was twelve ... but that I wouldn't have to do the ironing," she added hastily.

Sheelagh remembered Ellen's conversation with Paul, and had to smile at the child's logic. "Yes, I know he did ... but ... even though you *are* very grown up, and you sometimes behave like you are twelve, we know you're really only six, so it's just not going to be possible, sweetheart."

The child's face crumpled. "But you promised," she cried.

Sheelagh tried to reach for her again, but Ellen stepped back, tears welling in her eyes. "I want to see my Mammy."

"Yes, I know you do, Ellen, but you can't, not right now."

"I don't care. I want to." Ellen's fists were now clenched stiffly at her side. Tears fell unheeded as she stared angrily at her aunt. "You promised me, and I have been a good girl like Mammy told me, and you said she was coming here, and she didn't. I want my Mammy, and I want my Daddy, and I want to go home. I hate you."

She snatched up her doll and ran from the room.

Sheelagh stood to follow the little girl. Brendan abandoned his thumb and began to cry, and Sheelagh heard Richard call, "What the hell is going on up here?" as he came up the stairs.

She passed her husband in the hall. "Look after Brendan, please. Ellen's upset," she said to him as she hurried up the stairs.

The child had thrown herself face down on her bed, her pillow now muffling her sobs. Sheelagh sat beside her. She rested her arm across the little girl's shoulders. Ellen shrugged it off. "I'm so sorry, Ellen. I really am. I hate to see you so upset."

"I want my Mammy, *and* my Daddy."

"I know you do, sweetheart, but you just can't, not for the moment. I'm so sorry."

Sheelagh felt so helpless, the child was inconsolable. She leaned forward to hold the little girl, rested her head beside Ellen's. It was impossible to hold back her own tears any longer. It was all too much. She remembered, so vividly, how scared *she* had been, when she first came to live in England, how strange everything had been.

She was crying for herself. She was crying for Ellen, and she was crying for poor little Brendan, who was so like his father. She was crying for Michael too ... she hadn't understood until now how frightened he must have been back when they first came to England. He was her baby brother and she hadn't helped him.

"You know your Mummy is in the hospital, Ellen," she tried to steady her voice. "She has to get better, and then she can get out of the hospital and you can see her. I promise you, Ellen, truly I do. I'm not lying. You will see your Mummy again, very soon. I promise."

"Then I want my Daddy," the girl wept.

Sheelagh pulled up and away from the child as if she had been hit. She sat upright, sobbed into her handkerchief.

"You have to tell her."

She looked up to see Richard standing in the doorway.

She shook her head. "I can't," she whispered through her sobs, "I gave Beth my word. I just can't." She was crying as bitterly as her niece.

Richard put his arms around her shoulders and eased her to her feet. "You go and look after the boy. I'll stay with her."

"But ..."

"Go! She'll be fine."

Sheelagh didn't want to leave, but she knew she was no help to Ellen like this. She nodded, stepped back, and Richard took her place on the bed. She dabbed at her eyes with her handkerchief. "Are you sure?"

He nodded.

"Thank you." She left.

* * *

"Ellen."

The child turned away from him, toward the wall.

"Ellen, I need to talk to you."

She didn't want to talk to him. She didn't want to listen to him either. She shook her head.

He rested his hand gently on her shoulder. "Look, Ellen, I know I don't know you very well, and I know you don't know me very well, either, but I'm very sorry you are so sad and angry right now. And I need to talk to you. Please."

She tried to cry a bit quieter.

"I would like you to look at me while I try and explain something to you."

She thought about it for a minute, then slowly she turned to look up at him. His face was very serious, but he gave her a tiny smile.

"Thank you." He wiped her tears with his thumb. He did it softly, he was very gentle. Then he took both her hands in his. "Ellen, you have to be a big, brave girl when I explain this, All right?"

He'd never been as nice and gentle as this before. Most of the time he seemed to pretend Brendan and her weren't there, unless they made too much noise, then he would just throw down his paper and leave, or frown really hard at Aunty Sheelagh. He seemed nicer now.

She nodded.

"You can't see your daddy because there has been a big accident, and your daddy was hurt."

She sniffled and nodded. "I know, Uncle Paul told me."

"Well, yes, I know he did. But, little one," he took a deep breath, and squeezed her hands a little tighter. "Your daddy died."

She looked hard at him, tried to understand what he said.

"Do you understand, Ellen?"

She continued to look up at him.

"He didn't want to leave you, or Brendan, or your mother, but it was an accident. He didn't know it was going to happen."

She pulled her hands away from his. She didn't want to hold his hands any more, she wanted to hold Mandy.

"Do you understand what I am saying, Ellen?"

She pulled Mandy to her, squeezed her tight. She had seen a dead cat on the road one day a long time ago, and its mouth was wide open like it was making a loud noise, but all its teeth were showing too, like it was snarling like a lion, but there was blood all around it and Mammy had said it was dead. Was daddy's mouth open?

She heard her uncle talking to her again. "Do you understand, Ellen?"

She nodded and bent her face into the doll's hair. It was soft and warm. She tried to think of her daddy's face, but the only picture in her head was the cat that was trying to make a noise.

"Do you have any questions you want to ask me?"

She shook her head.

He waited for a while. Then he took another deep breath and said, "I don't think we should tell Brendan yet, do you? He's a bit too young to understand right now. Is that all right?"

She nodded. Brendan didn't see the cat either; he was only a baby really.

"Would you like me to sit here with you for a while?"

She nodded again.

"All right." He settled himself a little more comfortably on the bed. "I'll stay here as long as you want me to."

She just wanted to be quiet, and still.

After a long time, when Mandy's hair was tickling her nose, she put her doll on the bed and snuggled over to her uncle. He lifted her into his lap and put his arms around her. She leaned against him and hugged him tight. He seemed a bit stiff, like he wasn't used to hugging, but she didn't want to see the cat in her head any more, and Uncle Richard smelled nice, a bit like daddy.

Confessions

Sheelagh stood in the hall, took time to compose herself before she went in to Brendan. His earlier cries had subsided to whimpers, but as she stood there she heard several strange thuds. She stepped quietly to the doorway and peeked in. He was kneeling at the table, where she had left him, but now his building blocks were scattered all over the floor and, unaware that she was watching him, he threw the last one toward the armchair.

His ammunition all gone, he sat back on his heels, a sad and confused bundle of misery, staring at the table, still whimpering.

"Oh, you poor baby," she said going to him, arms out-stretched. This time he didn't reject her but raised his arms in response. She picked him up, and hugged him close.

"There, there," she whispered as she rubbed his back, "You poor, poor love. I know just how strange it must be for you, my sweet, and I'm so sorry. I promise everything will be better soon."

She continued to hold him close as she eased herself into an armchair, settled him comfortably on her lap, and rocked him back and forth. He leaned in toward her and rested his head on her shoulder. Sheelagh said nothing more. His crying finally stopped, and he made only the occasional sob. After a while, he slept.

It was some time before Richard came downstairs.

"She's calmed down. Said it was all right for me to leave her. She's been sitting on my lap, believe it or not!" He smiled, looked a little abashed. "But my back started to stiffen up, so I asked her if she'd like to rest for a bit. She's lying on the bed, hugging her doll. Poor kid."

Sheelagh was surprised at the softness in his voice. She nodded. "This little man is exhausted," she whispered, "Cried himself out". She looked ruefully up at her husband. "I think I have too. Sorry about that. You're sure she's all right?"

"Yes ..." he hesitated.

"What?"

He looked a little awkward.

"What's wrong, Richard?"

"Nothing's wrong, dammit," he said, though he kept his voice low. He looked around at the blocks scattered on the floor, then shrugged and said, "I told her."

"What? ... About Michael?" Her whisper became a hiss. "You told her about Michael?"

"She needed to know. You know she did, Sheelagh. Don't go all righteous on me. We both agreed Beth should have told them right away. We couldn't go on lying, pretending he was still alive, for God knows how long, while Beth is in hospital. Someone was bound to tell her. Better she hear it here, than in that damn school. The poor kid deserves to know what's going on. It's not fair on her."

Sheelagh's anger flared. She bent her head to the boy so Richard wouldn't see just how angry she was. Furious! Yet she knew he was right. She had no right to be angry. Ellen *did* need to know. It was becoming almost impossible to keep it secret. And it's not as if *he'd* promised anyone he wouldn't tell! No, that wouldn't be Richard; he was always honest, however much it hurt. But at least this time it seemed like he'd spoken because he cared. He'd called Ellen a 'poor kid'. Why was that a surprise? She thought he didn't like the children, positively disliked them in fact. Had she been wrong? She looked up at him, tried to smile. "You're right. Thank you. I'm sorry. She did need to know." She nodded down to the boy, "but not this little lad, he's too young, he wouldn't understand."

"That's fine with me. I already said that to her." He picked up one of the blocks. "It wasn't the easiest thing I've ever done!"

"And she took it all right?"

"Seemed to me like she knew already, took it very quietly. She's a bright child, Sheelagh; she has to have known something was up with everyone bawling all the time."

She nodded.

"Right. ...I think she will be all right now." He waited for her to agree. "I'll go on downstairs then. Unless you need me up here?" He put the block on the table.

"No, I'm fine. I'll let him sleep for a while. It'll do him good."

"All right." He turned to leave, stopped, and turned again. "Oh, by the way, I forgot. The reason I was coming up, Colm called. I actually left him on the line, thought I was just coming up here to get you. I suspect he's long since hung up!"

"Oh, Richard, I need to talk to him. Did he say anything? Did he tell you where he was?"

"No. I told him I'd come up and fetch you, that's all. I'm sure you can call him back at home."

"I suppose so. I'll do it as soon as this little man wakes up. If he calls again will you ask him where I can get hold of him?"

"I will."

Richard left and Sheelagh very slowly and carefully disentangled herself from Brendan, stood, and gently laid him in the armchair. She took off her cardigan and covered him with it, tucking it under his chin. She picked up the rest of the bricks and put them on the table. When she was quite sure Brendan was still asleep, she went up to Ellen.

The little girl was lying back on the bed, doll tucked in beside her, and staring at the skylight window.

"Hello, Ellen. Are you all right, darling?"

The child nodded, indicated the window. "Is my Daddy in heaven, like Mammy's daddy?"

Beth must have told her about her father. "Yes, sweetheart, he is. He surely is."

"Are they together?"

"Yes, Ellen, I'm sure they are, and with my mammy and daddy."

"So, Daddy won't be lonely without us, and Mammy?"

Sheelagh could feel a lump forming in her throat. She mustn't start crying again, that wouldn't be fair to the poor child. "He will always love you, and I'm sure he will be minding you, Ellen. He's like your guardian angel now; you just can't see him anymore."

"I miss him."

"I know you do, darling. So do I. You know he was my brother, my baby brother, like you and Brendan."

Ellen nodded.

Sheelagh took one of Ellen's hands, "Are we friends again now?"

Ellen looked a little doubtful, but didn't pull her hand away.

"I will do my best to look after you," said Sheelagh, "until your mummy comes home. And I promise you, she really will be home, as soon as she can."

Ellen thought about this, before nodding again.

Sheelagh tried to smile. "How about we go shopping for that school uniform for you after lunch? Then we could take a picture of you in it and I could get it printed and take it in to mummy. You could write a letter to her as well if you like?"

"I can't do writing yet, only a bit. I can't do joined-up writing."

"That's not a problem, I can help you. What do you think?"

Ellen looked doubtful, but she said, "Yes, please".

"Good. Well, perhaps I'll get some lunch first, and then we can get going?" Sheelagh stood and helped Ellen to scoot herself off the bed. The child reached back for Mandy. They made their way downstairs to the still-sleeping Brendan.

Colm would have to wait, at least until later in the day.

The Truth

Both children were calmer by the time lunch was finished, though Ellen had become as quiet as her brother. Sheelagh was glad she'd suggested the outing for the new school uniform. It would be a much-needed diversion.

After they had visited a shoe shop, and the school outfitters, and once there had been a great deal of measuring, and trying on, everything was wrapped and Sheelagh took the children, as promised, to the portrait photographer. In the cramped changing room at the back of his studio the bags and parcels were unpacked and Sheelagh helped Ellen struggle into the several layers of her uniform; maroon underpants and socks, cream shirt, maroon tunic, maroon and cream woven sash, maroon overcoat, and a velour hat with a wide, turn-up brim, its crown ringed with a striped, grosgrain ribbon and the school badge stitched center front.

Once she was dressed the photographer helped fashion a thick Windsor knot in her tie, and Sheelagh tied the laces on her new brown leather shoes.

"I can do that myself, my Daddy showed me."

"Well, this will just be a bit quicker, because the man is waiting."

Ellen complained that the belted overcoat was heavy and she didn't want to wear it, or the hat with the tight chin elastic. "It feels uncomfortable," she whined.

Sheelagh was losing patience. It had been a long day. To humor the child she stood back to get a better look. She had to admit the hat *did* look a little uncomfortable. It pressed down on the child's ears and made them stick out at the top, and the elastic dug a slight groove under her chin, but she was too tired to go back and change it, at least for today.

"You'll get used to it, darling. Perhaps I can put in a bigger piece of elastic. You'll only have to wear it to and from school, not in class. And you don't have to wear it now if you don't want to." she said as she tugged the hat from Ellen's head. The elastic caught on the child's ears.

"Ow! That hurt."

"I'm sorry."

"And I *don't* want to wear it."

"All *right*, Ellen. You're not wearing it."

"I don't want to wear the coat either."

"All right, all right, take it off then. I really don't care, Ellen. It's only so that your mother will be able to see a picture of you in your new uniform."

Ellen's bottom lip trembled and Sheelagh immediately realized her error. She shouldn't have mentioned Beth, especially with the children so tired and fractious. She felt a bit that way herself in fact. She bent and hugged her niece.

"I'm sorry, Ellen. I didn't mean to be growly. Let's just get these pictures done and we can go home. Look." She turned Ellen toward a full length mirror in the corner of the studio. "Look how smart and grown up you are."

Ellen studied her reflection. She smiled. "I look like the other girls."

Tears had been averted.

"Yes, you do. Now, let's get these pictures done, shall we?"

While Sheelagh had been dressing Ellen, the photographer had tried to keep Brendan amused by letting him play with his box of 'props;' an assortment of hats, stuffed toys, and even a large-piece wooden jigsaw puzzle. As soon as Ellen reappeared from the dressing room the props were discarded. They now lay strewn around the floor of the studio.

Sheelagh thought the photographer was probably as relieved as she was when the session was over. He promised to have the photographs ready for collection as quickly as possible.

* * *

When they arrived back at the shop Sheelagh left the children to play and went downstairs to telephone Colm. Richard was in the office, but said he had things to do in the stockroom, and left.

She waited on the line a long time. The phone rang and rang. She thought Colm might have been trying to ignore the call, suspecting it was her. She was determined to out-wait him. Eventually someone picked up the receiver.

"Yes."

"Colm?"

"Yes." The reply was clipped, tetchy.

"We need to sort out this insurance for Beth. Will you come over here, or will I come to you?"

She heard him sigh. "Could you leave it with me for another day or two, Sheelagh? I'm very tied up right now."

"No, Colm, I couldn't. You did get hold of them, didn't you?"

There was a pause. She thought she heard him light a cigarette before he answered.

"Yes." There was another pause before he added, "All right, why don't you come over here? About eight?"

"Fine." She was in no mood for Colm's game-playing. Whatever he was up to now was no concern of hers; she just wanted to get the insurance policy sorted. "I'll be there at eight. And Colm ...."

"Yes."

"Will your girlfriend be there?" Sheelagh hoped she wouldn't. She wanted family business to be private.

"I have no idea, Sheelagh, and she's not here now so I can't ask her. See you at eight."

He hung up before she could say anything else. She stared at the receiver, thought about calling him back, but decided there was no point in starting an argument on the phone. She went back upstairs to get the tea.

* * *

Colm took as long to answer the door as he had to answer the phone. When he did, he stood back, waved her in, said nothing. Sheelagh walked past him and up the stairs, choosing to be as silent as he was. She waited at the flat door until he joined her and pushed it open.

195

The blonde was draped over the couch, in a Marlene Dietrich pose. Artificial blonde, Sheelagh corrected herself. She shot a quick sideways glance at her brother, but he was taking his time closing the door and didn't look her way.

The woman eased herself off the couch, stood, and extended her hand, "Hello, Sheelagh honey, so nice to see you again."

Sheelagh glanced at the long, red-painted nails extended toward her ... claws! She shook the woman's hand as brusquely as was civil and turned to her brother.

"This shouldn't take long, Colm."

"Right." He went to the sideboard. "Well, you have time for a little drink, don't you? You're not in that much of a hurry, surely?"

"I promised Richard we'd go out this evening. He's waiting for me. Doris is babysitting the children."

"Well, you don't mind if *I* have one, do you? What about you, Margot, a little gin and tonic, perhaps? Or a whisky?"

"Manhattan please, sweetie, you should know how to make one by now." The woman sank back onto the couch. "Won't you sit down, honey? You look so uncomfortable standing there. Colm, you really are the most dreadful host. Why don't you offer your sister a seat?"

"She's my sister, for heaven's sake! We don't have to be on ceremony. Sit where you like, Sheelagh. I'll be with you in a second." He busied himself pouring the drinks, not even looking at her. Sheelagh sat in the nearest armchair and glanced around the room; it was certainly much tidier than the last time. Her eyes met the woman's, who continued to smile at her. Sheelagh noticed a smudge of red lipstick on her front teeth. The way she was making herself comfortable on the couch, slipping off her shoes and tucking her feet up, it was clear she had no intention of leaving. So, they would simply have to discuss the money with her sitting there, listening to everything. Sheelagh would have to do her best to ignore her.

"It's just that Beth is fretting about how much money she will have, once everything is settled. If I can just tell her how much the policy is worth? Did they tell you how much she will get, Colm?"

"Are you sure you won't change your mind?" he asked as he brought two drinks over and handed one to the woman. It was a dark brown color, darker than whisky, with ice cubes, *and* a bright red, preserve cherry. Sheelagh wondered where he'd got the cherries; she'd only seen them in drinks in films. Trust that woman to want a fancy American drink! She shook her head, again declining his offer of a drink. Her brother sat on the couch beside his girlfriend. She pursed her lips to him in a silent kiss. Sheelagh was seething. Colm smiled, took his time taking a cigarette from the packet on the table and lighting it.

"So?" Sheelagh was barely holding on to her temper. He really was such a self-centered, egotistical person; he'd never cared about anyone else, she thought, not even on the odd occasions she'd met him when they were children. He was always the same. Fine! To hell with civility!

"How much, Colm?"

"It ... would seem there has been a little bit of a mix-up," he said, slowly.

She sat forward in her seat. "What do you mean? What kind of a mix-up?"

"Well, ... it would seem they didn't get *all* the payments."

"What?" She almost shouted it.

He took a large swallow of his drink, then a deep draft of his cigarette. The smoke escaped in irregular puffs from his mouth as he continued.

" ... and when they didn't get them for a couple of months I gather they presumed the policy was cancelled."

"What?" she said again.

"Oh, for heaven's sake, Sheelagh. You look like a damned fish, close your mouth."

"Are you telling me there is *no* insurance policy? No insurance money?"

"That is certainly how it would seem. Bloody stupid really. Can't imagine what they were thinking."

"But you were the one who was supposed to be looking after it. Beth said Michael asked you to!"

"I know, dear woman, but I'm a busy man. Can't be here all the time, waiting for 'our man from the Pru.' to turn up, now can I?"

Sheelagh jumped up. "You didn't keep up the payments!"

"It just seems I wasn't here when he called, then some other chappie took over the round and thought it was cancelled or something."

She wanted to hit his smug, arrogant face. "You selfish bastard. You thoughtless, selfish bastard. What am I supposed to tell Beth?"

He looked up at her, shrugged, and took another deep draw on his cigarette. "Who knew Michael was going to snuff it at this point? When he'd got all the way through the war without a scratch? *I* certainly thought he was destined to die of old age, in his bed."

"Don't you dare talk about him like that!"

He leaned back, made a helpless gesture with his hands, drink in one, cigarette in the other. "Like what? Sheelagh, be reasonable, let's face it; I hardly knew him. Brothers?" he shook his head. "Not really. I could probably count on the fingers of one hand the times we even met, and one of those was carrying our dear father's splinter-filled, *nailed*-down coffin."

"Stop it, Colm. And don't make pathetic excuses." Sheelagh was almost choking on her anger. She remembered what Beth had said about the payments. "He sent you money. He never stopped. You didn't stop him! Michael was sending money to you right up until the accident." She stepped back, horrified. "Where's the money, Colm?"

He seemed about to speak when the woman put her hand on his knee. "Oh, come now, sweetie, I hate to see family fighting like this." She turned to Sheelagh. "Why don't you two just sit awhile, honey, and we'll try and fix this little problem in a civilized manner?"

Sheelagh could feel her face burning with suppressed fury. She was so angry it was difficult to be civil. If that damn woman called her 'honey' once more she would scream.

But she sat, waited, and said nothing.

"It would seem my sweetie has been more than a little careless in this matter. From what he's told me it would certainly seem he owes your brother." She paused, "Well ... your brother's widow I suppose it is, a reimbursement." She bent and reached for her handbag, on the floor beside her. Sheelagh noticed with some satisfaction that there was a dark line at the parting in her hair. Not that the blonde looked natural anyway. It looked brassy, common!

The woman took out a cheque book. "I don't suppose you have any idea how much that would be, do you?"

Sheelagh shook her head in disbelief.

"No, I didn't think so, and I don't expect the poor widow knows either?"

Sheelagh just stared at her.

"So, I thought, perhaps, if I gave you a cheque for two hundred pounds that would help compensate her for Colm's carelessness."

Sheelagh found her voice, "But it was a life insurance policy. I'm sure it would be worth far more than that. It's all she'll have, and she'll have three small children to look after. She won't even be able to go out to work until the baby is older."

"Oh, for goodness' sake, Sheelagh!" Colm leaned forward and mashed his cigarette out in the ashtray. "She'll get the house money when she sells the Dublin place, which will probably be a tidy sum. She'll have plenty left over if she buys a smaller place this time; and with the money Margot is giving her, she should be fine."

"Irish law says two thirds of the house money will go to the children, and that's *after* the mortgage is paid off. Their money will be held in trust until they're twenty one. The law is not the same in Ireland, Colm. She'll have almost nothing."

"Then their law truly *is* an ass. Not a surprise really, is it?" he said. "Anyway, I'm sure she's entitled to a widow's pension or something. She'll be fine."

"You're telling me there is no insurance money? None at all?"

"I did go to see them today," he said defensively, "asked them why no one had been around to collect for so long. Couldn't get any sense out of them, except that they weren't going to shell out, not a single penny, even though I'd certainly paid some of it, and Michael had. I'd quite a ding-dong with them, in fact. But no change."

"When did you stop paying?" She stopped and stared at him.

"What did you do with the rest of the money Michael sent you, Colm?"

She was icy calm now. Furious, but icy calm.

"Good lord, woman, anyone would think it was a fortune. I don't know what I did with it, probably bought cigarettes!" He shrugged again.

She couldn't believe he truly didn't care.

"So *you* walk away with Michael's money, and Beth is left with nothing."

"Look, Sheelagh," he said, then glanced at the woman sitting beside him, "Margot has been kind enough to offer to help. It's the best we can do, I'm afraid. Damn glad she's here." He reached over and took the woman's hand. "In fact, I've decided to up stakes and go back to America with her. She's anxious to go home."

The woman leaned conspiratorially toward Sheelagh, "What he's trying to say, honey, is that your brother and I are going to get married."

Sheelagh was speechless.

The woman scribbled on a cheque, blew on the ink to ensure it was dry, and offered it to Sheelagh. "I've made it three hundred. That's three hundred *pounds*, dear. Bless your English money; I am so glad now that I transferred some emergency money to one of your quaint little banks. Anyway, that should help, shouldn't it?" She smiled and Sheelagh again noticed the red lipstick smeared on her teeth.

"You're what?" Sheelagh looked from the woman to her brother.

"I know," he said, and smiled. "Generous isn't she? ... Oh, ... you mean about getting married? Yes, who would have believed it? Me ... getting hitched! Don't worry, it's not going to be a big affair. In fact we're getting married over there; saves a lot of fuss, and it will be easier for Margot's family and friends to be part of it." He looked around the room. "Not a lot of point hanging around here, actually, in hock for most of this stuff. No! New beginning, New World, all that sort of thing."

The same old Colm. She should have realized. Even his home was a lie. All the elegant furniture, the beautiful flat; all show, no substance.

The woman was still holding out the cheque.

Sheelagh took it.

"What will you do there?"

"Actually Margot has a nice little business, a new way of printing and developing film, photographs. Well, it was her second husband's business actually. But he died and Margot inherited the lot. I expect I can find a little niche in there, some little job to keep me busy. A bit like you and Richard in fact, isn't it?"

She looked down at the cheque. Three hundred pounds! A pittance, and it was clear that was all she was going to get. She stood again.

"I kept thinking you would change, Colm, maybe get more like Michael, or even Pierce, but it's never going to happen is it? You're selfish and thoughtless, and you don't give a damn about anyone else." She looked at the woman. "I wish you well of him, and good luck on your marriage. I can't imagine he'll ever change."

She turned and left the apartment.

"Make sure the door is closed as you go, Sheelagh," he called as she hurried down the stairs.

She opened the front door, intent on slamming it, changed her mind, left it wide open, and walked away.

Letters

When he heard the front door open Richard hurried to the stairs. He stopped when he saw Sheelagh. "I was going to say you're late; we've missed the start of the film, but I suspect that would not be a good idea." He went down toward her. "How do I know the meeting didn't go well?"

Sheelagh shook her head. "It was a disaster. There's no money."

"What?"

"That bloody awful woman."

"*What* woman?"

"Three hundred pounds! That's all. Three hundred pounds!"

"So you *did* get money?"

"Only from that horrible woman with the red teeth."

"Sheelagh dear, you're not making an awful lot of sense."

"And *don't* call me bloody 'dear.'" Sheelagh stopped, realized she was shouting, that she must sound hysterical.

Richard looked confused, raised his hands as if to fend her off. "All right sweetheart, whatever you say. Perhaps we could skip the film, go for a drink, maybe? And you can tell me all about it."

She took a deep breath. "I think a drink would be a very good idea. Is Doris here?"

"She is, and I'm very glad *you're* finally here. We ran out of things to talk about an hour ago. Come on, let's go."

"I'll just go up and ..."

"No, you won't go up and do anything." He turned and called up the stairs. "All right, she's here, Doris. We're off, see you later."

"Very well, Mr. Hudson," came the distant response.

"You see? No reason to go up. Now, let's get going. You can tell me all about it in the club."

* * *

Once they were settled in the bar, Sheelagh explained what had happened in her meeting with Colm.

"So, he's getting married, is he?" Her husband chuckled. "Now there's a turn up for the books. Never would have believed that of your Colm; too fond of the wild life I would have thought. Hope she's got enough money to keep him in the style he likes."

Sheelagh had not mentioned Colm's final snide remark about marrying into a business, like Richard. He'd clearly implied that was a large part of the reason Richard had married her, and the comment made Sheelagh almost as angry as him stealing Michael's insurance money. And that's what it was, stealing!

"So, now what happens to Beth?"

"I've no idea, Richard. I don't know *what* she's going to do. I don't even know what *I'm* going to do."

"It's not really your problem Sheelagh; you've done everything you could. You went over as soon as you heard about Michael. You brought the kids back, took them in. What more can you do?"

"But she has nothing, Richard. Where's she going to live?"

"I suppose she'll have to move in with her mother and her new husband."

"I know that's what she was going just until after the baby is born, but then get her own place. She can't go on living there, Richard. There isn't enough room."

"They'll have to make room, won't they?"

She wanted to hit him. "That's not going to work! Evelyn's still living there. They only have three bedrooms. She and two children and a new baby can't all crowd into one bedroom. I have to think of something."

"For God's sake, Sheelagh, stop it. You don't. It's *not* your problem." He waved to the barman and indicated he should bring two more drinks. "When you have another one of those, you'll feel more relaxed."

Sheelagh sipped at her drink. Was there any point in trying to discuss it further with him? If she suggested giving Beth money he would probably go crazy, rattle on about profit margins, over-investments, liquidity issues. She did wish she hadn't invested so much money in renovating the shop. They were pretty tight for cash right now, she knew that. It's part of what had Richard so jumpy. But she didn't want to upset Beth, didn't want to tell her about the insurance, not until she could think up some kind of solution.

She'd tell Mary and Pierce, they were family; perhaps they would have some ideas. She would have to write. They still didn't have telephones, even though there was electricity in their villages now. Both of them insisted telephones were not necessary. "Sure, doesn't bad news travel fast enough without that ould bell jangling its arrival," had been Mary's response, and Pierce said word of mouth had suited his father, and himself, for long enough ... why would he change now? Both of them said that Sheelagh was probably the only person they knew that owned one anyway, so who would they be talking to?

Her! That was the point; they could talk to *her*, and *she* could talk to them. And that was exactly why they should have one! But there was no point in getting cross with them now. Too late! Thinking of her brother and sister, she had to smile. They were so content with the old ways. And probably better for it, she thought. The bartender arrived with their drinks. Still, using the mail, it could be a week or two before she would hear back from them.

She hastily finished her first drink, handed the empty glass to the barman, and took the fresh one. She thanked him, leaned back in her chair and stared into the glass, watching the thin slice of lemon circle slowly in the bubbles of tonic. She would just have to lie to Beth in the meantime, pretend everything was all right, that the insurance company would be giving her the money.

"You've gone very quiet."

She looked up from her drink. Richard was watching her.

"I'm not going to tell Beth."

He slammed his almost empty glass down on the table, splashing whisky over his hand. "Oh, don't be so bloody stupid, Sheelagh. What choice do you have? She has to be told. What is it with all of you women not wanting to tell things?"

She glanced around at the scattering of patrons. "Keep your voice down, Richard."

"*You* keep things in perspective! You've done all you can, it's up to her family now."

"Well, well, well, look who it is." A large man in a loud check sports jacket, blue shirt, cravat, and slacks was coming toward them. "Thought we were never going to see you again, old thing," he bellowed, waving at Sheelagh. He arrived at the table and struck Richard on the back with his open hand, "Hello Richard, old man. Finally let the little lady out of the kitchen then, did you?"

His loud laughter caused a few people to turn in their direction. Richard stood, shook the man's hand, and turned to Sheelagh. "You remember Arthur Pettifer, don't you, Sheelagh? Think you met him at the New Year's Eve party here."

"And very fetching you looked too, my dear, if memory serves." The man released Richard's hand and grasped hers. His hand was warm, and damp. Sheelagh managed a half-hearted smile.

"Mind if I join you, always nice to see a friendly face in the place, very bad to drink alone, eh?"

He gave another loud laugh and without waiting for a reply pulled out a chair, sat, and waved at the barman. "Usual please, Bill, and whatever these lovely people are having."

Sheelagh glared at Richard. Why didn't he get rid of this horrible man? They had come here to talk, that's what Richard had said. So get rid of this man! Richard sat, looked across at her and gave a slight "what can I do" shrug. She frowned and gave him an almost imperceptible shake of her head. He put his hand over his glass.

"No, no, we're fine for drinks. Thanks, Arthur."

The man waved away Richard's protests. "Nonsense old chap, can never have too much of a good thing, what?"

Richard leaned back, pulled a helpless face at her.

So much for trying to talk things through. Now she would have to listen to this bore for the rest of the evening. Well, she would write to Mary and Pierce as soon as she got home. They would understand how she felt. And she would have to decide, on her own, exactly what to say to Beth tomorrow. She only knew she couldn't tell her any more bad news, not now anyway.

Communication

Brendan, Ellen, and Sheelagh were at the dining table. Brendan had recreated yesterday's miniature roadways with his building blocks. He was making subdued car noises as he navigated his toys through the multi-colored twists and turns. Ellen, the tip of her tongue just visible at the corner of her mouth, was absorbed in keeping her crayoning within the lines. The coloring book and the pencils had been purchased at Peacocks Bazaar earlier that morning, to add to the collection of toys, books and novelties that already littered their bedroom and the living room.

Sheelagh's head was throbbing. She hadn't written to Pierce and Mary when they got home the previous evening. Her head felt too addled. She was not used to drinking, and had clearly had a glass too many. Damn that man anyway, though she had to admit to herself that she didn't have to drink it!

This morning, she'd thought the gifts might bribe the children into a peaceful silence while she wrote. She'd been right. Brendan had chosen a bright red fire engine to add to his collection of cars, vans, and lorries. The engine was presently parked in a garage of red building blocks and she was grateful it was finally silent, at least for the time being. All three sat in companionable quiet, except for Brendan's occasional "Beep, beep, beep."

Sheelagh struggled to phrase the letters, as absorbed as the children in her task. The letter to Mary was the most difficult. Her sister never wanted to hear, or believe, ill of any of her siblings. "We have to stay close, Sheelagh," she always insisted, "I couldn't bear for us not to be close; we have so many years to make up for."

Any time Sheelagh tried to complain to her older sister about Colm's excesses or poor behavior Mary always excused it as the way he was brought up by the Sinclairs. "Sure they spoiled him rotten, Sheelagh, 'tis no wonder he's a bit wild. He'll settle eventually, you'll see."

Sheelagh tapped the top of her pen on her teeth and wondered if Mary would consider him 'settled' now he was partnering with a twice-married, divorced and widowed, American lady with artificially blonde hair and red-painted nails!

She felt her anger against her brother rising again. She knew he wouldn't tell the rest of his family about his up-coming departure for the USA, or his marriage. Too thoughtless. *She* would have to do it; *knew* that she would. He was nothing but a coward, running away from his responsibilities. Probably afraid he might get into an argument with Pierce about his neglect of Michael's affairs, too.

Sheelagh put down the pen, leaned back in her chair. How could he be so unlike his brothers? Even though Michael and Pierce were different they had become so close. Pierce's wife, Maeve, had written only a week ago to say she still found Pierce crying about Michael's loss when he thought he was alone, despite the many weeks that had now passed.

She and Mary were close too, even though they too were so different in almost every way. Colm was definitely the odd one out. And it was of his own choosing. Lord knows they'd all tried. She sighed, read her most recent letter attempt, tore the page from the pad, and screwed it into a ball.

Oh, Michael! What are we going to do? We have to look after your children, and your wife.

She began to write again. She had to get this done. Pierce and Mary had to know how hard-up Beth might be now; that to a large extent it was Colm's fault, and that they would have to make it right, for Michael's sake. She hoped Mary and Pierce would agree, though she had no idea if they would be in a position to help very much. They both had a clutch of small children of their own to care for.

"When is Uncle Paul coming to take us to the zoo?" Ellen had stopped coloring and was watching her aunt.

Sheelagh put down her pen. Brendan stopped his play too, and watched her.

"In the morning, sweetheart, remember? He said he would come on Saturday, and that's tomorrow."

Brendan's forehead creased in a frown. He took a deep breath. "Effalunt," he said.

Sheelagh stared at him in amazement for a moment, then began to laugh, "Yes, elephant! You are right, Brendan, my sweet; he promised you are going to ride on the elephant. Aren't you a clever boy that you remembered that?"

The frown disappeared. Brendan's lips slowly parted into a wide smile, and his head bobbed back and forth in agreement. "Effalunt," he repeated grinning broadly.

"It's elephant!" his sister corrected him.

"Oh, Ellen, he's only four. He's a very clever boy to be able to say such a big word. I think he deserves a reward, don't you." She pushed her chair back from the table and stood.

Ellen pulled a disdainful face. "I can say bigger words than that!"

"I know you can, darling." Sheelagh patted Ellen's shoulder. She opened the cabinet and took out the brightly painted biscuit tin, embossed with pictures of horses, and ladies in full-length, hooped dresses, and men in red soldier's uniforms. She opened it and offered the contents to Brendan. He considered for a while, and selected a round, chocolate-covered biscuit with a hole in the center, and immediately stuck his thumb into the hole. Sheelagh didn't take the tin away, he looked up, hesitated, then grinning, put his other hand in and took out a long, thin, chocolate finger.

"Thank you," he said, his voice soft, quiet.

Sheelagh had to blink back tears. He was starting to talk again. Thank goodness. She offered the biscuits to Ellen, then put the lid back on and put the tin back in the cupboard.

Before she sat down again she hugged them both, then returned to her letter writing.

Things were going to get better. They would work things out, somehow. She knew that they would.

But, she still had to talk to Beth.

Delays

Sheelagh called in to the office to tell Richard she was going out for a while. "What about the children?"

She glanced into the shop. "The staff doesn't seem to be too busy down there. I was going to ask Doris if she'd watch them, if that's all right with you? They like her, they're used to her, and Ivy can always do the cash."

"Fine. Where are you going?"

"I'm going to post these to Mary and Pierce." she indicated the two letters, "I *know* I can leave them in the out tray," She hurriedly continued before he could say anything. "But then it would be late this afternoon before they went ... and it's Friday. They might go a bit quicker if I take them to the post office." She felt like a child, making excuses, defending herself. She knew it was stupid, but he made her feel like that sometimes. "Then I'll go on in to see Beth," she added, as if to clinch the non-existent argument.

He looked up at her, nodded, but said nothing. Sheelagh knew what he really wanted her to say. He wanted to know what she was going to tell Beth. But she didn't know herself yet, so how could she tell him? So, she too was silent. A maelstrom of thoughts flew through her head, different ways she might be able to help Michael's family, some barely possible, some totally impossible. They couldn't come and live with her and Richard, not enough room; and the business wasn't doing so well that she could promise to fund Beth, even if Richard were to agree. And he would have to agree; he was her partner, despite what he said sometimes.

She wished he'd show more support, come up with some kind of helpful suggestion. Even if he was just prepared to talk things through with her, but last night proved it was probably never going to happen. He'd even chosen to talk to that loud, drunken fool rather than talk to her. They had driven home in silence.

Sheelagh shook her head. The walk to the Post Office was a good idea, would give her thinking time, to decide *how* she was going to tell Beth, *and* how she could help.

She realized she and Richard were staring at each other, each waiting for the other to speak.

"I won't be long."

He nodded, but still said nothing.

"See you later."

* * *

It was only when she had left the shop that she realized she'd forgotten to take stamps from the desk drawer. Well, she wasn't going back. She'd get them at the Post Office.

It was busy and she had to join a long line of people in front of the STAMPS window. She stood, deep in her own thoughts for a while, automatically shuffling forward when the others did. Her gaze wandered to the other line, parallel to hers. Their sign said PENSIONS. They were all women in that line, many of them young women. Widows, she thought, war widows probably. There were so many from the war, too many. One woman, who looked about the same age as Sheelagh, had her arm around the shoulders of a young girl as if to protect her. The child looked ill, ashen faced, circles of grey-brown shadows around her watery blue eyes. The girl was not much older than Ellen. The mother saw Sheelagh's glance.

"She's sick. I didn't want to leave her at home on her own; she gets nervous. I had to get my pension … have to feed her up." She gave a helpless shrug and held the child closer. "Don't I, lovvie?" The girl looked up at her mother, smiled, nodded, and broke into a paroxysm of coughing. Her mother looked at Sheelagh again. "Asthma."

Sheelagh nodded in understanding, though she didn't. Her line moved forward and the brief exchange was over.

That could be Beth, and Ellen. How did these women cope? Paying for Ellen's school wasn't enough. It wouldn't really help Beth; it just meant Ellen would get a slightly better education. It's only what Michael would have done anyway.

She bought the stamps, dropped the letters into the box by the door, and walked the rest of the way to the hospital.

Of course she was happy that Brendan had started to speak again, so no one would think he was slow, or stupid. Once was enough for *that* terrible mistake. She still felt much closer to Ellen. The child reminded her so much of herself at that age, though Ellen was probably a bit brighter, Sheelagh thought ruefully, and probably less spoilt than she had been.

By the time she arrived at the hospital the idea was full-grown. There *was* a way she could help more, and Beth would probably be quite relieved and, hopefully, pleased.

Awkwardness

Sheelagh walked down the ward toward Beth. Some patients were sleeping, or resting, others were already chatting to visitors. A few watched Sheelagh's progress down the ward.

Beth saw her, and waved. She waved back.

Her stomach tightened. Why did people call it butterflies when you were nervous? It was more like a slow cramp. Like someone had sewn running stitches around your stomach and was slowly pulling them together.

"Hello, Beth, how are you? How's the baby?'

"We're both fine." Beth sat up. They kissed. "I've been a bit down. They told me the children won't be allowed in. I miss them so much; I want to hear all about them, Sheelagh."

Sheelagh nodded. She was relieved the nurse had done as she promised, and Beth seemed to have taken it better than she expected.

"I nearly signed myself out, I was that down. Marcie, here calmed me down" Beth indicated the woman in bed beside her, "And she gave me her newspaper a while ago. Look what I've been doing!" She grinned and held up the paper so that Sheelagh could see. It was open at the 'Houses for Sale' columns, and several of the advertisements were circled. "I know it's a bit early, but I can get Mum to have a look at some of them … to get an idea what I can afford. Of course I don't know how much I'll have yet but …" She put down the paper, "Just tell me you have been talking to Colm, Sheelagh? It would be so nice to start planning. It might stop me feeling so sad and miserable."

The running stitches in Sheelagh's stomach pulled tighter.

"I did. I saw him yesterday."

"Oh, thank goodness. From the look on your face I thought you were going to say no. Pull up that chair, Sheelagh, sit down. Tell me."

It was no good, she would have to tell her; she couldn't lie, Beth would have to know. Richard was right.

"I'm not sure how much you were expecting, Beth." She rooted in her handbag and produced the folded piece of paper. "But I have a cheque for three hundred pounds."

"Three hundred?" Beth's grin faded, she looked puzzled. "... Three hundred? But it's a life insurance policy, Sheelagh. There should be more than that. I'm sure there should."

"Please don't get upset, Beth. I know there should probably be more, but there was a bit of a mix up about paying in the money."

Beth sat forward in the bed, reached for Sheelagh's hand. "That won't be enough, Sheelagh, I can't buy anything with that. What happened?" Her voice had risen.

"Please, Beth, relax. We just need time to work some things out. It will be fine, I promise. The children will be fine. You were going to stay with your mother anyway until after you had the baby. We have time to sort things out."

"Sheelagh, stop it, tell me what happened. Why is there only three hundred?" Her voice was getting louder. "I don't have any other money. I won't be able to work. Not for a while, at least. What am I going to do Sheelagh?" This came out as a loud wail. Several patients, and their visitors, turned to look. Beth didn't notice. She was bent forward, her hands on her stomach, wincing in pain.

Sheelagh glanced around to see if a nurse had heard her, was coming. No nurses, anywhere. She looked back at her sister-in-law. "Beth, what's wrong? Oh, God, Beth, please! *Please* don't get upset."

"Are you all right, Beth, will I call someone?" It was Marcie, the woman in the next bed.

Beth shook her head.

"Can I get a nurse? *Please,* Beth. Look, I have an idea, let me tell you. Relax, please, Beth, for the baby's sake."

The pain seemed to be easing. Beth slowly leaned back into the pillows, closed her eyes. She took a deep breath in, then exhaled slowly. She did this a couple more times before opening her eyes. Sheelagh was afraid to say anything, even to call the nurse.

Eventually she opened her eyes. "They told me to do that; they said it would help me relax."

"Well, does it? Lord, Beth, you frightened me. I'm sorry, I didn't want to upset you, are you all right now?"

Beth nodded, but Sheelagh saw tears welling in her eyes. "I can't manage with three hundred pounds, Sheelagh. What am I going to do? What went wrong?"

"I can explain that later, and I've written to Mary and Pierce. We'll work something out, I know we will. Give us time. But can I tell you about my idea? It may help?"

Beth brushed away tears and nodded.

"You probably didn't know, but Richard and I have been talking about having a baby."

Beth frowned, "That's nice, Sheelagh. You'll love having children. We do ..." She squeezed her eyes tight shut again. "I mean we *did*. I mean ..." she looked at her sister-in-law. "I'm sorry, Sheelagh, sometimes I still forget it's not 'we' anymore."

Sheelagh felt the too-familiar lump in her throat, but she didn't want to start crying, she had to finish what she wanted to say.

"Yes, well, Richard is not actually that keen. But it's the baby I think he's against, doesn't like the idea of dirty nappies, bottles, and all the time and attention that babies need."

"I can understand that. But he'd get used to it, Michael did." Beth's look clearly showed she didn't understand what Sheelagh getting pregnant had to do with her.

"But Ellen isn't a baby," Sheelagh continued, "And she doesn't need attention like a baby does, and anyway she will be at school a lot of the time, and I know he's getting fond of her, Richard I mean, even though he hasn't actually said it. But that's typical of him."

Beth sat up, looked like she was going to say something. Sheelagh wanted to finish before her sister-in-law could speak, maybe put arguments in the way, say no before she realized what a good idea it was. She hurried on... "I love her Beth, I really do, and I would look after her, and care for her, and make sure she had the very best of everything. I wouldn't let her get sick, and she could see you as much as you want, but please, Beth, could we adopt Ellen?"

"What?"

"I've always wanted a little girl, and Ellen is beautiful. And then it wouldn't be so crowded in your mother's house, and you could stay there a bit longer, until we can sort something out. But you'd have Brendan, and the baby, and that would probably enough for you to cope with. And we would have a beautiful little girl. And you wouldn't have to worry about feeding her properly, or buying clothes, or dentists, or medicines, or her getting sick with asthma, or anything."

"Have you lost your mind, Sheelagh. Stop it, Sheelagh. No!"

"Don't say 'no' straight away, please, Beth. Think about it. I was adopted, and I was so much better off, you know I was. I could still be living in a cottage in Glendarrig, making my own bread. I haven't actually spoken to Richard about it yet, but I know he'll agree. He was really so good with her when he told her about Michael. *I* couldn't do it, even though she kept asking for him ..."

Beth was staring at her in horror. Sheelagh realized what she had said. She covered her mouth with her hands.

"He told her?" Beth's voice was quiet, hard. "Richard told her? About Michael?"

Sheelagh reached for Beth's hands, but she pulled them away.

"She had to know, Beth. I know you said you wanted to tell them yourself ..."

"You told Brendan too?"

"No, no, we didn't. He wasn't asking questions. Ellen knew there was something wrong, and you were in here, and they couldn't come in, and we didn't know how long you were going to be here. She's starting school next week, and someone was bound to let something slip, and Richard thought it was better she hear it from us, rather than a stranger."

"But I was going to tell her. It was my place to tell her." Beth was crying. "She's my daughter, and Michael's. How on earth did you think I could ever give her up?"

The drawstring in Sheelagh's stomach tightened to a knot. She had handled *everything* wrong.

It had all seemed so straightforward in her head, so logical, as she was walking from the Post Office. Of course she hadn't meant to say Ellen knew about Michael. Not today anyway. That was going to be a conversation for another day. And now she had done everything wrong, and Beth was angry with her, and Richard would probably be as well, because she hadn't talked to him about her idea of adopting Ellen. But she didn't think he would mind, she really didn't. As long as his life wasn't disrupted too much, he would be fine. At least she had hoped he would. What a mess she'd made of everything.

She could only look at Beth, mute. She had no idea how to rescue the situation. Beth was trying to stifle her tears.

The nurse rang the bell for the end of visiting time.

"Oh! Beth, I can't leave you like this. I am so sorry. I didn't mean it all to come out like this."

Beth didn't even look at her.

"Please, Beth, please don't be angry. Will you just think about what I said, about Ellen? I was only trying to help, and I would truly love to have her, but it was most of all to help you, Beth, *really*."

Still Beth was silent.

"Can I at least get the nurse for you, before I go?"

Nothing.

"Oh! God." She lifted Beth's limp hand and kissed it. "I'll come back in this evening. I'm sorry, Beth, I'm so sorry."

The bell rang again. Sheelagh waited a minute longer, but she knew Beth wasn't going to speak, or even look at her.

"I'll be back, I promise. I'll make things all right. I'm sorry."

She rushed from the ward, her face burning with embarrassment, eyes stinging with unshed tears. She felt everyone was staring at her. How could she have been so stupid? Have handled things so badly?

Please God, don't let anything happen to Beth, or the baby.

Admitting Mistakes

Sheelagh rushed through the shop, not really caring what customers or staff thought. She hurried up the short flight of steps to the office, burst through the door, and dropped into the seat in front of the desk.

Richard pushed his seat back from the other side of the desk, startled. "Good Lord, Sheelagh, what happened?"

She buried her face in her hands. "I've messed up everything, I did it all wrong, and now Beth won't even talk to me, and she might have the baby too early, and if anything happens to her, or the baby, it will all be my fault. And I didn't mean to tell her about you and Ellen, and I really did think my idea was a good one."

"Stop! Sheelagh, stop! For God's sake woman, take a deep breath and tell me what you're talking about. I swear you've been like a mad woman since those children arrived."

"I'm sorry."

"I don't give a damn about sorry. Would you just pull yourself together, tell me what this latest outburst is about, and while you're at it, would you please remember that everyone in the damn shop can see you."

"I'm sorry." She turned away from the window, took a deep breath, and tried to calm herself. "You're right." She straightened her back "I don't know what's got into me, I seem to be either angry or crying all the time. Sorry."

"That's the last damn 'sorry' I want to hear. Now will you please tell me what happened?"

She was hesitant to explain everything, including her idea about adopting Ellen.

"Please don't get angry with me."

"Why should I get angry?"

"Well just let me explain everything first. Don't jump at me until I explain."

He tugged his chair back to the desk, screwed the cap on his pen and tossed it onto the desk. "All right, I'll try. Go on."

Sheelagh repeated her conversation with Beth, about how she had been looking at houses advertised in the newspaper, about there being no insurance money, "Though I told her there was three hundred pounds, which was *something*." Richard snorted at this, but said nothing. Sheelagh went on to say about Richard's part in telling Ellen about Michael's death, and about Beth knowing the children were too young to visit, and being depressed about it. She told it all in a rush, barely stopping to take a breath, and Richard sat, impassive, throughout.

She had kept the bit about Ellen and adoption until last and now she wasn't sure how to begin that part of the awful visit, but she gathered her thoughts and started with when she was in the Post Office and about the widow with the sick child standing beside her, about how she could imagine Beth and Ellen in the same situation, and how it upset her so much she decided she had to find a way to make sure it didn't happen, especially to Ellen.

She paused. Richard only raised his eyebrows, waited for her to continue.

"Well, I know we've spoken about having children … and I know, and fully understand, that you aren't keen on babies and everything," she continued before he could interrupt, "But you really were very good with Ellen, when she needed it, much better than me, and it's not as if she's a baby." She saw his eyes had opened wider. She hurried on, "And I really have grown very fond of her, I think I would really miss her if she were to go, and I know she wouldn't be much trouble, and it would help Beth because she would only have two children then, and it would be easier for her to stay with her mother …" She took a breath.

Richard quickly leaned forward and said, "Are you out of your mind?" his voice was calm. Too calm, she thought.

"You promised you'd let me finish."

He leaned back, "Well then, *do* go on."

Sheelagh stared at him. She felt afraid. And what more was there to say really?

There was silence. Her husband looked at her expectantly, lips pursed, eyes flint-hard. She shrugged. "I thought it would be nice." She shrugged again, "I thought it would be a way to help. I thought it was a way we could have a child of our own, without having a baby."

"But you *didn't* think to mention it to me before you went off half-cocked in the hospital. No wonder Beth is upset. ... What if she had said 'yes'? ... And then what if I didn't think it was a very good idea at all? ... Did you think about any of that, Sheelagh? Don't tell *me* you thought! You didn't think at all. It is one of the stupidest, hare-brained ideas I have ever heard." He stood. "I really am beginning to think you have *totally* lost your reason, woman. You are besotted with your bloody family. God knows where *I* fit in, because at this point *I* surely don't."

He rounded the desk and headed for the door.

"Richard, don't go, I'm sorry."

"Yes, of course you are Sheelagh, now that it's all blown up in your face. Like I said, I've had enough of the apologies. Get yourself together, for God's sake. And let someone else look after your bloody sister-in-law."

He left, slamming the door behind him.

Sheelagh sat, stunned. She was shivering, though she didn't feel cold. She turned in her chair to see Richard storm out of the shop, staff and customers watching as he did so. Once the shop door closed behind him, several of them turned to look up at the office window. She hastily turned her back on them.

Within moments there was a soft tapping on the door. Before Sheelagh could say anything, Doris had opened it. She came in and closed it quietly behind her. She put her arm around Sheelagh's shoulder.

"It's alright, Miss Sheelagh. He's just a bit hot-headed, bit like your father, if you don't mind my saying so. He'll calm down." She gently patted Sheelagh's shoulder. "Whatever you two were arguing about, it can be sorted out. How about I take you upstairs and make you a cup of tea. Always a good picker-upper, a nice cup of tea."

Sheelagh leaned in to the woman's ample bosom. She nodded. Just to have someone put their arm around her felt so comforting.

"Come on then, Miss." Doris gently helped Sheelagh to her feet.

* * *

The old lady asked no questions. Upstairs, she settled Sheelagh in her arm-chair, made her tea, and played quietly with the children. After a while Sheelagh sighed and put the cup on the table.

"Thank you, Doris, I think I needed that."

"You do seem to have been getting yourself in a bit of a state recently, Miss Sheelagh. I know you're grieving for your brother, and looking after two little ones isn't easy, but you have to look after yourself too, you know ..." She paused, seemed uncertain as to whether to continue.

"And ..." Sheelagh prompted.

"And ... well ... it's not really my place to say, Miss Sheelagh," she looked back at the children, lowered her voice, "you have to look after your husband too. Husbands can be the biggest babies you know, if they feel they're being neglected."

"Oh! Doris, I wish I'd had a mother like you. Maybe I wouldn't have got myself in all these messes."

"I'm sure they're no real disasters, Miss. It's just a bit of a stressful time; and Mrs. Porter was a lovely lady, from what I remember."

"She was, but she seemed so scared of everything, and she always agreed with Daddy. I think I got to be more like him."

"That you did, Miss." Doris smiled. "Well," she went to Ellen and Brendan who were playing quietly. "I think I should get back downstairs now. Before Mr. Hudson comes back." She tousled the children's hair. "Bye, bye, you two." She turned back to Sheelagh. "You're sure you are all right now, Miss?"

"I am, and thank you again, Doris."

Confrontation

The next morning the children were awake early. Sheelagh could hear them moving around upstairs as she prepared breakfast. Richard was already down in the shop. He'd come home late the previous night, long after she was in bed. She'd woken, and snuggled into him, but he didn't responded, and was soon fast asleep. This morning he'd made himself tea, declined breakfast, and said he had things to do in the shop.

Sheelagh went the bottom of the stairs. "Breakfast!" she called, "Come on you two. Wash your hands and come on down." She heard their bedroom door open and their scurrying footsteps racing to the bathroom before she left the hall. Two pairs of feet drummed on the stairs as she fetched their toast and porridge from the kitchen. "Stop running, you'll fall," she called as she put the tray on the table.

The children burst into the room. Both were fully dressed, though Brendan's sweater was on backwards and his shoes were on the wrong feet.

"Oh! Good heavens, Brendan, you're lucky you didn't break your neck on the stairs!"

Ellen grinned. "I dressed him, all by myself. And me!" She twirled to show her aunt.

Sheelagh had to laugh, the child was so proud of herself. And Brendan looked almost as proud as his sister. His dark brown eyes sparkled, and his grin was as broad as his face. Sheelagh couldn't *ever* remember seeing him this happy.

"Well, well done, Ellen. You *should* be very proud of yourself. Now, come and sit down and have your breakfast."

She sat to watch them, cutting Brendan's toast into fingers, putting a tiny sprinkle of sugar into Ellen's tea. Brendan still preferred milk.

"And what, may I ask, is the reason for all this helpfulness?" she asked.

"Uncle Paul is taking us to the zoo."

Brendan had been carefully raising his mug with both hands. He nodded in confirmation at Ellen's statement, milk slopped over the rim of the mug. Sheelagh reached over to steady it.

"Of course! I'd completely forgotten." She looked at her watch. "It's a little early yet, but well done for getting ready on your own."

She watched as they finished breakfast, put Brendan's shoes on the correct feet, turned his sweater around, then sent them back upstairs to wash their hands and brush their teeth. "And would you make sure Brendan does it properly for me Ellen, please? Brush all the way to the back, Brendan, remember?"

He nodded and Ellen said, "I will. Come on, Brendan." She seemed to be enjoying being in charge.

Sheelagh closed the door behind them, and had started to clear the table when she heard footsteps coming up the shop stairs. Maybe Richard had changed his mind. She would make him scrambled eggs, with grilled tomatoes; he liked that.

It was Paul who opened the door.

Sheelagh put down the tray.

"Hello, Paul. My goodness, you're early." She glanced at her watch again. "I wasn't expecting you for an hour at least."

"I wanted to have a word with you before we went. Where are the children?"

He looked very serious, not like the usual, smiling Paul.

"They're upstairs, brushing their teeth. Why?" She recalled the dreadful conversation she'd had with Beth the day before. "Don't tell me something has happened to Beth." She sank into a chair. "Oh, *please*, tell me she's all right."

"She's all right, though she has been pretty upset after your visit yesterday."

Sheelagh felt the color rise in her face. "I'm sorry; I didn't mean to upset her. I was trying to do what I thought best."

"Sheelagh, we all appreciate you having the children, we really do. But you seem to have lost sight of what's going on here. You are *not* Beth's family; *we* are. You offered to take the children, and because Mum was staying over there with Beth she thought that was a good idea. But they are *Beth's* children ... Mum's grandchildren. And, I think you might have forgotten that Michael was my best friend."

He stopped, gripped the back of the dining chair, his knuckles white. It was a while before he continued, but Sheelagh didn't dare interrupt.

"It is not *your* place to decide what happens to these children. You are *not* responsible for my sister, *or* her children. Your help and support is very much appreciated, but what the *hell* did you think you were doing offering to adopt Ellen?"

His voice had risen.

"Please don't shout, Paul, the children will hear you." She felt sick to her stomach, she was shaking. "I was only trying to help."

He was quieter when he spoke again. "I understand that, Sheelagh, but, if you'll excuse my saying so, what you did was more like something your father, or Wyn Porter, would have done. You didn't consider anyone else. Don't you think my family should have a say in what happens to Beth and her family? She's my sister! They are my niece and nephew! Don't you think we've been thinking about it? Talking about it? Not wanting to go to Beth with half-cocked, half-cooked ideas?"

"I ..."

He raised one hand to stop her.

"Of course, we had no idea Colm could do something that despicable, cheat Michael and his family.

"He ..."

"I don't need to know the details. Nothing that man could do would surprise me. Sorry Sheelagh, I know he's your brother, but I don't suppose he's changed much all the time I've known him. That's beside the point. We're not paupers, Sheelagh; we can look after our own. Just because you have the children *now* doesn't mean you have taken control of the rest of their lives, though you seem to think you have."

"I am so sorry."

"I'm sure you are, Sheelagh. And I know you were well-intentioned, but you just took over. You said nothing to any of us. First we hear about what's been happening is when the hospital calls us saying Beth is very upset and could mum go in. Not even at visiting time, just straight away. Mum was in a terrible state".

Sheelagh jumped up, "Is she all right, Beth I mean, and your mother?"

"It would seem so, but this secretive planning of yours has got to stop, Sheelagh."

"I wasn't being …"

"You didn't think you were, but it certainly seemed like it to us."

"I am so very, very sorry, Paul."

He did not acknowledge her apology. The silence in the room was palpable.

"I wanted to do it for Michael's sake."

"We all do, Sheelagh, *and* for Beth's!"

"Uncle Paul, Uncle Paul is here."

Sheelagh and Paul turned to the door. Sheelagh's cry of, "Don't run, you'll fall," was automatic. Paul hurried into the hall and caught the two children as they launched themselves off the stairs and into his arms.

"Hey, you two are far too heavy for me; you nearly knocked me over." He was laughing, and so were they. Sheelagh watched from the dining room door. He turned to her as he lowered the children gently to the floor.

"Are they ready to go, Aunty Sheelagh?"

She nodded.

"Do they have bread for the ducks?"

She shook her head. "I'll get some."

The children followed her, their liveliness somewhat subdued, as if they felt the tension. Sheelagh put the remainder of the toast into a paper bag and handed it to Ellen.

Paul reached across to her, put his hand on her arm. "We know you mean well, Sheelagh, and we appreciate what you've done, but we have to all sit down *together*, and decide what's best."

She nodded.

"OK, kids, let's go." He looked at her over their heads. "We'll talk when I get back, all right?"

She nodded again, and they left.

Reconciled

Sheelagh spent the morning catching up on all the housekeeping, neglected over the last few weeks since the children's arrival. She dusted, swept floors, washed and ironed clothes, and tidied up the children's toys, but there were so many thoughts racing through her head. She thought about her disastrous visit to Beth, and how much she had upset her. She would have to go back to the hospital, apologize again, make things right. She thought about what Paul had said too, and especially about Doris' advice.

Maybe she and Richard didn't have the perfect marriage, but maybe it wasn't all his fault, or hers; they were probably equally to blame. If she was honest with herself, it's not as if she didn't know what he was like before they married. She knew he was vain, and that he could be selfish, and stubborn. If she was being honest she would have to admit that so was she. She tucked the abandoned Mandy into Ellen's freshly made bed and smiled ruefully. Paul was right, she *was* inclined to make decisions that suited her, then try to persuade everyone else to see them her way. He'd said she was like her father, well, stepfather really, she acknowledged, though she never thought of Jim Porter that way. The Porters were the ones who had reared her, educated her, and looked after her, even if they had left a lot of the ordinary, day to day, care to Martha.

As she dusted down the stairs Sheelagh remembered watching Martha do the same thing, every day; always the same way, banister, railing, step, banister, railing, step. She wondered where the maid was now. She left to marry that delivery man; that was the last time she saw her. The man had seemed nice. Sheelagh met him in the kitchen one day, but her father had told her it wasn't seemly to be friends with 'people like that' when you were adult. "A totally different class of people", he'd said "working class. Common!"

Sheelagh sat on the bottom step. And what was *he?* she thought, becoming aware as she remembered that conversation, just what a snob, and a bigot, he'd been. She was momentarily stunned by the realization. He was as bad as his sister! Just as much of a bully as she was to Michael!

Why hadn't she realized that before? But she knew why. He loved her, and spoiled her too; private education, expensive clothes, even if many of them came from his own store, and the wonderful holidays they enjoyed. All the things she wanted to give Ellen, to do for Ellen.

Still, she didn't want to be like him! Not the bully part of him anyway.

And Doris was right too, you *did* have to look after your husband. Sheelagh sighed; she had probably been neglecting Richard for a long time now, even before the children came. She was so focused on developing and modernizing the business. Maybe it was time to make it up to him, she could at least try.

She stood, looked at her watch, and hurried to the kitchen.

* * *

By the time Richard came up at noon she had prepared a Toad in the Hole, one of his favorite meals, and had a jam tart in the oven for dessert. She was bringing the dish to the table as he came in.

He stopped in the doorway. "Good lord! What's happened here? Did I come up the wrong stairs?"

She put it on the table, "This is my way of saying, I'm sorry."

He sat. She filled his plate and handed it to him.

"Not sure what this particular apology is for, and I know I'd said I'd had enough of them, but under the circumstance, you're forgiven." He poured so much gravy over the pie it was in danger of overflowing the plate. "I don't remember the last time you made this," he said, taking up his knife and fork.

She sat opposite him, smiled and served herself. "I've turned over a new leaf."

He stopped eating and looked at her. "Is this what happens when those two kids are out of the house for a couple of hours?"

"No, though it did give me time to do a bit of thinking. I've been a bit scattered for the last few weeks."

"A bit?"

"All right, a lot."

"Hmm. Well, let's see if this magical change sticks when they get back this evening."

"I'm going to try, Richard. I don't want to be like my father, not in some ways, anyway."

"Wow. What brought that on?"

Sheelagh put down her cutlery. If she wanted to make amends, try and change, then perhaps she'd better start by being a bit more honest and open. "Paul gave me a real telling off this morning. Worse than you! He made me feel like I was five years old. But he was right. I've been very selfish, so I'm going to try and change."

He too put down his cutlery. "That sounds good." He shrugged and returned her smile. "I've not been that happy with all this damned fighting either ... and if we're being honest, I'm sick of eating at the club."

They both laughed. The tension of the last few days and weeks eased. They continued their meal talking more comfortably together than they had for a long time. Sheelagh promised she would do her best to include him *before* she made any more impetuous decisions, and he promised not to be so sensitive to imagined slights or perceived exclusions.

"It's not going to be easy. I've only realized today how spoiled and selfish I am."

"Good lord, Sheelagh, this is a bit like the road to Damascus. I'll have to ask Paul around more! Ha, Paul, that's funny!"

She looked puzzled.

"Paul! The road to Damascus!"

"Hmm. Anyway, that was one of the things he said, that we should all get together and see how we can help Beth and the children."

"Some sense at last. I'm glad to hear it, Sheelagh. Really I am."

"And I'll try not to go on about having a baby."

"And how about I see if I could adjust to the idea?"

"I love you."

"I love you too."

"We seem to have lost sight of that a bit."

"Well, I'm definitely getting refocused." He stood from the table. "Do you think Doris could cope in the shop for a while if I didn't go straight back down?"

"I made a jam tart."

"We can have that later."

She nodded.

As they went out into the hall she couldn't help silently thanking Doris, and not just for looking after the shop.

* * *

That evening, while Richard babysat, Sheelagh returned to the hospital, and Beth. Their conversation was tearful and Sheelagh was humbly apologetic. Beth said they should do their best to forget what had been said, though she did want to know more about Colm, the insurance, and where the cheque, with a woman's name on it, had come from. Sheelagh explained, and told Beth all about "That Woman" as she continued to call her.

Sheelagh was relieved that they parted on good terms.

Family Meeting

Paul suggested she and Richard join the family on Sunday evening "for a pow-wow". Sheelagh pressed the ever-willing Doris into babysitting and, once Ellen and Brendan were in bed and Ellen's uniform was laid ready at the bottom of the child's bed, they set out.

"I'm terrified I'm going to get scolded by the whole Howard clan. I'm not at all sure I'm ready to face them en masse."

Richard reached for her hand. "You'll be fine. And they'll have me to deal with if they start on you after all you've done."

"*We've* done."

"Umm, well I think I probably set out to make things more difficult, if the truth were told, so let's not mention my part in this."

She squeezed his hand then released it. "How about you just keep your hands on the wheel for now. We'll talk about your contribution later."

He laughed and continued driving in silence.

* * *

They were first there, Margaret and Bill greeted them warmly and hugged Sheelagh, who started to cry and apologize until Margaret hushed her, said bygones were bygones, and they had more important things to talk about now.

Bill was taking their coats as Ev arrived. "Sorry, late as usual, haven't missed the Big Confab, have I?"

"No, we've just arrived." Sheelagh again started to explain when Margaret interrupted her.

"That's enough, Sheelagh. You don't have to do any more explaining, or apologizing. You have been wonderful, taking the children, offering to pay for Ellen's schooling; I don't know where we would have been without you. Now, come on in, sit down, and I'll put the kettle on. Maggie said she might be a while getting her children to bed, so you can tell me all about those two little angels. Ellen starts school tomorrow doesn't she? Is she nervous? Did she go to bed all right?

The next half an hour passed with small talk about Ellen, Brendan, and their excitement at starting school. Sheelagh told them about the trip to the zoo, the children's delight at having ridden on a camel *and* an elephant, and their disgust at the smell of the lions and tigers. Margaret said she missed them, and wished she could have seen them more since she returned from Ireland, and how time seemed to fly by. Sheelagh asked about Beth, and Margaret said she was doing fine, that the doctors were pleased with how the baby was developing and how Beth was coping. She had a few phantom contractions, but no real sign of the baby coming early.

Paul arrived, then Maggie and her husband. Margaret made a fresh pot of tea. When everyone was settled, they addressed the issue they had gathered to discuss.

"Beth had been doing a lot of talking about having her own house." said Margaret. "I saw a newspaper when I was in there on Friday, with different places circled. Of course she did that before she knew about the insurance."

Sheelagh felt her face redden, but Margaret was quick to forestall any awkwardness.

"Sheelagh, no saying could be more true that that you are not your brother's keeper. There was no way you could have known, and whatever Colm has done certainly doesn't reflect on you."

"Hear, hear," said Ev. "You've been a treasure, Sheelagh."

Sheelagh felt her blush deepen. She bent her head in embarrassment.

"Anyway," continued Margaret. "I brought the paper home with me. I went to look at one or two of the houses after I visited Beth yesterday. Bill and I looked at another three this morning. Two of them seem perfect, and they're quite close to here."

"But ..." Sheelagh began, but Paul gave her the faintest of frowns and she said no more.

"Now, what you don't know, Sheelagh, is that we have been concerned about whether she would have enough, even with the insurance, to buy a house, so ..." she beamed at her husband and her three children, "we've been trying to see if we could help."

Sheelagh felt so uncomfortable. Of course this wonderful family would have been thinking about all of this. She knew they were close, Michael had always said they were his real family, the only family he had when he was growing up. Why hadn't she thought of all that when she was trying to single-handedly 'fix' everything?

"Between us we are sure we can come up with a goodly deposit," Margaret continued, "and we have all said we will chip in on Beth's day to day expenses, until she is better able to cope on her own."

"I enquired and, because she is a British citizen, she will be entitled to a widow's pension." said Ev, helping herself to another slice of the apple cake. "They said she will start getting that very soon, paperwork takes time."

"And the RAF Benevolent fund have been in touch with me," Paul added. "They said they can't do an awful lot, too many widows, sadly, after the war, but they said they will certainly help with incidentals, "paying for her furniture to be shipped over, giving her a few bob extra at Christmas and the children's birthdays, that sort of thing."

"And I can help looking after the children when she needs a break or whatever," added Maggie.

Margaret smiled. "I hope to be doing a lot of that myself once the baby is born and she is out of hospital."

Bill had been sitting back puffing on his pipe, silently watching and listening as each member of the family contributed to the conversation. Now he smiled across at wife. "You are good people; I'm a lucky man to have inherited a family like this."

It was Margaret turn to blush, but she returned her husband's smile and only said, quietly, "You are my rock."

"Well, you certainly seem to have it all worked out," said Richard, breaking the moment.

"Michael was right about you," added Sheelagh, "You are a very special family."

"No" Margaret shook her head as she replenished empty teacups, offered more cake. "This is what family does. Especially when they are needed."

* * *

The rest of the evening was lighter in tone. It was agreed that a friend of Bill's who "knew about houses" would go and look at the two he and Margaret had singled out.

"And if he says they are sound, no hidden damage or whatever from the war, then we can maybe talk to Beth about them."

It was settled, and Sheelagh left with hugs and promises of updates from the family. It was agreed that the children would spend the following weekend with their grandparents, and she saw Richard give a slight nod to Paul at this. She had not felt so relieved, or relaxed, for some time. She just hoped that both children would settle in to school without too much fuss.

First Day

Both children were awake but still in bed when Sheelagh went into them on Monday morning.

"Good morning, sleepy heads, I thought you would both be up and dressed already this morning." She sat beside Brendan. "Hello, sweetheart, are you all excited about going to school?"

He stared up at her eyes wide, thumb firmly stuck in his mouth, said nothing. She kissed his cheek and looked over at Ellen. "What about you, Ellen? I'm sure you're looking forward to making new friends; getting away from your Aunty Sheelagh for a while."

"I don't want to go."

"Ellen! Don't be silly, sweetheart! Don't you remember how you said it would be nice to make new friends?" Sheelagh kissed Brendan again, went to the bottom of Ellen's bed and took up the neatly ironed cream blouse. "You looked so nice in this the other day. So very grown up."

"I want Mammy to take me."

"Oh! Ellen, you know she can't do that right now. She will, when she can, but just for now I have to take you."

"I don't know any of them."

"No, I know you don't, but Miss Singleton will help you make friends, and they all looked very nice little girls." She put down the blouse. "How about I take Brendan to the bathroom and get him washed and dressed. Then I can make a special First Day at School Breakfast for you when you're ready?"

Ellen's eyes narrowed. "What kind of breakfast?"

"What would you like?"

"Sugar sandwiches!"

"Sugar sandwiches? I didn't know you liked those. I never heard of anyone having sugar sandwiches."

"Daddy made them for me."

Sheelagh's breath caught in her throat. Ellen hadn't mentioned Michael since the day she found out. "Did he darling? Well then, that is an *extra*-special breakfast. What about you, Brendan, would you like sugar sandwiches too?"

He nodded, but kept his thumb in place.

"Right then, let's get going. Come on Brendan, let's do you first." She pushed back the covers and helped him scramble to the floor. "Will you wash and dress yourself Ellen, while I get breakfast, or will I come back and help you?"

"I can do it."

"Good. Then I'll do your hair, but don't take too long; we don't want to be late on our first day, do we?"

She took Brendan's hand and they left.

* * *

Sheelagh sat Brendan at the table, tucked a large napkin into the neck of his shirt, and draped it across his chest and stomach. "We don't want any accidents before we leave, do we?"

He waited patiently until she finished, then took one of the sandwiches from the plate she'd put in front of him. He separated the slices, examined the filling, smiled up at his aunt, and began to eat.

"I spoiled it."

Ellen was standing in the doorway, her tie in one hand, Mandy in the other. She held up the tie "I tried to put it on and it opened, and now it won't work."

"Never mind, we can get Uncle Richard to do it up again. He'll be down in a moment."

"And I can't do this either." Ellen indicated the sash that hung from the waist loops on her tunic.

"Ah, that's easy. Don't forget I used to have the same uniform. I know how to do that. Come over here and I'll show you."

"Did Uncle Richard do your tie?"

Sheelagh laughed. "No, darling, that was a little before his time. My father used to do it." As soon as the words were out of Sheelagh's mouth she regretted them.

"But I don't have a daddy."

"Oh! Ellen, my sweet." Sheelagh hugged the child close. "All right, let me tell you a secret. I think the knot in my tie was probably only ever done once, then I never, ever, had to do it again."

"Never, ever? How?"

"I'll show you when Uncle Richard comes down, but then it's a secret, all right, we won't tell anyone, and everyone will think you are very clever to make *exactly* the same knot every single day. What do you think?"

"All right."

"Good, now, why don't you sit and have your breakfast and I will re-plait your hair and finish getting you ready afterwards."

Ellen did as she was told and Sheelagh breathed a sigh of relief. Yet another crisis had been averted.

"My goodness, everyone is up early this morning." The children looked around in surprise. Uncle Richard didn't usually talk to them that much, especially in the mornings.

"Ellen would like you to do her tie when she has finished her breakfast."

"That would be my pleasure, Ellen. Have to have you looking smart for your first day, don't we?"

He gave Sheelagh a peck on the cheek, sat opposite the children and poured himself a cup of tea. They eyed him warily. He was not like he usually was at all. He seemed nicer.

When breakfast was over Ellen stood, somber-faced, in front of her uncle. She studied his moustache; she'd never been this close to it before. It looked like it went up inside his nose. She wondered if it tickled him. His eyes had tiny golden dots in them, in the blue bits. They were like the tiniest stars.

"There you are, Ellen. A perfect knot, even if I do say so myself."

"Now I have to show you the secret," said Sheelagh.

Brendan hurried over to get between his sister and his aunt, so as not be excluded. Ellen roughly pushed him to one side. "Go away Brendan; it's my secret."

Brendan whimpered.

Sheelagh sighed and looked to Richard.

"Hey, young man, come here for a minute. I think you've something strange in your ears."

Brendan's hands went to his ears. He found nothing so remained where he was, but his Uncle stared at his ears with such puzzlement and curiosity that the small boy finally relented and left his aunt and sister to themselves.

Sheelagh showed Ellen how to carefully loosen the loop to slip the knotted tie over her head, and how to tighten it again when she put in back on. Meanwhile Richard 'magically' produced halfpennies from both of Brendan's ears, and presented him with the money.

It was time to go. Sheelagh fetched Ellen's coat and a jacket for Brendan. She tucked a neatly folded linen package into their satchels. "Now, there's a snack for each of you." She took two apples from the fruit bowl, "and these should keep you going until you come home. Kiss Uncle Richard goodbye and we'll be off."

At the top of the front door stairs Ellen stopped so abruptly that Brendan bumped into her.

"I forgot Mandy."

"I don't think you're allowed to have dolls, Ellen."

"But I want her."

Sheelagh struggled for an excuse. "I don't think Mandy is old enough to go to school yet, Ellen; she's not as grown-up as you."

Ellen didn't move.

"What about if we bring her in the car, and then she will be waiting for you when I collect you."

Ellen thought about this for a moment, then nodded.

"Go on then, go and get her, quickly. We don't want to be late."

Ellen ran upstairs and returned with the doll under her arm.

They were ready to go. Sheelagh led the way down the stairs.

* * *

When they arrived at the Sacred Heart Ellen shed a few tears, but seemed resigned enough to stay with Miss Singleton. At Saint Nicholas School it was a little different. Brendan gripped tight to Sheelagh's hand as they crossed the school yard. Sister Thomas stood at the double doors into the school, greeting the students. As soon as she saw Sheelagh she went forward to meet her, then she knelt to Brendan. She wrapped him in her arms and Sheelagh was astonished to hear her crying. Brendan stood very still, looking at his aunt over the nun's shoulder, his face expressionless. Sister Thomas released him, stood, and fumbled a handkerchief from her pocket.

"What a silly nun I am," she said smiling down at the little boy, and dabbing at her eyes. "A silly goose of a nun! Or do I look more like a penguin?"

There was a faint flicker of a smile from Brendan.

"You are very welcome to Saint Nicholas, Brendan Kelly. I am so very happy to meet you. Would you like me to show you your new school?"

He glanced back at Sheelagh. She nodded.

The nun held out her hand. He took it.

Sheelagh said, "Will I come?" as they walked toward the doors.

Sister Thomas looked down at Brendan. "I think we'll be all right for a while, won't we Brendan? We're friends already aren't we?"

His face remained serious, but he nodded and kept hold of her hand.

Sheelagh was astonished at the child's acceptance of the nun, but she smiled at him, blew him a kiss and said, "I'll see you later, sweetheart."

Sister Thomas and Brendan waved, turned their backs on her, and went in through the battered double doors.

A Quiet Time

The first week of school passed without incident for both children.

Within a few days Ellen had made a new friend called Rebecca; by the end of the week they were inseparable. Her first elocution class went well. When she came home Ellen proudly recited a little poem about a cat, to her aunt. Sheelagh took her down to the shop and asked her to do it for Doris and Ivy.

They stood her in the middle of the aisle. She stood very stiff and straight and began,

"I have a little kitty," She made her fingers into ears,

"He is as quick as he can be," she ran in a small circle, nearly bumping into Brendan who stood, fascinated by his sister's performance.

"He jumps upon my lap," She sat on the floor and stroked an imaginary cat on her lap.

"And purrs a song to me." She looked up at her tiny audience. "I can't make that noise yet, but Miss Pollard said that didn't matter."

The women laughed and clapped and Doris gave her and Brendan, a sweet.

"Can we have a cat, please, Aunty Sheelagh?"

Sheelagh laughed. "You'll have to ask your mother about that. I think I have enough on my hands."

* * *

By the fourth day, when Sheelagh parked at the school gates, Brendan climbed out of the car and ran across the school yard to Sister Thomas, without a backward glance at his aunt.

Sheelagh was relieved to discover that both children seemed happier.

As the first week came to a close she found, once the children were out of the house for a few hours each day, that she had time catch up on a backlog of paperwork in the office, and to meet with staff, and work on the more changes she had in mind for the interior of the shop, *and* for the window displays. It was good to get back to work, without distractions.

"I hadn't realized how far behind I was," she told Richard as they ate an early lunch on the Friday. "I feel so much more relaxed, even though I'm working harder."

"You're doing what you enjoy," he said as he folded the newspaper, put it beside his plate and stood. They heard a downstairs door open, and Doris' voice calling.

"Mrs. Hudson, there's someone here to see you."

Sheelagh glanced at her husband, people usually knocked on the front door if they were family or friends, not come through the shop.

They heard footsteps on the stairs and hurried into the hall. It wasn't like Doris to let anyone come up without checking with her bosses first.

"Hello, Sheelagh. How are ye?"

"Pierce!" Sheelagh ran to her brother, threw her arms around his neck, and hugged him tight. He laughed, and muttered, "Will ye get off me, woman. Sure ye'll suffocate me before I'm in the door." She finally released him.

"Well now, isn't that's a grand welcome. Hello, Richard isn't it. Delighted to meet you, at last" He held out his hand, Richard shook it. There was a brief, awkward pause. Sheelagh caught his arm and hugged him to her side. "What on earth are you doing here? Why didn't you telephone us?" She stopped, frowned. "Is there something wrong?"

Pierce laughed again, "Would you give me a minute to get my breath, woman. Sure aren't I only just off the boat and train. That's the very devil of a journey! My mouth is parched and here's you with a dozen questions before I've even been offered a cup of tea." He smiled down at her. "And no! Nothing is wrong." Looking across at his brother-in-law he added, "Don't they always be expecting the worst?"

Sheelagh couldn't stop smiling, "Oh, Pierce, it is so good to see you. Come in, come in. I'll make you a fresh pot of tea. Are you here to stay for a while?"

She looked behind him to where a beaming Doris was standing, close to the top of the stairs. "Do you have any luggage?"

"I do, Sheelagh, I've a small bag. I left it downstairs when this good woman said she'd show me up.

Sheelagh's mind was racing, where could she put him up? The children had the only spare bedroom. She could worry about that later. Now she just wanted to sit and talk with her brother. She turned to Richard, "Would you get it, while I put the kettle on please, sweetheart?"

Richard nodded.

"Come in, Pierce, come, in." She glanced over at the still-smiling Doris. "Thank you Doris, thank you." The woman dipped her head and turned to go back downstairs. Richard followed her smiling and shaking his head. Sheelagh led her brother into the back room.

* * *

As she puttered in the kitchen she bombarded Pierce with questions about Mary, Joe and their children. She asked after his own wife, Maeve, and the children, and finally, when they were settled at the table, cups of tea in hand, Sheelagh asked him again the reason for his visit.

His smile faded.

"I got your letter, Sheelagh. I'm not at all sure what bothered us more, the troubles that poor Michael's wife is having, Lord rest his soul, or that fact that Colm is going to America. *America,* Sheelagh! That's an awful long way away. We might never see him again."

Sheelagh smiled. He was such a gentle man, such an innocent man.

"But it's not difficult to travel to and from America now, Pierce," she said. "It's not like the old days. I'm sure we'll see him again." She pulled a face, "Not that I feel I'm going to miss him all that much, right now, and after what he's done."

"He's still blood, Sheelagh. I couldn't let him go, not without saying good-bye to him, despite the terrible thing he did. Mary wanted to come too, but isn't she expecting again, and Joe thought the journey might be a bit too much for her." It was Pierce's turn to pull a wry face, "though I'm not sure he wanted to be left to look after the four they have already, if the truth be told."

"Another one? She's expecting another one?"

Pierce nodded and smiled, "She said I could tell you, though it's early days yet." He took a sip of his tea. "And anyway, I thought I should come over and see Beth, to apologize for Colm, and maybe make some amends, if I can, for what he did." He stared into his tea, then looked back up at his sister. "It's been nearly two months since the funeral service. Is she doing all right, Sheelagh? I know she's in the hospital and all, but will she and the babby be all right? It must be due soon?" He looked around, "And where are the other two. They're awful quiet if they're here, not a bit like ours."

Sheelagh jumped up, "Oh, my goodness." She looked at her watch. "I have to collect them from school. Will you come with me, Pierce?"

Richard stood in the doorway, Pierce's bag in hand. "The poor man would probably like a chance to freshen up after his journey, Sheelagh. He can see them when you come back."

Sheelagh ran a hand through her hair. "And I'm not sure where we can put you up, Pierce. We've only the one spare room, and the children are there."

Her brother raised his hand to wave off her concerns. "Sure, I thought maybe I could stay with Colm for the day or two, get to know him a bit better before he goes."

Sheelagh was horrified at the thought of Pierce meeting the Margot woman, but now was not the time to talk about it; they could cross that bridge later. Right now she had to go.

"All right, I won't be long. Look after him, won't you, Richard? I'm thrilled you're here, Pierce. I'll be back soon." She snatched up her handbag and fled the room.

Colm

"Colm? Sheelagh here. I have a surprise for you." Sheelagh had no idea how he was going to take the news, but she couldn't avoid it. The children were upstairs playing with their Uncle Pierce. He seemed to have a natural way with children. Sheelagh wished she did.

"I trust it's a pleasant one."

She had to smile to herself. She suspected it wouldn't be, and that pleased her, though she felt some sympathy for Pierce. He had no idea just how self-seeking Colm was. He and Mary were so trusting, believed the best of most people, and especially wanted to believe their own brother was a good man.

"Pierce is here."

"What? Why?" his voice was wary.

"It seems he wants to see you before you go."

There was a pause. "Not sure if we can do that; pretty busy you know, and we leave in a few days."

She could hear the uneasiness in his voice. He was afraid! Probably afraid Pierce had come to confront him about Michael's insurance. Well, she didn't feel like telling him the real reason, didn't want him to get off that lightly.

"He is actually hoping to stay with you."

"He what? Don't be ridiculous, Sheelagh."

"Well, *I* can't put him up. The children are in our spare room and you have that huge flat. I told him you'd be delighted."

"You did *what?*"

He sounded truly panicked now and Sheelagh was enjoying this.

"You wouldn't have your brother stay in a hotel would you?"

"Stop playing bloody games, Sheelagh. I don't think this is funny."

"No, neither do I, Colm. But it's *not* a game, Pierce *is* here, and his reason for coming *is* to see you. And he did say he thought he might spend a little time with you, stay with you. But I decided not to inflict that on him, so I've booked him into a B and B near us."

"That makes more sense." She could hear his relief.

"So do you want to come here this evening?" She didn't mention the woman. If he did come, she hoped he would come on his own.

"Ah, ... not sure about that ... lot of things to sort out. I'll get back to you, Sheelagh. Have to go, I'm late already." He hung up.

Sheelagh stared at the dead receiver. Why didn't it surprise her? Damn him anyway! He had no intention of coming over, with or without his blonde. What could she do? She certainly didn't want to explain to Pierce that Colm would try and avoid a meeting.

She went back upstairs. Pierce was sitting in an armchair, Brendan on his lap and Ellen sitting on a cushion at his feet. All three looked up as she came in.

"Uncle Pierce is telling us the story of a leprechaun named Brendan," said Ellen, smiling up at her aunt.

"Is he now?"

Pierce winked at her, and she smiled. "Well, do you think I could spend some time with my brother, or are you going to keep him prisoner all the time he's here."

Ellen looked disappointed. "Can he finish the story?"

"Of course he can, and I will make our tea. Then it's bath and bedtime. You are off to Granny Margaret's tomorrow, for the weekend, don't forget."

"I don't want to go. I want to stay here with Uncle Pierce."

"He has a few things to do, Ellen, so he won't be here tomorrow anyway, and Granny Margaret is looking forward to having you." Sheelagh didn't want to mention he was visiting Beth. "Your cousins will be there too, and he'll be here when you come back on Sunday." She glanced at Pierce again with raised eyebrows. She hadn't actually asked how long he intended to stay. She'd only booked the bed and breakfast for one night, just until she had time to sit and talk with him.

He nodded.

"All right."

Ellen turned back to her uncle. "Did he catch the goat, did he?"

Pierce smiled and continued the story.

* * *

"I'm so glad you and Richard have finally met," Sheelagh said as they sat around the fire that evening. "I've tried to bring him to Ireland, Pierce, but it's just never happened.

Richard shrugged. "Someone needs to stay and mind the shop. I can't imagine your family would be too thrilled if I turned up instead of you."

"Someday, perhaps. Mary is anxious to meet you." Pierce looked over at his sister. "Never happier, that woman, than when she's surrounded by family. The more the merrier. She's even taken to Joe's brother and family, despite them owning the bar! And you know what a demon of a woman she is about the drink!"

"She doesn't approve?" Richard sounded a little surprised. "Then I should probably stay away. Wouldn't want to shock your favorite sister, Sheelagh."

"My only sister."

The conversation was light and easy. Sheelagh was glad the two men seemed to get along, and she looked forward to surprising Beth tomorrow when she brought Pierce into the hospital.

She wasn't surprised that Colm didn't arrive. But she'd promised Pierce they would see him tomorrow, and she wasn't going to disappoint him.

Visiting

By the time Sheelagh had the children ready Pierce had walked over from the Bed and Breakfast. The children begged him to go with them in the car. Margaret was surprised and pleased to see him and insisted they all stay to lunch. The children ran off to play with their cousin's toys.

"Paul is working today, and Ev went into town early to do some shopping, then she's going over to sit with Beth, but Bill will be home from the allotment soon. He will be delighted to meet you too, Pierce. I barely got time to talk to you at the funeral, and we've heard so much about you from Beth over the years, and from Michael of course." No one spoke for a moment, then all spoke at once, then stopped.

"That would be lovely, Margaret. I'm taking Pierce in to visit Beth this afternoon too. I know she will be just as surprised as we all were.

Lunch was a chaotic affair. Brendan, Ellen, their cousins, and the four grown-ups all chattered, laughed, passed dishes and plates. It finally came time for Sheelagh and Pierce to leave. All the children were playing Simon Says in the back garden and barely acknowledged their departure.

* * *

Ev saw them first. She, too, had only met Pierce at the funeral, but she recognized him immediately and pointed him out to her sister. As soon as Beth saw him she began to cry. Walking towards her bed, Sheelagh glanced sideways and saw Pierce, too, was crying though doing his best to smile and look happy.

They hugged for a long time. Ev said she would leave them to talk, before the nurse came to give another lecture about only two visitors being allowed at once. She said her goodbyes, urged them to sit, and left.

Over the next half an hour there was more animated conversation. Pierce spoke about the family's concern for Beth's condition. There were messages from Mary, and he gave some explanation for his visit, mentioning Colm's engagement and imminent departure.

Sheelagh was impressed that Beth refrained from any angry or unpleasant comment about Colm in front of Pierce. She felt she would be perfectly entitled to.

Finally there was lull in the conversation. Pierce cleared his throat.

"There was another reason I came, Beth, apart from saying goodbye to Colm."

He looked, uncomfortable, awkward. He leaned forward in his chair, gripped his hands tight together until the knuckles were white. "I can't say how sorry I am for what he did, Beth. I can't believe the man could stoop so low, but Sheelagh told me all about it, and I believe her. I can't help that he's my brother, and I couldn't let him go to America without saying goodbye, but I'm mortally ashamed for what he did."

He unclenched his fists, reached into the inside pocket of his jacket and tugged out a large brown envelope.

"You know that Mary's Joe and myself have the business together?" Beth nodded as he continued. "Well, we both decided, along with Mary of course, that we should try and make it up to you." He handed her the envelope. "I'm afraid I'm still not all that trusting of the banks, Beth, though Joe tells me they're safe enough, so I don't have any of them cheque book things." He looked at her, half-shamefaced, half-smiling, "But the money's good, and it might help you get the house you and the babby need."

Sheelagh and Beth looked at him in astonishment.

"You didn't tell me," Sheelagh said.

He turned to her, with a sheepish grin, "Ah, well, no. I wanted it to be a bit of a surprise, and if you're anything like your sister you'd have the news blurted out before I could take my first breath."

Beth had lifted the flap of the envelope. It was not sealed. "Oh, my goodness, Pierce, there's hundreds in here!"

He glanced quickly around "Be careful now that you don't be showing that to the world, Beth. You never know who you can trust, you know."

Beth reached for his hand. "Thank you, thank you so much, and please thank Joe, and Mary."

"And my Maeve, of course, I forgot to say our Maeve. She was all for it too, Beth."

Beth frowned, "But what am I going to do with it?" She smiled "I can hardly hide it under the mattress in here now, can I."

"I can look after it for you. We can put it in our bank until you need it, Beth." Sheelagh glanced at her brother. "I've a bit more sense than my brother here. I *do* trust the banks. Are you mad, Pierce, bringing all that money in your pocket?"

"There! You see, I said you were like Mary!"

They were laughing when the bell rang to signal the end of visiting time. He kissed her goodbye. "I'll be in to see you again, Beth, Mind yerself."

There were more hugs, and heartfelt thanks from Beth, and they left.

* * *

"So, where now?' Asked Pierce, once they were outside the hospital.

"Now I think we'll go and visit Colm."

"Grand. I wasn't sure if you were talking to him at all, Sheelagh, when you put me in that bed and breakfast last night.

"Yes, well, I don't think I actually explained much about his girlfriend, Pierce. Fiancée, I suppose she is now, but I didn't think you would feel too comfortable staying with them."

"Them? What do you mean 'them' Sheelagh? Are they married already?"

"Let's get in the car, and I'll try and explain."

* * *

It took most of the journey to Colm's flat for Sheelagh to tell Pierce how, and where, she had met Margot, a little of what the woman was like, where she came from, and about her marital background. She didn't describe her appearance. Pierce had surprised her with the money. She wanted to see his face when he met his sister-in-law to be.

247

Moving On

A large van was parked at the entrance to Colm's flat. Sheelagh parked her car in front of it. She and Pierce got out and were about to ring Colm's bell when the door opened and two men carried out a couch. Sheelagh recognized it from Colm's sitting room. The men loaded the couch into the back of the van. They had left the door open behind them, but Sheelagh pushed the doorbell, and heard Colm yell, "Don't tell me they closed the bloody door after them," as he stepped out onto the landing.

He stopped when he saw his sister and brother at the bottom of the stairs.

"What the hell are you doing here?"

"You didn't come round last night, so I thought I'd bring Pierce over here."

"I told you I was busy."

"He came from Ireland, specially."

The two removal men squeezed past and continued up the stairs. Colm stepped to one side as they went into his apartment.

"Who are you talking to, darling?" Margot appeared beside Colm. He gestured toward the stairs. She looked down, saw Sheelagh and Pierce still standing in the doorway. "Ah!" She looked back at Colm and smiled. "Looks like you've been caught, sweetie." She gestured to Sheelagh, "Come on up honey, and I guess that's your brother. You come on up too, big man. Let's not air the family linen in public."

Sheelagh glanced at Pierce. His face showed his shock. "Come on," she said as she led the way upstairs. Colm scowled at them as they came.

The two men reappeared carrying the coffee table and a standard lamp. There were a lot of 'excuse me's' as they maneuvered their way around the small group of people now standing in the hallway, and negotiated the stairs.

Colm ignored Pierce's hand. "I suppose you'd better come in."

"Hello darling. My, but good looks run in your family." Margot clutched Pierce's hand. "Colm's probably just a little embarrassed, don't mind him. It is such an unexpected pleasure to meet you. Pierce, isn't it?"

"It is ma'am." Pierce shot a glance at Sheelagh. He looked very uncomfortable.

"I didn't know you were moving today." Sheelagh looked around the almost bare apartment. Even the beautiful curtains were gone.

"Yes, well, the bloody bailiffs decided that for me, didn't they?"

Colm lifted a half-full whiskey tumbler from the last remaining coffee table and drank its contents in one gulp.

"Your brother has been a naughty boy. Forgot to pay the landlord, *and* the furniture company, it seems. Such a forgetful man! I've only known him for six weeks, but he does seem to forget an awful lot of things. My wild, wild, Irish man." She went to Colm, snuggled against him. "Definitely needs a woman to mind him, don't you think, Pierce?"

"Yes, ma'am."

"You are a disgrace, Colm. What would your parents say?"

"Our parents, dear Sheelagh, are long dead. As you well know."

His voice was slightly slurred.

"I mean the Sinclairs. You know I do."

"Ah, dear Mater and Pater. Don't actually see a lot of them. Not since pop's business went bust." He almost seemed to be talking to himself. "Bloody demob suits pretty much did for him, not a lot of money left in bespoke tailoring now. Struggling themselves to put bread on their own table so far as I can gather. No bloody help to me."

"Six weeks?"

"What?" Colm looked at his brother, as if he were a fool.

"Six weeks! You have only known each other six weeks?"

"Amazing isn't it?" Margot nuzzled Colm's ear. "Love at first sight, wasn't it, honey?"

"Mmm." Colm jerked his head away. "I'd ask you to sit, but ..." He waved his arm around the empty apartment, "As you can see that would present a little difficulty."

There was silence as two men returned. One picked up the last remaining dining chair and the other took the coffee table.

"Maeve and I were courting for over two years."

"Really? Nice. Quaint!" Colm raised his empty glass. "Well we all know they do things differently in Ireland. Even give away their children to perfect strangers at the drop of a hat."

"Shut up, Colm."

"Nice! You come to visit, uninvited. Come in to my home, and then tell me to shut up!"

"I think maybe you've had a teeny bit too much to drink, sweetie." Margot took his glass. "Be nice to your brother and sister."

Pierce took Sheelagh by the elbow. "I think maybe I made a mistake, Colm. I thought *you* had made a mistake somehow, with Michael's money and insurance, I mean. I didn't want to believe you didn't care. And I wanted to say goodbye and wish you well. But it *was* a mistake. You're like Da. You're drunk, Colm. Just like Da. I can see how it makes Mary so upset. " He looked at the woman. "I'm sorry for your trouble, ma'am, for you'll have plenty of it, if he is as like our father as he seems." He turned back to Colm, "Goodbye, Colm, and good luck to you. You'll need it, I suspect."

He did not offer his hand this time. He guided his sister to the door. They stood aside for the two men, then left.

They were silent on the drive back to the shop. Pierce seemed engrossed in his own thoughts, and Sheelagh didn't know what to say. She felt so sorry for him, and angry, and disgusted, at Colm. It was only when they arrived and Sheelagh had parked the car that he spoke.

"I think I'll be going home tomorrow, Sheelagh."

"But you've only just arrived, Pierce. Stay a few more days, for me, for the children, please?"

He shook his head. "I don't think so, Sheelagh. I'm not feeling too comfortable here." He indicated the street, the bustling traffic, the people hurrying from shop to shop. "I'm more used to the quiet life."

"But it's just Saturday. The street is always busy on a Saturday."

He looked over at her. "I'm not just talking about the street, Sheelagh."

"I know, but I'm so happy to have you here.

He shook his head again. "I've done what I came to do. You know I'm always available if you need me, but 'tis better I go."

"Ellen and Brendan will be sorry."

He smiled, "Then we'll just have to make a grand day of it tomorrow. I'd like to see Beth again before I leave, and perhaps we can collect the children a little early and take them for an ice-cream or something. What do you think?"

"I think that would be lovely." She tried to sound cheerful. "Now, let's go on in. I don't want to waste a minute of the time we have."

* * *

With Sheelagh's encouragement Pierce hardly stopped talking, and she loved it. He told stories about the children, his own, and Mary's, and about the haulage business he had with Joe. He talked of the changes that were happening in Ireland, *even* in his own village. Glendarrig had a post office, and a police station, though Pierce said they were called Garda now, so it was rightly called a garda station. "Sure the crime is rampant," he said with a laugh. "Mossie Flannigan's pig has got out twice in the past week, and didn't it eat half the vegetables in Biddy Dunne's back yard the second time. 'Twas she who called the gardai, daft woman! Sure wasn't it only doing what pigs do? So, what with Mossie's pig, and the sneaky raids on the odd poteen still, the gardai are kept busy enough. Though in truth, the station is only an ould one-roomed cottage, and there's only the two of them, and Liam O'Dea is as likely to be committing the crime as policing it!"

"I'll have to come and visit, soon; it sounds like it's all changed."

"Sure we'll be as big as Bristol before you know it."

They laughed at the prospect, and continued to talk long into the night.

* * *

Beth was sorry Pierce was going home so soon. "I wish I could have spent more time with you. I hate being stuck in here, just waiting for visiting hours, and this darn baby." She rested her hands on her swollen stomach.

"Sure they take their own time, Beth, and my Maeve says you women should enjoy every minute of it. Aren't you busy enough when they're born?"

"I really can't wait." Her smile faded and Sheelagh saw she was close to tears again. "I miss the children, Pierce. It's bad enough that I miss Michael so much; it's cruel that I can't see them either."

Pierce nodded and glanced around the ward. There were high, thin windows along each side. He stood and went to the one nearest Beth's bed, looked out, then back at the two women.

"Are ye allowed out of bed at all, Beth?"

"Only for a few minutes."

"But you could get to this window."

She nodded.

He looked at Sheelagh. "I can see your car."

Sheelagh realized what he was suggesting. "Oh, Beth, you could see them!" she paused, "Of course it wouldn't be the same as having them close, but it would be something. Why didn't I think of that?"

Beth began to cry. "Oh, please! That would be wonderful."

"Whist now, woman, do you want to get us in trouble? Don't cry. We're going to collect them after this visit anyway, sure can't we drive back here? You can beep your horn, Sheelagh, and you can get to that window, Beth. So long as you mind yourself. I don't want to be the cause of any untoward problem with that baby." He was back at the bed now, and nodded at her stomach.

Beth nodded, scrubbed away her tears. "You are magic, Pierce. Why didn't any of us think of that?"

He looked a little embarrassed, but pleased with himself.

Sheelagh was almost as excited about the idea as Beth. "Would you like us to go and get them now?"

Beth looked from Sheelagh to Pierce and gave a slight nod. "It's lovely to see you both, but, oh! It would be wonderful to see the children. Would you mind?"

"I'll go, Pierce can stay with you. I'll be back as soon as I can. I'll beep the horn twice."

* * *

Ann O'Farrell

Visiting time was over by the time Sheelagh returned. Pierce was waiting for her in the car park. She had explained to the children what they were going to do. Ellen was excited, Brendan seemed to be confused.

"You understand that you can only wave at her? It's not like you can go into the hospital."

"Can I shout?"

"Well, the windows are closed, so I don't expect she will hear you, but you can try."

Sheelagh parked the car. She beeped the horn twice and they all climbed out. Brendan ran to Pierce who picked him up. They scanned the line of windows on the second floor until Ellen jumped up and down and pointed shouting "There she is, there she is!"

Beth waved as excitedly as her daughter and Pierce pointed out the window to Brendan. The little boy finally saw his mother. "Mammy" he said, beaming at Pierce, then up at Beth, "Mammy!"

"I love you, Mammy," shouted Ellen, and blew kisses at the window. Beth smiled and blew kisses back, though Sheelagh saw she was crying.

The children shouted and waved for a few minutes, then a nurse appeared beside Beth. They spoke, and Beth waved and blew kisses one last time before she stepped back out of their sight.

The children were quiet.

"Your mammy has to go back to bed now," Sheelagh explained. Ellen nodded and Brendan whimpered "Mammy." Pierce hugged him close and began telling another story about Brendan the leprechaun. They all climbed back into the car for the journey back to the shop.

* * *

That evening Pierce's departure was the source of more tears, but the children were tired and Sheelagh was soon able to persuade them upstairs for their baths, and bed.

Sheelagh kissed them goodnight. As she left Ellen called her back.

"Thank you, Aunty Sheelagh. I love you, and I love Mammy."

Time

Two weeks had passed since Pierce's visit. Sheelagh assumed that by now Colm and Margot had left for America, though he'd not contacted her to say 'goodbye'. The children had settled into school, and they had made a few more 'window visits' to the hospital. Sheelagh had collected the portrait photographs from the studio and helped Ellen to write Beth a note to take into the hospital with the pictures. She wrote about a new poem she was learning in her elocution class, and about her new best friend, Becky.

With more time for themselves, there was less tension between herself and Richard, and Sheelagh acknowledged, at least to herself, that perhaps children were a great deal more work than she had ever imagined. She didn't admit that to Richard, not just yet anyway. We'll just wait and see what happens, she decided.

It was good to be more involved in the running of the shop again. Doris was getting old and she really did need more help than Ivy could give her. Sheelagh noticed her giving the wrong change more than once. She would have to retire her soon. On the other hand she was a treasure at looking after the children and spent almost as much time upstairs now as she did in the shop.

It was as Sheelagh was helping Ivy with an order form for a new line in silk stockings that the phone call came.

"It's time, Sheelagh." Paul was almost shouting down the phone. "Mum and Bill have gone in, and I'm going now, once I've made a couple more calls."

"Can I come?" she said standing and pushing the order book away.

"Of course you can. There's a waiting room there, though it could be a long wait. We only got the call a short while ago."

"It doesn't matter. I want to be there. I'll just tell Richard and I'll see you there."

"Fine."

He hung up and so did she.

"It's time, Ivy; the baby's on its way." She waved down from the office. Richard was gazing absent-mindedly at a display stand. Sheelagh tapped on the window. He finally saw her and realized what was happening. He hurried up to the office as she came down the steps and into the shop. "The baby's coming. I just have to get my bag and a coat. Will you give Doris a hand, give the children something to eat, and help put them to bed?"

He hurried after her. "Like what?"

She was already halfway up the stairs, "It doesn't matter, anything, sugar sandwiches; that's a favorite. Doris will know. I don't know when I'll be back." She turned at the top of the stairs. "You don't need to bathe them."

Before he could say anything more, or follow her, she had grabbed her coat and bag and raced down the other stairs. The baby was coming!

* * *

Paul had arrived before her. Ev was there too, and Bill.

"Maggie's on her way, just waiting for James to come home from work. Mum's inside." Paul indicated the green double doors with the 'Patients and Staff only' sign. "You might as well sit. We're going to be here for a while."

Sheelagh looked around. The waiting room was large, could probably hold fifty or more people, but there were only three others there, sitting at the far end; a young man, sucking nervously on a cigarette. He was seated beside a woman who looked like his mother. She was knitting. An older man sat by himself reading the newspaper.

About nine o'clock Paul offered to try and find a cafeteria and get everyone sandwiches and tea. Bill offered to go home and make some and bring back a thermos, but Maggie said Margaret would want him there when it was all done, so Paul went and Ev said she'd go with him.

At ten thirty a nurse came out. They all stood, but she called to the older man. Paul asked her if there was any news of Beth. She said "Babies take their own good time," and ushered the man through the double doors.

It was long after midnight when Margaret came out. She looked exhausted, but happy. Bill immediately went and put his arm around her, the others followed.

"What it is, Mum?"

"It's a boy."

"Baby Michael!" said Sheelagh.

They all looked at her.

"That's what she told me, the day before the funeral. She said it was a boy; she said it was baby Michael."

"Is she all right Mum? Is the baby all right?"

"They're fine, Ev. They're both fine. He's seven pounds one ounce. They said that's very good, given that he's still a little early. The cord was wrapped around his neck three times, poor little thing."

"But he's all right?" asked Ev.

Margaret nodded and smiled up at her husband. "He's beautiful, Bill. He has a mop of dark hair, and dark eyes, just like his father."

They stood in a small circle, hugging, and laughing and crying, and asking when they could see the mother and baby.

"The doctor said it would be a good idea if she rested now. We can all visit in the morning. I said I would go back in and say goodbye, once I'd told you. Then we should all go home."

Bill gave her a quick kiss. "Go on then, love. You looked tired out, and I think we could all use some sleep. Go on, Grandma, say goodnight to your new grandson. See you in a minute."

Margaret went back through the doors. Sheelagh hugged everyone again, said 'goodnight', and left.

* * *

Once outside she stopped and looked up at the stars in the clear, black, sky.

"You have a son, Michael, another beautiful son. And we'll all look after him for you."

Made in the USA
Charleston, SC
10 March 2012